MADAME MOLL

BOOK 3

BETHANY-KRIS

ERIN ASHLEY TANNER

Published by Bethany-Kris and Erin Ashley Tanner

eISBN 13: 978-1-988197-42-5
Print ISBN 13: 978-1-988197-44-9

Cover Art © Jay Aheer
Editor: Eli Peters

DEDICATION

For all the fans of Mac and Melina. We thank and love
you.

CONTENTS

CHAPTER ONE

Very few things were held sacred to those who lived inside the suffocating world of Mafiosi. There were still certain things that would never be touched in such a way that it might hurt the foundation upon which *la famiglia* rested its most core values. Those values were handled with the utmost care, treated with the respect one might give their mother, and never did a made man abuse those traditions.

Mac Maccari took comfort in knowing all of this, if only because it guaranteed him and his wife, Melina, a few moments of peace.

Events like babies being born and lives being started were not simply passing moments in time to *la famiglia*. Rather, they were cornerstones that were always celebrated and protected amongst the men that made up Cosa Nostra. Because they were *the* family. It was not just one man, but every man and their wives and children. Their world and culture did not sit well with people outside of their circles, so they only truly had one another to fall back on when the time called for it.

It was important—no one, no matter how much they might dislike another made man, would step in to ruin one of those events for someone else.

So yeah, Mac was grateful that despite the uproar that was currently rocking the very ground upon which Cosa Nostra had been built, there were still some things that would always be left untouched.

One of those things happened to be his wife … and her pregnancy.

Her very *beautiful* pregnancy.

Mac smiled to himself, glancing to the side to find his wife sitting in the passenger seat of his Challenger, her hands resting on her thirty-six week swell. It wouldn't be long now, and their baby boy would be making his way into the world, ready to cause hell, probably.

After all, the baby was *his* son.

"What are you snickering about over there?" Melina asked.

Her head turned in his direction, but she couldn't see him. She hadn't been pleased when he'd shown her the black silk sash and asked if she would let him take her for a surprise, but Melina played along. She usually did, even if she did put up a fuss first.

"Thinking, doll," Mac admitted.

Melina's full lips curved into a soft grin, like she just knew what was in his head. "You're awfully proud of the fact you're having a boy, aren't you?"

"Would have been just as pleased had the baby been a girl."

"Yes, but—"

"But," Mac interjected, reaching over to place his hand on the crown of his wife's stomach, "I'll have some backup, at least for a little while."

"A little while? What is that supposed to mean?"

Mac chuckled deeply. "What do you think it means?"

While his statement was joking in nature, the suggestive undertone was still as clear as day. His wife certainly hadn't missed it if the way her cheeks pinked were any indication.

"God, Mac, you can at least wait until this one is out of my damn body before you start talking about more kids."

"That's debatable," he murmured.

Melina just sighed, shaking her head but still smiling.

She could act coy all she wanted, but Mac knew the truth. His wife was as stubborn as a mule, but so was he. The two of them were like peas in a pod, and she threw just as much at him as he tossed at her.

It made their marriage interesting.

And he so loved his wife.

"I'm just saying. A little friend might be nice for the baby," Mac suggested.

Melina scoffed. "Stop it."

"Well—"

"Like I said, at least wait until *after* this one is out of my body."

"Fine," Mac muttered, "since you want to be that way about it."

Melina smirked. He swore if that sash hadn't been covering her eyes from him, he would have seen she was rolling her damn eyes. She was not so coy that he couldn't see right through her act. Despite her loud and repeated protests from the very start of their relationship that she absolutely in no way would become the Susie Homemaker sort of wife, Melina was certainly enjoying the perks of being at home more often with the only responsibilities being to take care of her pregnant self and stay happy.

Of course, she still had The Dollhouse to run, and she did.

Thankfully, Melina had knocked down her time from several hours a day to two or three times a week. Mac knew there was no way on fucking earth that he would be able to convince his wife to hand the business over to him, so that she could focus on her pregnancy and the baby when he was finally out into the world. Somehow, they were just going to have to figure it all out and make it work.

Melina was nothing if not a fighter and a survivor.

Mac, too.

Surely they could figure out something as simple as this.

"Timothy," Melina suddenly said.

Mac knew exactly what his wife was saying because they had been playing this game for months now. "No, it doesn't have …"

"What?"

"Pizzazz."

"Did you honestly just reject a baby name because it doesn't have *pizzazz*?" Melina snorted indelicately. "We're not in the Dirty Thirties, Mac."

Melina couldn't have sounded more patronizing if she had tried.

Mac only laughed. "Well, it's true. It's not very noteworthy of a name. It's a fine name, doll, just not what I want."

"Why don't we just go with your name?"

"Because my name isn't actually *my* name," Mac explained, probably for the fifth time since they had begun the process many months earlier of trying to pick a name for their baby boy. "My name is James, not Mac."

"We could start the tradition of using Mac instead of James," Melina suggested.

"Mac isn't really Italian, doll."

Melina conceded to his point. "And you're a definite no on James."

Mac scowled, thankful his wife couldn't see it. "Yeah, that's a big, fat fucking no."

"He's going to be born nameless."

"So what if he is? Maybe he will, maybe he won't."

"We don't have a name."

"Stop panicking," Mac said, reaching over to place his hand on his wife's thigh, and stroke her skin with his thumb. "We'll find a name."

"You're too picky."

"Doll, I love you. You know that, right?"

"Of course," Melina said.

"You're making it hard right now."

Melina wacked him hard in the arm. Even though she

couldn't actually see him, she still had a pretty damn good aim. "Watch it, Mac."

"We'll pick a name," he assured.

She still didn't look convinced, but she didn't argue.

Mac figured they didn't have a name for their baby already because he wasn't born yet. How could Mac possibly say yes to a name when he hadn't even gotten to lay eyes on his child in the flesh? Seeing the baby moving around on a gray and black screen was not enough for him. He wanted to know his baby first—see his little face and learn his features.

Then, and only then, Mac would pick a name.

A name that fit.

A name that was *right*.

"Are you going to tell me where we're going?" Melina asked.

"Nope."

"I'm getting a little car sick."

"Liar, you just want to peek."

Melina pouted at having been caught in her lie, and Mac squeezed her thigh in response. He still loved her pouts. It still made him hotter than ever.

Really, her whole pregnancy had done that for him. Something about his wife growing with their child, glowing and beautiful, just *did it* for him. That was the best way he could explain it, really.

Mac had no shame.

And he'd take his wife whenever, wherever.

As long as Melina was willing.

"Almost there," he assured.

Melina made a disgruntled noise under her breath. "Better be worth it. I had to cancel my appointment at the spa today."

"You'll be there tomorrow instead." Mac cupped his wife's cheek, keeping his eyes on the road at the same time. The last thing he wanted to do was get them into an accident. "And Vic will be able to go with you; she'll keep you company and tell off the masseuse when they don't listen to what you want."

Melina smiled at that, especially the mention of her sister-in-law. "Vic is good for that."

"Good for annoying the hell out of me."

His statement had come out too low for his wife to hear, but it wasn't any less true. Victoria Maccari was an adult, sure, but she was still Mac's little sister. He tried to look out for her as much as he could, but sometimes she made it hard. He was pretty fucking sure she did that shit on purpose, too.

"Hmm?"

"Nothing," Mac said. "And we're here—no don't take that off yet, doll."

Melina huffed, her hands lowering from the sash and resting back on her swollen stomach. Mac parked the car in the paved driveway, thankful someone had thought far enough ahead to leave a clear and open spot for him to drive straight into. This had all been a little last minute. He'd tried his hardest to make sure everything was done on time, and in doing so, managed to get things done a little early for his wife.

Melina didn't know.

It was the perfect chance for Mac to give her one of his surprises.

"Sit tight," he told her.

Melina's mouth opened to speak, but Mac was already getting out of the car, slamming the door behind him. Just as fast, he jogged around the car, came up to her side and waved to the people waiting on the front steps.

Mac opened Melina's door, and took her hands in his. "I'm going to help you out of the car, doll."

"If you would just let me take this off, then—"

"The answer is still no."

Melina's lips pressed together in a thin line, her silent displeasure clear. While she didn't mind indulging his games and surprises, he wasn't shocked that she didn't have a lot of patience for it right then. Being heavily pregnant and tired because she wasn't sleeping well, Mac really didn't blame his wife.

But he wanted to make her smile.

He wanted to see her happy.

She would only be pissed for a few more seconds, he knew, and then it would all be gone.

"Careful," Mac said as Melina got out of the car, still holding tightly to his hands. Once he had her standing right in the middle of the driveway where he wanted her, where she would be able to get a clear view of her finished surprise that she had waited months for, Mac let his wife go. "Okay, doll, take it off."

Melina didn't need to be told again. She pulled the sash from her face to let it hang loosely around her neck. It took her all of ten seconds to blink at the large Victorian-style home staring back at her to realize what she was seeing. Mac saw the realization dawn. People standing on the front steps, ready to welcome her into their home for the first time since building it had officially finished a couple of weeks before.

She had been here before, of course. They had both made their way out to the plot of land they owned to check up on the build and how it was going. But over the last couple of months, Melina hadn't wanted to make the drive because it was a good thirty minutes from their current apartment. Thirty minutes out and thirty minutes back just to check on how things were going was tiring, so he had used that to his advantage, telling her some things had come up that put the build a little bit behind.

Not by much, he had promised, but a month at the most.

Melina never questioned him.

The last two weeks had been a bit of a rush to decorate and style the inside, to make sure the rooms were painted with the colors Melina had picked when the contractor first made the plans on the blueprints for them to look over.

She had purchased furniture over the last several months, keeping it locked away in storage until they were ready to fill their home with it. Mac had gotten a few of the guys from his crew to help move the furniture in and place it where it needed to go.

If Melina wanted any changes, they could do it easily enough.

"Oh, my God," Melina whispered. "It's done?"

Mac nodded, coming up behind his wife to wrap an arm around her waist. His hand rested on her stomach, and he felt the gentle prods of his baby as he kissed his wife's cheek. "It's been done for a couple of weeks."

"It looks amazing."

"Wait until you see the inside."

Melina wiped at her eyes, and smiled sweetly. "Okay, the blind folding and driving was worth it."

He grinned, smug as fuck. "Thought you might say that. Now …"

"Now what?"

Mac pointed at the people waiting on their front steps. His mother, sister, a couple of Melina's friends she had made, and some of his guys. "Time to have a house warming party, doll. I think we've earned it, don't you?"

Melina's laughter was a balm to his soul. "Yeah, I think we did."

As she walked forward, ready to greet and thank the people waiting, Mac stayed a little bit behind, enjoying the scene. After all, this wasn't so much for him as it was for her. All too soon, their baby boy would make his presence known to the world, and things like house warming parties and time to spend eating good food and laughing with family and friends would have to take a back seat for them both.

At least for a little while.

He wanted Melina to have some fun before that.

She deserved it.

All over again, Mac was reminded how grateful he was that there were still things that were untouchable to *la famiglia*. While the family was important, and their crime family was struggling between the official attention from the Feds and the police, *his* budding family was something else entirely.

Sacred, he knew.

These moments were not to be sullied by problems of made men.

No one would dare do that to him or his wife.

He would get back to the grind tomorrow, get his guys back on the street, and hope to hell another street war didn't break out with another Capo's crew. With no boss heading their family at the moment, petty feuds had become all too common.

No one really trusted anyone.

But today?

Today would not be dirtied with any of that.

He was grateful.

Mac stepped into the warehouse, letting the creaky, heavy door close behind him. The audible click of the door latching stopped the murmuring conversations happening between the young and older gentlemen of his crew. There was a misinterpretation that all the men in a crew were young guys picked up off the street because they were easy to manipulate—that couldn't be less true.

If anything, young guys were harder to handle. The older crew members had been in the game long enough to know better than to stir the pot of shit or do something that might earn them a bullet, while the young guys were more likely to push against whatever authority stood in their way of getting what they wanted. Older guys usually liked where they were and the position they had, so they didn't have much interest in getting higher in the family. Younger guys always wanted to be more—get more.

It was one of the benefits of being a younger Capo like Mac was. He supposed he related to the younger guys in his crew which meant they didn't mind shutting up and listening to him. Not that the situation was always the case—it wasn't—but almost always was better than nothing.

Mac had a fuck lot less problems with the guys in his crew than other Capos had with their crews.

He wasn't about to complain.

"Skip," came a collective greeting from twenty different voices as Mac stepped out from the entrance.

He waved a hand in greeting and leaned against the wall. "Any news for me?"

His gaze skipped over familiar faces, checking for any sign of a lie as several "nopes" rang out from most of the men. He didn't want to have to look for lies at all, or think that maybe, possibly, one of his guys might not be telling him the truth. Too much police and FBI attention left Mac more paranoid than he usually would be.

No Capo wanted to wake up one day to find out his crew had a rat.

A rat meant jail time, especially if it happened to be close.

"Anyone get pulled in for another talk?" Mac asked.

"Just Enric," said one of the older guys sitting off in the corner with a cigarette hanging from his lips. "But he isn't in the mood to talk today—never is lately."

The guy nodded in the direction of the office Mac used to do work when he wanted privacy from the rest of the crew as they did their work.

Mac would deal with Enric later. He was all too aware it wasn't Enric Pivetti's fault the officials wouldn't leave him alone. The bastards had his father locked up, and he'd been the recipient of several bullets to the back months ago when he'd been acting as a guard for Mac's wife. No one was looking at Enric like he was talking to police for his own gain because everybody knew he didn't have a choice.

Still, Enric was hiding himself away.

For more reasons than the obvious, Mac knew.

Right now, though, Mac had to deal with his crew. Morale was low because business was *shit*. Working was damn near impossible when every job was like sticking your hand in a roaring fire pit. With so much official attention on them, even the smallest job was dangerous and carried great risk.

But no work meant no money.

Money was the reason these men were here.

"All right, listen up," Mac said, his tone rising to get all of the men's attention on him. He really hadn't needed to bother, as they all looked to him when he started speaking, anyway. They were good that way—he figured it was a check on his good side, too. "I know everything has been slower than death lately. We don't have a lot of cash flow coming in. I'm working to fix that."

"How so, Skip?"

Mac smiled. "Different ways, but what I want to focus on first is making sure all of you are safe when you go out to do a job. That starts with the other crews, so I'm going to work on that and making some peace. As for money, I have another idea other than the usual deliveries, boosts, or heists that take a lot of attention and might be too dangerous for you all right now."

He could tell he had his guys' attention.

Money was on the table, after all.

"I have money to be collected all over the city—some rackets, a few loans that are owed, and bookies' payments that come in pretty regularly depending on the game the night before. Even some of the businesses that still pay for their place, so to speak, come in on a weekly basis. It's not a lot—not what you usually make, but it's something."

Mac shrugged, adding, "And something is better than nothing."

A few murmurs—some confirmative, some grumbling—passed between the guys. Mac let them have their moment, and when they all quieted, he spoke again.

"You can take fifty percent of whatever you pick up for me and deliver *without* issues. No violence to get the payments, and definitely *no* bodies. These aren't those sorts of payments, all right? So that we don't have guys acting like petty bitches, I'll be the one to divvy up who picks up what and when." Mac chuckled, saying, "It'll change from week to week to make it as fair as possible, but this is the best I can do for now to make sure you're all looking at decent cash to get you through whatever fucking spell this is and however long it might last."

Because *that*, Mac didn't have an answer for.

He didn't know how long any of this was going to last, and he didn't want his guys to suffer because of it. With no boss running the family and taking payments from his Capos, Mac wouldn't need to explain the drop in cash. He could afford to lose some income for the benefit of his crew.

Other Capos wouldn't do or say the same thing. Others would probably be too concerned about keeping up their lifestyle and banking more money as the dry spell went on.

Mac knew better.

When all of this was said and done, his crew would still be there waiting to get back to work. His guys would still be loyal and honorable to him. All because he took care of them when they needed him to.

That was what a good Capo did.

"But for today," Mac continued, "just relax. Go chill. And stay the fuck out of trouble, huh?"

"Got it, Skip," came the confirmative, collective reply.

Mac waited the guys out, leaning against the wall, as

one by one they passed him to leave. He could tell they were a bit lighter on their shoulders with his promise of making sure they would be looked after, so that gave him a sense of relief. Once the warehouse was empty but for a few familiar faces, one being his longtime friend, Bobby, Mac headed for the office.

The guys were handled.

One thing checked off his list.

Now, he could deal with Enric.

Mac quickly slipped into the office, letting the door close behind him. He turned the blinds on the window, hiding the inside of the office from the few men who had remained behind. Enric sat behind the desk, his back turned to Mac, and tossed a small red ball against the wall. The rhythmic smack of the ball as it bounced off the wall and hit Enric's skin came in perfectly timed intervals, and the guy never once turned to greet his Capo.

Not even after Mac said his name.

"Enric," Mac said a second time, slightly louder.

Nothing.

The ball kept moving.

Enric stayed just like he was.

Mac didn't let his frustration take over because he knew Enric Pivetti had a great deal more to be frustrated over than he did in the grand scheme of things.

"Heard you got pulled in by the cops," Mac said.

Enric shrugged. "Nothing big—the usual "do you remember anything" spiel."

"Nothing new, then?"

"Nope." Enric laughed. "I did go see Dad a couple of days ago."

Now, that *was* interesting to Mac.

Nobody had heard anything from the boss or his underboss since both men had been locked away. Some of the Capos in the family surmised that Luca and Enzo were being refused phone calls because of their statuses and the influence they could have on their men with a single order.

Mac didn't know if any of that was true, but even getting *some* word or kind of order from the boss was better than the silence they were getting now.

"And?" Mac asked.

"Neeya is moving out, I guess," Enric said quietly. "I've never been close with his wife—my choice, not hers. He wanted me to head over there, see if she needed any help or if the girls needed something. He said not to bother her too much. She's allowed to do whatever the fuck she wants to do."

Mac took a few seconds to digest that information. "Wait, you mean she's moving out of their mansion?"

"Selling everything she can."

Holy fucking shit.

The boss's wife was *leaving* him?

That didn't sound right.

Mac had seen Neeya and Luca Pivetti in more than enough situations to know they were a power couple to strive to *be*. Nothing and no one was going to separate them, and that was fucking admirable.

Except … had something done that?

Mac wasn't sure.

"Thought maybe you and Melina could take me over," Enric said, spinning slowly to face Mac. "You know, the city bus only goes so far and whatnot."

Mac's gaze darted down to the seat Enric was sitting in—his wheelchair that had been a constant since he was released. Slight spinal cord damage and two surgeries later, Enric had some feeling in his legs. He also had little muscle and nerve control, but his four-times-a-week physical therapy would get him walking again.

Eventually.

He needed to put in the work, though.

Mac figured that was half of Enric's problem.

And he hadn't found a reason to do the work, yet.

He would, someday.

"Yeah, we can get you over there to see your sisters,"

Mac assured.

Enric nodded. "Dad wanted one other thing, too."

"What's that?"

"He wants a meeting with you after you get this handled."

Now, Enric really had his attention.

CHAPTER TWO

Melina opened her eyes and smiled. Every morning that she woke up to the tall vaulted ceilings and the wide bay windows in her bedroom was a good one. She groaned as her son shifted in her belly none too gently.

"All right, munchkin, take it easy on Mommy."

As usual, the baby ignored her and continued doing whatever he liked. That was a definite trait their unborn child had inherited from his father. Speaking of his father, Melina sighed and pulled the pillow closer from the empty spot beside her. Mac had left the house hours ago.

She hated that it seemed his days were getting longer and longer with the current unrest in the Pivetti Organization. It was astounding to her that Luca was still in jail. She had no idea what the Feds thought they had on him, but it had to be bad. The man hadn't even been allowed bail. Enzo either. The whole thing was surreal.

A family without a boss.

What would happen now?

Throughout her pregnancy, Melina had tried not to think about Cosa Nostra. It had nearly ended her life and her son's once not that long ago. But she couldn't stick her head in the sand and pretend everything was perfect. It wasn't. She worried for her husband. Mac was the most hardworking, honest man she knew and in the back of her mind she wondered if that would ultimately lead to more trouble in their future.

Melina winced as a sharp pain pierced her belly. Involuntarily her hand moved to the place where the pain had come, but just as quickly it was gone. Perhaps she'd imagined it. No reason for concern. Moving back the covers she got out of bed and slowly made her way into the adjoining bathroom. She caught a glimpse of herself in the mirror before getting into the shower. Her belly was huge. At one time she'd wondered if there were two babies inside her instead of one, but her OB doctor had quickly put that idea to rest. She was just carrying a big baby.

Turning on the shower, she stepped inside and allowed the triple heads to rain water down on her body. This shower was amazing. Large enough to accommodate four people, with crisp, black tile and fog proof glass doors it was easily one of her favorite things about her new home. Lazily she scrubbed her body with the loofah sponge as she stood under the warm water.

Minutes later as Melina toweled off her wet body, her son changed positions and another sharp pain hit her belly. Ignoring it, Melina brushed her teeth and finished getting ready for her day. It was damn near eleven when she finally entered the kitchen and grabbed a snack before setting the alarm and leaving the house.

It didn't matter if her belly was as big as a beach ball or if the swelling in her feet was so bad somedays she didn't even want to wear shoes, sitting at home was just not an option. For any business to be successful, you had to put hard work into it and pregnant or not there was business to be done at The Dollhouse. It seemed dissension and despair lead to the increase of certain appetites. Who knew?

Melina ignored the pain in her lower back as she talked to some of the women currently awaiting patrons at The Dollhouse. No doubt it was just the kitten heels she'd insisted on wearing catching up with her. She was nearly nine months pregnant, after all.

"No. She's not the kind of girl I'm looking for," Melina said.

"But, Boss Lady…"

Melina shook her head, cutting off the rest of Amina's sentence.

"I can appreciate you wanting to help your friend out, but The Dollhouse is not the place to do that. No. I'm sorry."

She turned away before the young woman could plead with her again. Since her business had become such a success, her girls were always approaching her seeking employment for friends and family. So far she'd turned everyone down. It took more than just a pretty face to be a Doll at The Dollhouse. A woman had to have a certain charisma. She had to know how to handle herself, but most of all she had to be all business. Too much could go wrong otherwise.

Needing a minute to herself, Melina headed back to her office. Dropping down onto the small couch, she took off her shoes and rubbed her throbbing feet. The dull pain in her back was still there, but she felt better now that she was off her feet. Maybe if she laid down for a quick nap she'd feel even better. Stretching out on the couch, Melina closed her eyes and was soon asleep.

When Melina opened her eyes again, she didn't know how long she'd been asleep. But she knew why her dress was wet, and it wasn't because she'd peed on herself. Sitting up slowly, she cried out as a stabbing pain hit her. She took a breath hoping that it would soon pass. It did and then another pain hit her just as sharply.

Fuck. She was in labor.

Her son was ready to make his way into the world.

Gingerly getting up from the couch, she walked over to her desk and searched through her purse for her phone. When she found it, she quickly dialed her husband. His phone continued to ring, and she doubled over as another contraction hit her.

"Hey, doll."

"I'm in labor," she panted.

"You're in what?" Mac yelled.

"Damn it, I'm in labor. Are you deaf?"

"Where are you?"

"At the club. In my office."

"How long have you been in labor?"

"Like I know. I just took a nap, and when I woke up my water had already broken."

Melina clutched the desk and gasped as another pain tore through her.

"I'm on my way, doll."

"Hurry, Mac."

Melina ended the call and waddled back to the couch. Just as she sat down, Erika entered her office.

The tall, pixie-haired Doll rushed over to her. "Oh, my God. Melina, are you all right?"

She shook her head. "No. My water just broke."

"Shit. We have to get you to the hospital. I'm going to call an ambulance."

"No. Mac is on his way."

Erika put her hands on her hips and frowned. "We don't have time to wait for Mac. You need to get to the hospital now."

"I'm fine. I can hang on until he gets here."

Erika sat down beside her on the couch and placed her hand on Melina's stomach, while glancing at her watch. "How far apart are the contractions?"

"I don't know. I haven't been paying attention."

"Melina!" Erika shrieked.

"I told you, I'm ..."

The rest of her sentence was cut off by another

contraction. Melina grabbed her belly and sucked in a breath to keep from crying out.

"You are not fine. You need to be at the hospital getting your ass an epidural before it's too late for you to have one."

Melina glared at her former cellmate and now employee. "When the hell did you get so bossy?"

"When my friend's pregnancy brain is making her act foolish instead of cool-headed like she normally is. If your husband isn't here in the next ten minutes, I don't care what you say, the ambulance will be called."

Melina gritted her teeth. Erika was being pushy as hell, but she understood why. This was her first birth. Anything could happen.

"Fine. Ten minutes."

Melina closed her eyes as another contraction hit, and sent up a silent prayer that Mac would be there soon.

"Doll, are you sure about this natural birth?"

Melina glared at her husband. "I think it's a little late for you to be asking me that now, isn't it?"

By the time Melina had finally made it to the hospital, she was already dilated five centimeters. That was hours ago. Mac paced the length of the hospital room, and for every step he took Melina's aggravation increased.

"I can't help I got held up in traffic. You should've let Erika call an ambulance for you."

Melina opened her mouth but quickly closed it as another contraction hit her. She bit her lip. They were coming together, closer and closer. It wouldn't be long now.

"I didn't want to ride in the back of a bumpy ambulance. And besides, this is the most important day of our life together. I wanted to wait for my husband."

Mac finally stopped his pacing and took a seat in the chair next to her bedside. He took her hand in his. Melina tried not to grimace, but she couldn't help the whimper that escaped her lips as another wave of pain hit her body. They were silent a moment, watching the various monitors she was connected to that monitored her vitals and their son's heartbeat.

"We still haven't decided on a name," Mac said quietly.

"I know, but I think once we see him we'll know."

"Yeah?"

"Yeah."

Melina smiled at Mac. Though he hadn't said anything, she could see worry etched in the lines of his face. Her pregnancy had been a normal one, but there was always risk associated with childbirth. She knew that was what had her husband concerned now.

"Both of us are going to be all right. You don't have to worry," Melina assured him.

"Who said I was worried?"

"I know you better than anyone."

"Yes, you do and I couldn't ask for a better partner in this life, Melina."

Melina cocked a brow. "So does that mean I can count on you to give me a spectacular push present?"

"What's a push present?"

"Husband of mine, you really are living in the dark ages. A push present is a really nice gift a husband gives to his wife for having his child."

"You definitely deserve one for what you're enduring. Anything you want."

Melina laughed. "You know I'm just jerking your chain, right? The only things I need in this world are you and our son. That's all that really matters."

Mac leaned over and kissed her softly on the lips and just as he pulled away, Melina screamed.

"What's wrong?"

"I need to push."

Quickly, she pressed the call bell that would bring a nurse to her bedside.

"What can I do?" Mac asked. He looked helpless.

"Just keep holding my hand."

Less than a minute later, nurses and a doctor rushed into the room.

"Mrs. Maccari, let's see how far you're dilated," Dr. Adams said.

"I'm ready. I need to push now," Melina told him.

The doctor ignored her and lifted the sheet off her legs, but Melina couldn't hold back any longer. As another contraction hit her, she pushed as hard as she could. She tried to maintain the deep breathing exercises that she'd been instructed were so helpful, but the force of the first push left her gasping for air.

"All right, Melina you're doing fine. Give me another push," Dr. Adams said.

Melina looked at her husband and squeezed his hand tighter. He offered her an encouraging smile.

"Right here with you, doll."

Melina nodded and pushed with the next contraction. Her body felt as if it was ripping in two. Her vagina hurt in a way it never had as she continued to push with the contractions.

"Almost there, Mrs. Maccari. I can see the baby's head," Dr. Adams said.

Melina rested back against the pillows as beads of sweat ran down her forehead.

"I just … need … a minute," she gasped.

Mac pressed a cool cloth to her forehead. "You're doing just fine, Melina."

"I'm so tired."

"You're almost done, Mrs. Maccari. A few more pushes, and your son will be in your arms."

Melina nodded, her body still in fiery pain as she

leaned forward and bore down as hard as she could. Her body begged for relief, and her lungs screamed for air but she couldn't stop. Not now.

"His head is out, doll. Keep pushing!" Mac said.

She looked down but the drape over her legs hid everything. She wanted to see their son so badly. With a final scream, Melina pushed again as hard and as long as she could. She fell back against the pillows and closed her eyes, completely exhausted. And she heard her son's cry, loud and lusty.

"Congratulations, Mr. and Mrs. Maccari. You have a beautiful, healthy baby boy."

Hours later, Mac and Melina were enclosed in a private room. Though her body still ached, with a dull pain, it didn't matter. She'd do it all over again if it meant having this precious angel in her arms. Swaddled in a soft blue blanket, Melina held her son. He was the most precious thing she'd ever seen.

"Melina, he's perfect," Mac said.

She looked at her husband and wasn't surprised to see his eyes glistening as well.

"Yes, he is."

Melina gazed at her son, noting his head full of black hair and small perfect features. He had her nose for certain, but the curve of his lips and the shape of his brow were all Mac. She wondered what color his eyes would be.

"He looks like you, Mac."

Her husband took their son's tiny hand. Reflexively, the little hand curled around Mac's pointer finger.

"Yeah, but he has your nose."

"That's about it though."

The baby stirred in her arms, and Melina smiled as

she noted the baby attempting to open his eyes. Melina held her breath as she continued to watch her son ever so slowly open his eyes.

"I'd say his eyes are all yours, doll."

Melina couldn't help the smile that crossed her face as she gazed into eyes so much like her own. Deep, amber pools of light met hers.

"Hi there, handsome," Melina said to the baby.

"Now being handsome, he got from his dad," Mac said.

Melina elbowed her husband. "Smartass."

"You love it."

Mac kissed Melina, and she responded easily. It was amazing the connection they had. The ease in every touch, every look they exchanged. Mac was her soulmate now and always. She was as sure of that as she was of her name. Speaking of names.

"Mac, we still haven't decided on a name. I think I have one in mind," she pointed out.

"Well don't keep me in suspense."

"How about Marquise? I know it's not a common name, but it's still Italian."

Melina bit her lip as she glanced at Mac, gauging his reaction.

"Marquise, huh?"

"Marquise Maccari," Melina said softly.

"It does have a certain ring to it. I like it."

"You hear that, Marquise? Your dad is in agreement for once in his life."

Marquise seemed to smile at her comment.

"Happy wife. Happy life. I learned that lesson a while ago."

"I'll make sure to remind you of this conversation ten years from now," Melina said.

Smiling at her son, a fresh wave of tears blurred her eyes. She tried to hold them back. This was a happy day. The happiest day of her life, but yet she suddenly ached for the voids that couldn't be filled.

"Melina?" Mac put his finger under her chin. "Talk to me."

She wiped her face before the tears could fall on Marquise. "I'm not sure how to put it into words."

Mac pressed a kiss to her forehead. "Try."

Melina chewed on her lip for a moment before she spoke. "I don't think there could be anything more wonderful than having you and Marquise. I know it's selfish for me to take anything away from this moment, but … my parents … I wish they were here."

Her tears flowed anew, and Melina could've sworn baby Marquise frowned as she cried. She smiled at him through her tears as Mac pulled her into the circle of his arms. His chin rested atop her head.

"You don't have a selfish bone in your body and on a day like this, I'd be worried if you hadn't thought about your parents. There's nothing wrong with you wishing they were here."

Melina looked at her husband. "You really don't think I'm spoiling our son's birth with all this crying? I'm not usually like this."

"Of course not, doll. I was just thinking why don't we give him Daniel as a middle name?"

"I think I'd like that," Melina said softly.

Mac was such a dichotomy of a man. Strong, but yet loving in a way others could never truly understand or appreciate. His acknowledgment of her pain, and his heartfelt desire to honor her feelings only made her feel as if she was falling in love with him all over again. Before she could say anything, the door to her hospital room burst open. She couldn't see who had entered behind the masses of balloons and gifts.

"All right, give him up. Let me see my first grandchild."

As the balloons were carefully herded into a corner, Cynthia Maccari and Mac's sister, Victoria, crowded around Melina's bed.

"He's beautiful. Finally, bro, you did something right," Victoria said.

"Stop being such a smartass," Cynthia said.

Melina laughed. "Wow. I think that is the first time I've ever heard you curse."

"Me, too," Mac said. "Wonders never cease."

Cynthia waved her son away as she reached for the baby. Gently, Melina handed her mother-in-law her precious bundle. Marquise wiggled as he was handed off to his grandmother. Melina held her husband's hand as his mother cooed and awed over their son.

"He looks so much like you, Mac. The resemblance is uncanny," Cynthia said.

"The Maccari genes are strong, but at least he has Melina's eyes," Victoria said.

"With babies this beautiful from the two of you, I'm definitely going to be looking forward to more grandchildren."

Mac coughed. Loudly. "Me too."

"You two are really full of it. I just had a natural birth where I cannot even begin to describe the amount of pain I endured, and you two are already planning for more babies."

"Melina, you really are a wonder woman. Natural? No, thank you," Victoria said.

Cynthia smiled down at Marquise. "Point taken. How about I mention it again in about six months? This little angel is going to need a sibling."

Despite the absurdity of the situation, Melina laughed. For better or worse, this was her family. No matter what happened tomorrow or the day after, nothing in the world could spoil this magical moment

It had been three days since Melina was released from the hospital, and little Marquise had surprisingly given her and Mac very little trouble. At first she'd wondered if their son was going to be one of those babies that cried all the time and refused to sleep like some of the horror stories she'd heard about new babies. So far that hadn't been the case. Marquise seemed to sleep in two hour intervals and awakened promptly for his feedings. They'd tried breastfeeding in the hospital, but her milk hadn't come fast enough to satisfy her son, so he was now happily bottle-fed.

Mac was equally sharing all of their parental responsibilities and for that she would always be thankful. Sleeping in intervals was a new thing for the both of them, but they were managing the new change in their lives well. Marquise not only had his father's looks but Mac's temperament as well. Rarely did their son fuss or cry. At the moment, their little bundle of happiness was curled in Melina's arms staring at her intently.

"Mommy's not getting any of these thank you cards written because she can't stop staring at you, Marquise. You're too precious for words."

She loved talking to him like this.

Holding him like this.

Watching him grow day by day.

Melina felt fulfilled in a way she'd never thought could be possible.

"I don't think that anyone will hold it against you, doll."

Mac entered the living room dressed in a tailored black suit and sat down beside her on the couch.

"I don't know. Some might say having a baby doesn't excuse good manners," Melina teased.

"With the mountain of gifts we've received, I'm positive the people will understand."

"To be honest I might be procrastinating a bit with

the thank you cards."

"And why is that?" Mac reached for Marquise's hand and allowed the tiny fingers to curl around his own pointer finger.

"I thought some of them might come by and I could thank them in person, especially Neeya. I haven't seen or heard from her at all."

Mac took Marquise from her arms and held his son, but Melina didn't miss the subtle tensing in his shoulders.

"Mac, what do you know?"

"What makes you think I know anything?"

Melina cocked a brow. "You tensed up when I mentioned her. Now spill."

"Neeya's been busy as of late."

"Luca is still behind bars. I'm sure she's working with lawyers trying to get him out. I can understand."

Mac shook his head. "It's not that."

"Then what is it? Why are you being so cryptic? Is she all right?"

"She's fine, if you consider selling everything she owns and liquidating her assets fine."

"What?" Melina asked.

"Yeah."

Melina frowned. What Mac was saying didn't make any sense? The Neeya she knew would be fighting tooth and nail to get her husband home and fighting anyone that got in her way. What Mac was telling her sounded like … no …

"Is Neeya leaving Luca?"

Marquise made a noise, and they both looked at him. Mac rubbed a thumb across their son's cheek.

"I don't know."

"I see."

Melina was quiet as the possible ramifications of a Pivetti split ran through her mind.

"So what happens now?" she finally asked.

"I don't have any answers right now, but maybe my

meeting will shed some light on things."

"Meeting with?"

"Luca."

"Mmhmm. I knew there was a reason you were extra snazzy."

Mac cocked a brow. "Snazzy?"

Melina rolled her eyes. "You've never heard that word before? Seriously?"

"No."

"It means dressed extra well. Looking extra nice."

"You learn something new every day," Mac said before he pressed a kiss to Marquise's cheeks.

"Yes. We do."

Mac looked at her, a small furrow forming between his brows. "I don't want you to worry."

"How can you expect me not to? It's not just us to consider. We have our son, too," Melina pointed out.

"Fuck, I know that."

In Mac's lap, Marquise whined. "I'm sorry, little man," he apologized before turning to her. "I'll be the first to admit things are a little shaky right now, but I live and breathe for you and our son. I will battle the Devil himself to keep you safe."

Melina leaned into her husband. "I know. I'm not doubting you. You know I'm always in your corner."

"Yeah. It's one of the reasons I married you. Love and loyalty like yours is hard to come by."

"Likewise. You go and handle your business. Marquise and I will be fine."

Mac nodded and gave her back their son before he pulled her close and kissed her. Their lips melded together in a kiss that spoke of love and a sweet, yet hot passion. When Mac drew away, Melina already missed the touch of his lips on hers.

"If you keep kissing me like that, doll, we're going to have a problem."

He stood up and looked at her with desire in his eyes.

"You and I have a while before we can engage in any of that activity again, Mr. Maccari."

He shrugged. "Doesn't mean I'm not thinking about it every time I look at you. Pregnancy has been exceedingly good to you, wife."

Melina made a shooing motion with her hands. "Stop making me horny and go to your meeting, Mac."

"All right. I'll see the two of you when I get back. Love you, doll."

"We love you, too."

Melina leaned back on the sofa as she heard Mac turn on the alarm before he exited the house. Alone with her son, Melina resolved to do her best not to worry. One thing Mac excelled in was handling his business. In retrospect, she had to wonder exactly how long he'd been sitting on this information about his boss's wife. She'd been so wrapped up in her bubble of happiness that she hadn't thought once about the Pivetti Organization. Perhaps she should have. Perhaps these few days were just an idyllic lull of happiness before another tsunami hit their lives. For once, she hoped she was wrong.

CHAPTER THREE

The jail was cold from the outside looking in, but it was far colder the very second Mac stepped foot inside the building. It was a simple, yet effective, reminder to Mac, how fragile a person's freedom really was in the grand scheme of things. In an instant, and without any sort of warning, that freedom could be taken away.

Luca certainly hadn't been given any warning before his arrest.

The thought bothered Mac more than he was willing to admit.

Mac's mind traveled to his wife and newborn son at home, and for a split second, he wavered in his desire to go further inside the jail. His boss was his boss, no doubt about it. Mac always followed the rules of Cosa Nostra, which included never shunning a boss when he called on a man. The moment Mac had gotten word from Enric that Luca Pivetti wanted a meeting, then he had no other choice but to follow through.

He had to see the boss.

But Mac had never been more aware than he was in that moment of just how much of his own freedom he was risking to be there.

As it was, Mac was already on the officials' radar.

All the Pivetti men were.

It was a major source of discontent between the men

in the Pivetti Organization. With a likely rat amongst their ranks, trust between any of them was a beautiful myth. It was no wonder that not a single Capo was willing to work with another, and that the men took any chance given to point out another man's flaws or culpabilities.

Despite how uneasy it made Mac to be at the jail, he walked further inside, strolling up to a waiting receptionist, sitting behind a Plexiglas window. The woman barely glanced at Mac as she typed on a keyboard and snapped a wad of gum in her mouth.

Mac's patience wore thin the longer he waited on the woman to, at the very least, acknowledge him. "Hello?"

The woman cocked a brow and looked up at Mac. "Visitation or request?"

"Pardon?"

"Are you visiting a detainee, or requesting a meeting with a detective on the Precinct level?"

"Visiting a detainee."

The woman shoved a clipboard through the rectangular shaped hole in the bottom of the Plexiglas window, pushing through a pen to drop on top of the papers. "Fill out the paperwork. You can sit over there."

She pointed to a small waiting area that sported hard chairs, one coffee table, and magazines that looked to be older than the fucking hills.

"Don't ask me for help," she added, "because I don't have time."

Well, what the fuck was she even there for?

Mac didn't bother to let the woman's attitude bother him, instead snatching up the items and making a beeline for one of the many chairs in the waiting area. Once seated, with his back turned to the woman and her snapping gum, he looked over the papers.

Pretty standard shit.

ID information.

Visitation request information.

It was basically a log of who he was, where he could

be found or contacted, and who he was there to visit. Mac didn't understand why the woman had made such a big deal about someone needing help because it was pretty basic nonsense. Or maybe he found the form easy to fill out because this wasn't his first rodeo with jail or prison visitation.

Mac went down through the questions, filling them out rather quickly. It didn't even take him ten minutes before he was back in front of the Plexiglas window and pushing the clipboard and pen back through. He pulled out his wallet, providing picture ID to be taken and photocopied, as the form requested.

Silently, the woman went to work inputting the information onto her computer and photocopying his ID before handing it back.

Mac shoved the license back into his wallet just as the woman pointed to the waiting area again. "It'll be a few minutes."

Wonderful.

Mac waited another thirty minutes, long enough for more people to file in, wanting visitations themselves, and filling up the seats all around him. A guard came through a large metal door, calling his name and waving him in.

Security in the jail was not as tight as security in a prison, he found. He still went through a metal detector, and had to give up his wallet and coat. His shoes were also taken and put through the metal detector before he was allowed to put them back on. But, it was easier and quicker than getting checked at security in the prison … or even an airport, actually.

Mac was directed to yet another seating area, only the chairs faced Plexiglas windows where empty seats waited on the other side of the glass for the inmates. Small, thin separator walls were erected between each section as if to give some sense of privacy, although Mac figured that was more for show than anything else.

There were cameras all around. He had zero doubt

that the phones provided to talk into would also record their conversation. No one expected privacy in lockup.

It was yet another reason why Mac felt this meeting was a little strange for Luca. The man was more than capable of putting out information through his new lawyer to pass along to his men, if needed. He didn't need face to face meetings that would be recorded for the officials' benefit.

Nonetheless, Mac took a seat and waited for the boss to show up on the other side of the glass. It wasn't long before Luca came into view, shadowed closely by a guard with keys in his hand that he used to unlock the boss's cuffs before he was allowed to sit on his chair, facing Mac. The drab, gray uniform and five o'clock shadow Luca sported was an unusual sight for the normally well-dressed, clean-cut Cosa Nostra Don.

The man looked tired, his eyes dimmed, and the lines on his aging face far more prominent than they had ever been before. He moved a bit slower than he normally would, too, another sign that something was off with Luca Pivetti.

This was not the boss Mac was accustomed to.

He wondered if it was jail that was taking its toll on Luca, or something else. Something like ... perhaps the man's wife appearing to rid her life of him and all the things they shared together, right down to putting their large mansion on the market, ready to sell.

That would certainly take a toll on Mac.

Luca nodded at the phone attached to the wall on Mac's side as he picked up his own. Mac put the phone to his ear, waiting for Luca to speak first.

"Congratulations are in order, or so I hear," the boss said, a slight smile warming his usually cold features.

"For what?"

"You have a boy, don't you?"

Mac smiled. "I do—just a few days old."

"Congratulations. His name?"

"Marquise Daniel."

Luca chuckled, the sound cracking through the speakers. "Certainly ... a different name than I was expecting."

"Melina wanted something special."

"Still Italian."

Mac nodded. "It is."

"I'm sorry I couldn't celebrate it with you properly—all made men should have the birth of their children celebrated by their boss." Luca's gaze dropped to the small ledge in front of the window that separated them as he added, "I remember my father celebrating my first daughter's birth; he made sure to tell me to make sure I planted the seed of a boy the next go-round."

"That didn't work out, huh?"

Luca had three girls with his wife, and his only son had come from a relationship with a woman that had come shortly before his marriage to Neeya.

Luca shrugged. "Thank God he died before my second daughter came along, so then I didn't have to hear him complain more. Do you have a picture?"

"Of what?"

"Your boy—what else? Show me."

Surprised that *this* was what his boss had called him to the jail for, Mac decided it wasn't his place to question it. He pulled out his cellphone from his pocket, bringing up the gallery and choosing from one of the many pictures he'd taken of Marquise since the baby boy's birth to show Luca.

Holding the phone up for Luca to see, the boss smiled again.

"Took after you, Mac," Luca noted.

Mac chuckled. "Everybody keeps pointing it out."

"You're awfully smug about it."

"Weren't you?"

Luca smirked. "It's a man thing. Healthy?"

"Big and loud," Mac assured.

"That's all that matters. It's the most important part, you know."

He did know, but he also had the feeling this whole conversation, this light banter and chatting about the newborn son Mac now toted, was just a prologue for the boss into a more … difficult topic. The shift in atmosphere became apparent the very second Luca turned quiet on the other end of the phone.

It took Mac less than a second to know exactly what was wrong with his boss. Here they were, discussing his newly growing family, while Luca was locked away from his own wife and daughters, not to mention Neeya's recent behavior.

"Sorry, boss," Mac said.

Luca glanced up, his gaze meeting Mac's unflinchingly. "For what? This was good—first time I've smiled in days, actually."

Still …

"Have your kids been around to see you?" Mac asked, carefully choosing his words.

"Enric has been here a few times."

"And the girls? Neeya?"

Luca frowned. "She came once with the girls."

The boss offered nothing else, and Mac chose not to push. Should Luca wish to discuss something particular about his wife, or the rumors floating amongst the Pivetti men that Neeya was selling everything she owned, he would bring it up.

"Have you taken Enric over to see his sisters yet?" Luca asked.

Mac shook his head. "Things got rushed with moving into the new house and then Marquise making his way a little earlier than expected."

Luca waved it all off. "No worries; take him when you can."

"He's not …"

The boss met Mac's gaze when he trailed off,

42

seemingly picking up on the hesitance in his tone. "He's not, what?"

"Keeping his appointments for his therapy. He works; he never complains about what I ask him to do. He's self-sufficient, even in his state. I can't make a fuss about that, you know?"

"But he's not putting in the effort elsewhere," Luca filled in.

"He could walk again if he just put in the effort, Luca."

"Enric is more like me than I realized—he's stubborn."

Mac nodded, agreeing. "Yeah, I know."

"Let him do these things on his own time, at his own pace."

Mac filed that advice away for a later date, hoping it would come in handy where Enric was concerned. It was one thing for Mac to tell Luca that his oldest and *only* son was too fucking stubborn to deal with the pain and emotion and dedication it would take to get on his feet again, but it was another thing to explain to the man that Enric's attitude and outlook was … bleak.

Depression was a bitch.

He didn't know how to help Enric claw his way out of it.

"Tell me about the streets, my people," Luca said.

Mac's stare flicked up to the security cameras trained on them, unease settling in the pit of his stomach. "It's a mess. Work is impossible. Issues are endless."

He figured that was the best, and cleanest, way of explaining the problems facing the Pivetti Organization and the men within its ranks, without outing all the dirty details for the officials to look over at the same time.

Mac had to be careful—so did Luca.

Luca scowled. "I bet."

"You can't expect them all to get along and work together when there is no hierarchy to keep them in line, boss."

"There is a hierarchy; they've simply forgotten we're just indisposed for a moment. That doesn't mean we're useless."

That was true enough.

"If even one of you was out—"

"Enzo might get a release when his bail hearing is refiled," Luca interrupted.

Mac's head snapped up at that with his concern growing. He already had enough problems with the men of the family as it was with Luca in lockup, and the other Capos causing issues with him at every little turn. Enzo certainly wouldn't help that situation if he was released, if only because he held a grudge for Mac, as he had been the one to kill his son and made no secret about doing so.

"I can see what you won't say written all over your face," Luca murmured into the phone. "Worry not—Enzo has much more to worry about, to deal with, than little old you, Mac."

"With you behind bars, he could do away with me before you even knew something had happened."

Luca smiled thinly. "Family before vendettas, Mac."

"To you, sure. For me, absolutely. We're not every man. We're only our own men, Luca."

The boss sighed heavily, and Mac took that as a sign of the man's agreement to what he had said.

"If he does get out—it's a long shot—do what you need to, be careful," Luca said. "As for the troublemakers still making it impossible to get anything done, remind them that their boss is watching. He knows what they are doing, and their mistakes will still be corrected when I am able."

Mac tipped his chin up. "You're asking me to deliver messages to the Capos?"

"Who better to do it?"

"Won't that …"

"Hmm?"

"It makes me a go-between for you and them."

Luca's brow raised. "It puts you in a better position than them, yes. As I said, who better to do it?"

Well ...

Luca said it.

Not Mac.

"Are you sure everything is okay, doll?" Mac asked as he pulled his car into a smooth parallel park on the side street.

Melina sighed. "He's just fussy, don't panic."

Well, he wasn't panicking, not really. But he could hear little Marquise wailing in the background, and Mac wished he was there to help his wife, and soothe his son at the same time. He'd been gone for most of the damn day, and it wasn't looking like he would be getting home anytime soon.

He'd gotten a call from another Capo—Carlos—that Anthony Corelli was holding a meeting at one of his regular haunts for the rest of the men, and Mac should be there. He had only just left the prison, with getting home to his wife and son on his mind, when he'd gotten the call.

Anthony didn't—and shouldn't—be calling meetings. He didn't have the pull to call men off the streets and bid them to show up wherever the fuck he wanted them to.

It just pushed all of Mac's buttons without even trying.

The *wrong* buttons.

Marquise wailed again, louder and fiercer, bringing Mac back to the call at hand.

"I'll be home as quick as I can," Mac assured. "Why don't you call Ma?"

"Because," Melina muttered, "I can handle a crying

baby on my own."

Sure, she could.

Mac didn't doubt that for a second.

But she was also alone for a large portion of her time, and she rarely asked for help. Mac fully believed sometimes, his wife just needed a few minutes to decompress, as all mothers did.

Good mothers.

"Call Ma," Mac said one final time, firmly, making sure not to give his wife more room to argue. "I know you can handle it, doll, but sometimes a break is just good for the soul. She'll have him happy, cooing, and sleeping in no time."

Melina sighed. "Fine."

"Thank you."

"I'm not cooking tonight, either," she added.

Mac chuckled. "I will bring something home."

"Works for me."

With a quick *I love you*, his wife hung up the call, and Mac shoved the phone into his jacket pocket before pulling the keys from the car's ignition. He eyed the small business across the street where he needed to go, taking in the spinning barber pole on the side of the front window.

Paul's Barber Shop, the window decals read.

Anthony owned a large stake in the place, while his old uncle was the man wielding the scissors and clippers. All over again, Mac found himself annoyed that Anthony felt he had any right to call a meeting of the Capos, as though he could shout for them to jump, and their only appropriate response was to clamor back by immediately asking how high.

It felt ... wrong.

Mac believed because the highest men in the Pivetti Organization were currently locked away, Anthony was making a move. The snake likely figured his age and time in the family gave him the pull to do whatever in the hell he wanted.

For now, Mac would play along.

If only to keep the peace.

But he wasn't guaranteeing how long that would last.

Mac slipped out of his car and quickly crossed the quiet street, entering the barber shop without so much as a look over his shoulder to see if someone was watching him. He doubted Anthony was stupid enough to call a meeting at a place that was watched by the Feds, but it was becoming all too common for them to have … eyes watching.

"Good of you to finally show up," Anthony said, passing Mac a dismissive glance.

Mac took in the scene in front of him, unsure of what exactly it was that he was currently seeing.

Nothing was right here, he thought.

It was all wrong.

Anthony sat in the barber's chair, a black cloak around his shoulders and white foam on his face as his head was tipped back, and an exceptionally sharp razor blade was brought down to his skin, starting at his jawline.

But that … that wasn't the problem.

The Capos stood around the room, a good half a dozen of them, with their hands at their fronts, clasped and waiting for the meeting to begin. Waiting, it seemed, on the man in the chair to finish his business.

Anthony looked to be a king sitting there, having his face shaved while his *people* waited on him to conclude before they inserted their presences.

No man in the mafia waited on any man like these ones were currently doing for Anthony. That sort of behavior was reserved solely for the boss, and his closest men, and not for anyone else.

What in the hell did Anthony think he was pulling here?

"Busy day," Mac explained.

Anthony looked over to him again, careful not to move lest his uncle's blade slit his throat. That wouldn't be such a bad thing in Mac's perspective. "Is that so?"

He owed Anthony fuck all.

Certainly *not* an explanation.

But for the sake of the other men in the room, Mac would talk, if only to get Luca's message out in the open while at the same time, reminding them all that they actually *did* have a fucking boss to answer to.

And it wasn't the king-in-pretending sitting in the chair.

"Luca called me in," Mac said simply, "and we had a good chat."

Silence filled the room, but Mac felt the gazes of all the Capos, including Antony, turn on him.

Mac continued speaking *before* Anthony could join in. "The boss isn't impressed with the nonsense that's been going on in the streets between the crews and Capos. He hears everything, even when we think he doesn't. The more problems that get made while he's away, the messier it's going to be when he gets out and decides to clean house."

Anthony pushed up from the chair, sitting straight, his face only half shaven. "Oh?"

"I didn't stutter, Anthony."

"Seems Luca thinks those RICO charges are just going to … fly away."

Mac refused to discuss Luca's legal problems—it wasn't his place. The man would have to deal with his charges and what he planned to do about them on his own time; the rest remained the same.

"He's still the boss either way—a Don is a Don is a Don, Anthony," Mac said quietly.

Anthony nodded once, and then rested back in the chair, letting his uncle get back to work on his face. "This is true, maybe the only thing that is true, actually."

Mac wasn't willing to argue that point, either. "Why are we here? You wanted something, what was it?"

"We can wait for my shave to finish, can't we?"

Like fuck.

"I have shit to do," Mac replied, "places to be, and it isn't here. I wait on one man and one woman, and you don't fit either of their descriptions."

There, Mac said it.

For himself.

For the other Capos.

Let Anthony make of that what he wanted.

A tic worked in Anthony's jaw. His only show of irritation.

Good.

Mac was pleased his point hit its intended target.

"Almost finished," the man wielding the razor said.

"Hurry it up," Mac urged with a smirk.

Anthony sighed harshly, trying to gain back some of his composure while his uncle finished the right side of his jaw, and Mac took his place against the wall. It kept his back protected, while he watched the rest of the men.

At least, the Capos finally seemed a bit more relaxed.

Mac mentally patted himself on the back for that.

Once Anthony had finally finished, his face was wiped clean of any shaving foam, and he was standing again, the older Capo straightened his suit jacket and nodded at a man waiting in the doorway that led to the private rooms in the back of the barber shop.

"Seems we're still having problems with men in crews being ... how shall I say it ... enticed by officials," Anthony said.

Mac's brow furrowed, but he chose to stay silent. It wasn't *news* that a lot of Capos were having problems with their young soldiers and the officials that were always on their asses. It was something they all had to keep an eye on just to make sure no one weeded their way into a crew for information.

They already had one rat to find and dispose of.

They didn't need more.

What was happening?

The man in the doorway turned and disappeared, coming back less than thirty seconds later with a bound, gagged, and blindfolded man that was dressed in only a T-shirt and boxers. Even his feet were bare, and looked to be raw, probably from being dragged around. Mac didn't recognize the young man at first, but once the blindfold was removed he realized it was a young soldier from Anthony's crew.

A rather disposable soldier, as most were, but still …

"I'm making an example for the rest of you," Anthony said, his tone ringing like a warning as he pulled a gun from his jacket pocket, and then a long silencer from his outer pocket. "Start cleaning up your crews. This is getting ridiculous."

The young boy's eyes flew wide, finding no sympathy in Anthony as the Capo screwed the silencer into the gun and stepped forward. He tried to say something behind his gag, but it was impossible to understand.

No one got the chance to move or say a thing before Anthony pulled the trigger, putting a bullet between the young man's eyes.

Mac's spine straightened as the body slumped to the floor, a small trickle of blood trailing down the cracks in the wood floor.

"What the fuck?" someone asked.

What the fuck was appropriate.

No one just *killed* someone, even if it was a solider, in a business out in the fucking open where anyone could see.

It was stupid.

Anthony didn't seem to care. "I am not going to jail because the rest of you idiots are too *affected* by the people in your crews to do what you need to do. If you don't start fixing the problems, *I* will."

Mac's jaw ached from clenching so hard.

He heard Anthony loud and clear.

The man was making moves—small ones, seemingly

unnoticeable ones in the grand scheme of shit that was happening, but he was still making the moves to appear in power.

Mac didn't like that at all.

He wasn't playing along anymore.

CHAPTER FOUR

Trouble was in the air.

Melina was certain of it.

Though Mac hadn't said much about the particulars of his meeting with Luca, when he had returned home, his mood had been off. He'd played with their son, given Marquise his bath and bottle before putting him to bed. She'd waited for Mac to say something, but he hadn't. He had simply pulled her into his arms as they lay in bed, while he half-heartedly watched a football game.

Part of her had wanted to press him, but she knew her husband. Mac would talk to her about what he could when he was ready. She just needed to give him time. That had been two days ago.

"Doll?"

Melina opened one eye and looked at her husband. The warmth and comfort of their bed made the thought of moving a distressing one.

"Yeah?"

"I just got a call. Your presence has been requested at the Pivetti mansion."

Melina opened both eyes and rolled over. "When?"

"At ten for brunch."

She groaned. "Not that I don't love the idea of seeing Neeya, but Marquise is still asleep. I was looking forward to attempting to sleep in today."

Mac ran his fingers through her hair, gently massaging her scalp. "I know. You've been absolutely amazing. It's like you're Superwoman or something."

"I'm glad you've noticed. That boy is your son through and through."

"Yes, he is. Our son is the greatest gift you could ever have given me."

Mac's voice was rich with emotion. Melina moved closer to her husband, cupping his face in her hands.

"Talk to me."

Mac moved his head so that he could kiss the palm of her hand. "I'm good."

She shook her head. "No, you're not. I've given you time, but your mood hasn't changed since you met with Luca."

"Things went fine with Luca," Mac said.

"Is that so?"

"Yeah. I showed him pictures of Marquise, and he offered me his congratulations. It made him reflect on some things."

"Like?" Melina snuggled into the curve of Mac's arm.

"The birth of his first daughter. Enric, too."

"It must be tearing him up inside to be away from his children, especially with everything Enric's gone through."

"He knows Enric is stubborn like him, but that doesn't make it any easier."

"Why don't you bring Enric to see his sisters while I visit with Neeya? I'm sure it would be good for all of them," Melina suggested.

"Yeah. I'll do that. It was in the plans."

Melina cleared her throat. "Well, if it wasn't your visit with Luca that changed your mood then what was it?"

Mac was quiet, and Melina watched the plains of his handsome face. He was waging a war internally with himself. There was a fine line between confiding in her, and betraying the confidences of what made the mafia the organization it was.

"Let's just say that in a truly loyal family, even if the boss was going away for a while, it wouldn't matter. There would be a natural order to things."

"But in this case, there's still unrest," Melina finished.

Mac nodded. "Unrest and greed corrupt even the noblest of men. At the same time, those with no regard for what someone else has built have no problems with tearing down an empire, no matter how fucking wonderful it is."

Her husband had said a mouthful.

"Someone's feeling themselves a little too much and ready to make a power grab."

"Yeah."

"Doesn't take a rocket scientist to figure out it's everyone's favorite Capo," Melina said. She sat up and crossed her arms. "What are you going to do about it?"

Mac frowned. "I'm not the boss."

"I never said you were. I just asked what you were going to do because you and I both know that man likes to deliberately push your buttons. The last thing anyone needs is more attention from the cops or the Feds."

"I won't disagree with you there. We're walking a fine line right now." Mac's brow knitted together.

"Exactly. So, as usual I am going to trust that you will continue to handle your shit, but make no mistake, if need be, I am ready, willing and able to go Bonnie Parker on somebody's ass."

Mac laughed, a large grin splitting across his face. "You don't need to remind me. I'm well aware I'm married to the best gangster moll a man could ever ask for."

"Yeah, and don't you forget it."

Melina kissed Mac softly before she pulled back to look at him. There it was. The fire in his hazel eyes that she loved. It was a fire that never ceased to scorch her soul.

"Never," Mac promised.

"Good, because with all seriousness, that is one *job* I

would be glad to do."

Mac kissed the bridge of her nose. "I didn't imagine motherhood would make you this antsy, doll. I thought you'd still be caught up in the glow of being a new mom."

"I am. Our son is the best thing I've done in life, and the reason why I'm extra concerned about any unrest a certain asshole is stirring up."

"I don't want you to worry. I'm handling things in the parameters I'm able to."

"Then that's all I need to know."

A loud wail drew their attention.

"Sounds like my boy is awake," Mac said.

He got out of bed and before Melina could say a word, he was heading to the nursery. She leaned back against the headboard as she waited for Mac to bring Marquise into their bedroom. Mac was downplaying things to a certain extent, but she trusted her husband. He would protect their family, while at the same time, maintaining his loyalty to Cosa Nostra. One thing Mac had always been was a man of duality. He could move between worlds and handle multiple situations.

"Look who's awake and happy to see his dad."

Melina smiled as Mac came into their bedroom, holding Marquise. Sure enough, their precious baby looked as if he was smiling at his father as Mac spoke softly to him. These were the moments she lived and would die for.

She knew how things worked.

She knew the role that she was supposed to play, and she would with a smile on her face.

She would love her son and support her husband.

But if the time came when Mac needed his gun moll back in action, she would be all too happy to fill that role again.

It was back to bodyguards.

At least for a while.

Though she didn't like it one little bit, Melina hadn't argued when Mac told her he was going to have a guard escort her to see Neeya while he picked up Enric. If that was what it took to put her husband at ease, she would not complain. Besides it was nice having someone around to help her carry some of the many bags and things you needed to have when you had a baby.

"We're here, Mrs. Maccari."

"Thank you, Samuel," she said to the older man before turning to her son.

Marquise stared at her with wide eyes. "You hear that, sweetness? We're here, so please be on your best behavior for Mommy."

Her son seemed to frown at her and she laughed.

"Okay. Message received."

The back door of the limousine was opened by Samuel, and Melina quickly unbuckled Marquise from his car seat. He squirmed in her arms as she exited the car.

"Would you get Marquise's bags for me?"

"Yes, ma'am."

Closing the door, Samuel got Marquise's things from the other side of the limo before he escorted them up the stairs to the front door. The Pivetti mansion had always been an imposing monstrosity in itself, but today things felt different. The winds of change were truly in the air.

Samuel knocked on the door. A few moments later it was opened by one of the same maids Melina always saw when she visited. Usually she was greeted with a smile. Today the woman simply opened the door and ushered them inside. Though for a moment, her eyes did light up when she saw Marquise.

"Melina?"

Striding into the foyer was Neeya Pivetti, dressed down in a way Melina had never seen her. At all of their meetings, the Don's wife was always wearing the height of fashion. Today she wore a simple pair of black slacks and a blue cardigan. Her normally well coifed hair was loose and kept off her bare face by a simple black headband. This was a Neeya that Melina had never seen before, and she honestly didn't know what to make of her.

"Neeya, it's wonderful to see you again."

"You too, dear. Now let me have a look at this handsome little man."

Neeya reached for Marquise, and Melina carefully handed her son to the older woman. In the back of her mind, she was silently praying her baby didn't burst into tears. Neeya's eyes lit up as she held Marquise.

"He's beautiful, Melina. I'm sure Mac is walking around like a strutting peacock."

Melina laughed as she followed Neeya down one of the large halls. Her guard followed discretely behind them.

"Maybe he's strutting just a little bit."

"And no one can blame him, dear. I knew you two would make some gorgeous babies together."

As they continued walking, Melina noticed the bare walls. Where there once had been photographs, beautiful paintings of the family, and stunning art décor, was now nothing. The mansion was eerily quiet as they went into the solarium located near the massive patio. A small glass table covered with food and four chairs was the only furniture in the room.

"Thank you for the compliment."

Neeya took a seat, still holding Marquise and staring at him intently. Melina followed suit.

"You're welcome, but I'm only speaking the truth. He has your eyes, but no one could ever doubt that Mac is his father."

"That's one less thing to worry about," Melina said lightly.

"Yes. Life does seem to have a way of giving us enough issues without us creating any unnecessary ones."

Neeya's eyes were momentarily downcast, but just as quickly as the look appeared, it was gone.

"That it does. I expected to see you at the hospital," Melina said.

Neeya held one of Marquise's hands. "I'm sorry about that, dear. I thought it would be a good time for you and your family to enjoy the blessed moment."

"You are family."

Reaching for her hand across the table, Neeya smiled. "As are you. I truly meant no offense."

"I know you didn't, but even if you didn't want to come to the hospital you could've come by the house later. Your presence was sorely missed."

Marquise started to whine, and Melina quickly grabbed a bottle from one of her baby bags, and handed it to Neeya.

"I apologize. I was sure with all the excitement of this little angel's birth, my presence wouldn't be missed."

"Neeya, I don't know what's going on, and I'm not going to ask because it's none of my business. What I am going to say is that in a lifestyle where friends are few and far in between and a real family is even rarer, you matter a lot to me. You've helped in your own way to fill a void."

Melina picked up a strawberry and bit into it. Her hostess was quiet for a moment as she gave Marquise his bottle.

"Your mother."

Melina nodded. "Yes."

"I'm honored that you would think of me that way. I've felt a connection to you since Mac first brought you around, and I'm glad to know the feelings are reciprocated. You are an extraordinary woman, Melina."

"As are you."

"Perhaps. Life has a way of reminding you that you are not as untouchable as you think."

"I'm sorry."

Neeya put Marquise's empty bottle on the table and

put him over her shoulder to burp him. "You have nothing to be sorry about, dear. We play the cards that we are dealt and hope for the best."

"Yes, but a wise woman once told me that perception is everything," Melina gently reminded her.

Raising a brow, Neeya offered her a small smile. "Indeed it is. But things are not always as they are perceived."

Before Melina could say anything the sound of girls' voices carried to them.

"Mom?"

"In here."

Melina turned as Neeya's three daughters came into the room. They too were dressed down. None of the *principessa* finery she had seen the girls in on several occasions adorned them.

"Mac just brought Enric. We're going into the theater room to hang out for a bit," the youngest said.

"Sounds like a wonderful idea. Make sure I see him before he leaves."

"Yes, Mother."

The girls left the room, but not before the oldest gave her mother the strangest of looks. Melina silently wondered what that was about.

"He's an exceptional young man. I hope he realizes his own resilience before it's too late," Neeya said.

"It's not awkward for you," Melina dared to probe.

"Not in the least. Enric was conceived before Luca and I even met. At first, I wondered if there was still some lingering feelings for Enric's mother, but once I realized that was not an issue, it was fine. It would be petty and foolhardy to treat my husband's only son as anything other than welcome."

"Not everyone would be as magnanimous." Melina took a sip of orange juice.

"Perhaps not, but the life I've lived has taught me a great many things. One of those being, you have to learn to pick and choose your battles. Why go to war over something not worth the bloodshed?"

"Especially when there are real wars brewing," Melina added.

Neeya smiled as Marquise finally burped. Moving to cradle him in her arms, she slowly started to rock him to sleep.

"Yes. The best way to win any war is to do the unexpected. There will always be vultures circling, ready to feed on the scraps. Simply don't give them any."

Melina finished a bite of the ham and egg quiche before she spoke. "Games of strategy have never been my preference. I prefer to tackle things head on, but sometimes that is not an option."

"Yes. You have an upfront personality, which is one of your endearing qualities, but there is a time and place for everything. You are in an even more important position now. Not only are you a rising Capo's wife, but you are also the mother of a made man's boy. Your worth has gone up exponentially, and that means the number of people seeking to undermine you has as well."

"I'm aware, and I'm doing my best to navigate this new role but the urge to do something is always there. Sometimes it's hard to just sit back and let my husband take the lead."

"I know that struggle well, but there are ways that women can get things done that a man would never even dream of. Take a good look at your chess board and utilize the pieces you have in play. I'm sure you'll realize you're not as powerless as you thought."

Marquise had fallen asleep. Both women looked at the deep, even breaths of the sleeping infant.

"From one strategist to another?" Melina asked.

Neeya smiled before leaning in closer. "From the best one you'll ever know. Now enjoy your brunch, dear."

Melina indulged in the lavish brunch laid out before her. Her hostess was silent, simply staring at Marquise and lost in her own world. Neeya Pivetti bore many burdens on her slim shoulders, but beneath it all the woman was a fighter. Perhaps not the in-your-face way Melina was, but a fighter nonetheless. Even better than being a fighter, she was a brilliant strategist.

For the first time, Melina considered that change could bring about something new and better than what was being left behind. The Pivetti mansion may have been empty, but the heart of its mistress was full. Of love, hope, or revenge, Melina couldn't honestly say. What she did know was that no matter what happened, Neeya Pivetti was a queen whether she had a castle or not. Somehow Melina was sure the coming days would be illuminating.

"I enjoyed your visit so much, Melina. It's a blessing to get to hold a baby in my arms again."

"I should thank you. You're a natural with Marquise. I might call you if I ever need a babysitter."

The two women walked towards the foyer with Samuel following behind them.

"I'd be happy to do it, dear. He's a delight."

"Thank you and thank you for all the wonderful gifts."

"I hope you enjoy them all."

"Because they came from you, I have no doubt she will."

The words came from Mac who was standing in the foyer. Beside him was Enric and his sisters. Her gaze flicked over her husband in a bold perusal for a brief moment. Though they'd woken up in bed together not long ago, she couldn't help the tug of excitement she felt at seeing him. Especially when the suit he wore was perfectly made for him.

"Mac, dear. Wonderful to see you as always," Neeya said.

She handed Marquise to Melina and enveloped Mac in a warm hug.

"You too, Mrs. Pivetti."

Neeya waved him way. "You know better. It's Neeya to you."

"Yes, ma'am."

Neeya moved to where her stepson sat in his wheelchair. Though he smiled often at his sisters and seemed to happily respond to whatever they said to him, there was a noticeable unease about him. As if sadness and anger were warring within him. Melina recognized and knew those feelings well.

"Enric, glad to finally see you. My girls have missed you."

The young man offered his stepmother his hand. "I've missed them."

Neeya ignored his handshake and hugged him to her instead. Somehow Melina felt as if she'd just witnessed a pivotal moment. Enric was wounded and uncertain of his place in either family right now. His stepmother's open embrace of him was a signal that he belonged. With everything he'd been through, Melina knew it meant something to him whether he acknowledged it out loud or not.

"Don't be a stranger." Neeya said as she pulled away.

"I could say the same thing," Melina said.

She moved closer to the young man and placed a kiss on his cheek. "Marquise and I have been waiting for a visit."

Enric regarded her with eyes so like his father. "Skip keeps me busy."

Melina cut her eyes at her husband. "Looks like I need to have a talk with my husband."

"Thanks, Enric. You just got me in trouble with my wife." There was a teasing lit in his voice as he regarded the young soldier.

"Sorry."

Melina shook her head. "No apologies. Just come by and see us sometimes. We owe you so much."

"I will," Enric said.

He looked away briefly in an effort to collect himself. A few minutes later, everyone had said their goodbyes and was leaving the mansion, when Melina had a thought.

"Do you have anything pressing you need to attend to right now?" she asked her husband.

Mac shook his head. "No. Why?"

"Would you mind taking Marquise back to the house while I take your car and drop by The Dollhouse?"

"I see that look in your eyes, wife. What are you up to?"

"Never speak about a move. Just put it in motion."

Mac lifted a brow. "Very sage-like advice. You constantly surprise me, doll."

Melina came closer and placed a hand on her husband's face. "And that's what keeps things interesting, don't you agree?"

Mac nodded before his lips captured hers. His tongue touched the seam of her lips, before he kissed her again. Hard. Her body ached for him. For the chance to be one with him again. A discrete clearing of the throat made them move apart.

"Sorry to interrupt, Skip. Would you like me to escort the missus to do her business?" Samuel asked.

"No, Samuel. That won't be necessary," Melina said.

"Melina?"

She handed their son to Mac. "Relax. I'll be gone less than three hours. I'll text you when I make it, and I'm ready to leave."

Mac hesitated, before he finally acquiesced to her wishes. "All right."

Marquise chose that precise moment to start wailing. She gave her husband a pitying look.

"It's your turn. Now, keys please."

Mac handed her his keys. She gave him and her son a quick kiss, before grabbing her purse from inside the limousine and quickly walking over to where Mac's Challenger was parked. Unlocking the car and sliding easily behind the wheel, Melina buckled up, put the car in gear and roared down the Pivetti driveway. Her conversation with Neeya replayed again in her mind. Idly sitting by had never been her style and just because it was required of her now, didn't mean she couldn't put some plans of her own in play.

It seemed every light was green as she drove the stretch of highway that would take her to The Dollhouse. Her purpose for stopping by was threefold. Ten minutes later, she pulled into her reserved parking space and texted her husband. Mac responded back instantly. She rolled her eyes at his instructions to keep him posted. Exiting and locking the car behind her, Melina walked inside and was mildly surprised to see the club at half capacity. This time of the day was usually slow before the evening rush.

She greeted one of her hostesses, and the men and women working the bar, before heading to her office. Once she was inside, she quickly looked over the books and did her own calculations. Though she had an accountant, Melina believed in being on top of her business. An hour later she was done and satisfied.

"Boss Lady!"

Melina looked up and saw Erika standing in the doorway.

"Well, hey stranger. Nice to see you," Melina said.

She came from behind her desk and hugged Erika. The two women had been through an ordeal together. In the ensuing happiness of her son's birth, she hadn't seen or called her friend.

"I could say the same about you. Domestic bliss has taken over everything, huh?"

Melina drew back. "No. I still have a business to run

and interests to protect."

"I heard that. How's the munchkin?"

"Perfect. Every day he does some new little thing that makes my heart melt."

Melina sat back down behind her desk.

"I bet. You better watch him. Marquise is going to be a lady killer like his daddy."

"I don't even want to think that far ahead."

Erika laughed as she sat on the edge of the leather armchair in the room. "Get ready for it, mama. You're going to have little girls sending home notes asking, *Do you like me?*"

"And they will be going straight into the trash. Nope. Not having it."

"You look really happy, Melina. I'm glad."

"I can say the same about you. Not to mention the type of money you've been bringing in. I'm incredibly impressed."

"Don't be too impressed. Two thirds of it is from one particular patron. You know him pretty well, actually."

Melina leaned back in her seat and crossed her legs. "I do."

"Yes. Anthony Corelli."

Internally, Melina smiled. For once maybe her plans and Fate's were going to line up.

"I don't think anyone really knows Anthony Corelli."

"Well, he usually has something to say about you," Erika said.

"Really? I can't imagine why."

"To be honest, I think he has a hard nut for you, and I'm just a poor substitute. But I'm all right with it. As long as he keeps the green flowing, you'll get no complaints from me."

"I can imagine the two of you get along very well."

Erika plucked a stray eyelash from her eye. "We do. Sometimes we talk for a bit. I can tell his work stresses him out."

"Is that so?"

"From what I gather. Is there a reason you're so interested in Anthony Corelli all of a sudden?"

Melina had to think and think fast. She and Erika were friends. She'd invited the young woman into her world and so far that gesture hadn't been misplaced. But she also didn't need Erika to be privy to anything that might come back to haunt her if things went sour.

"Actually there is."

Erika's eyes stretched. "Oh. Do tell?"

"I just feel like knowing Anthony a little better might help ease some tension. All I really know about the man is that he is a business associate of my husband's. Other than that Anthony's a blank slate."

"I sort of get the feeling he might not be too fond of Mac." Erika bit her lip.

"I do too, and I want to do something about that. Maybe if I knew a little more about the man, the two of them could come to a meeting of minds on certain things."

"It's a good idea, I think."

"I'm glad because you are in a unique position to help me, and I can assure you I have no problem making it more than worth your while."

Her petite friend regarded her with a shrewd gaze and for just a moment, Melina feared that she might have made a mistake. Perhaps she'd said too much or tipped her hand.

"I'm in, although let me warn you, sometimes he doesn't say too much. Or if he does it's some crass remark about how sexy you are or how big your tits have gotten with the pregnancy and all."

Melina wrinkled her nose. "Why am I not surprised? Men."

Erika shrugged, a half-smile on her face. "Hey. All I can say is you've made quite the impression on the man."

"I can assure you it wasn't my intent."

"Oh, I know. Even Ray Charles could see how in love you and Mac are. So when do you want me to make a report?"

"Only if you have something. Other than that business as usual. You can look for an extra incentive with your next paycheck."

Erika stood up. "Yes, ma'am. Anything else?"

"Yeah, now that you mention it. I'm thinking about having a private get together for my husband and a few friends. Find out how many of the girls would like to participate."

"Will do. I'll talk to you soon," Erika said before leaving.

When she'd shut the door behind her, Melina smiled. Perhaps this might go off without a hitch. She didn't know how Mac would feel about her plan as far as Anthony was concerned, but he'd surely agree to doing a little something for his guys. The idea had come to her when she saw Enric. The young man had nearly lost his life trying to protect her. Marquise might not be here if it wasn't for him. The same could be said of Giuseppe, who was still being treated for the terrible burns he'd gotten from a car bomb meant for her.

Melina understood that this lifestyle was a choice. The men who become a part of it were no angels, but that didn't mean that they didn't deserve to know their sacrifices were appreciated.

After all, what good was status and money if you were dead? Yes, a nice get together for Mac and his crew would probably do wonders for morale. Besides that, if word discretely got out, there was no doubt it would raise her husband a head above the other Capos. And ensure the continuing loyalty of his crew.

The game was in motion.

CHAPTER FIVE

"This is fucking undignified," Enric grumbled as Mac helped to pull him from the vehicle and into his waiting wheelchair.

"Next time I can build a ramp into the back of the SUV, shove the back seats down to give you some room, and you can just wheel yourself in and out, how's that?" Mac asked.

Enric glared up at his Capo, his hands already clasping tightly around the wheels of his chair, looking ready to get the hell away from Mac as soon as he possibly could. "Was that serious or sarcasm?"

"Bit of both."

Enric made a disgusted noise under his breath. "Of course, it was."

"Depends on how you like the idea."

"I'd *like* to be able to drive myself around."

Mac's brow raised at that statement. "Really, the man who refused to even buy himself a shitty little second-hand car a year ago now wants his own vehicle, with all the bells and whistles for someone in a wheelchair, so he can drive himself around?"

"Self-sufficiency, Mac."

Perhaps.

Or perhaps Enric was just in one of his moods, and this was the easiest thing to moan and groan about.

"It'd be nice, that's all I'm saying."

"Do you even have your license?" Mac asked.

Enric shrugged. "Somewhere."

Mac decided to indulge Enric's anger and whining, if only because the young man had been so focused on that instead of their arrival at their destination; he knew all too well how Enric would react once he figured out Mac had gotten ahold of the schedule for his physical therapy appointments. Not to mention, with a few phone calls, Mac had managed to get Enric into a *new* program and facility with great faculty, one of which, he knew personally.

A man in Enric's position couldn't ask for more than the best of the best to get him back on track. Mac had decided that regardless of what Enric felt at the moment, eventually on the outside *and* on the inside, he would be better for making the effort.

Even if he bitched a lot along the way to get there.

Eventually, when he was on his feet, walking, and back to his normal self, Enric would be grateful. Mac had a feeling it was still going be a hellish road to get there.

After all, the road to Hell *was* paved with good intentions.

Enric surveyed the clinic's parking lot. His gaze narrowed when his attention fell on the sign above the front entrance. "Physical therapy?"

"You have appointments four days a week."

"Yeah, but—"

"You haven't been going to them at all, Enric."

"I don't—"

"Want to walk again, apparently," Mac interrupted.

Enric's mouth snapped shut audibly before his burning gaze turned on Mac. "I want to fucking walk again, Mac."

"Then you don't want to put in the effort because sometimes you need help, and you get tired; sometimes it hurts, or it's just too much; maybe your body aches, and you need a rest, or you feel like giving up, but saying *any* of that is undignified to you. Humiliating, even. Degrading as a man to admit you're scared to do something because you believe that maybe—fuck, just maybe—you *can't* do it."

Enric didn't say a word.

Mac didn't really need him to.

"Come on," Mac urged, "tell me how wrong I am, Enric."

Stubborn as a fucking mule, Enric didn't speak.

"This is going to take work," Mac told Enric, quietly but firmly. "It's not going to be easy. It's going to take a long time. You have to want it more than anything else in your life, so that you can truly appreciate it once you have it back. Most of us are born with the ability to learn how to walk and run, and we don't understand how easily that ability can be taken away. You're *lucky*, Enric, because you can get up and walk again if you just put in the fucking effort. There are people who would give anything for the chance you have—stop wasting it.

"What if your father never gets out of prison, huh?" Mac asked sharply, never once allowing Enric to look away from him. "Who is going to help your sisters move into new apartments for college, or move out of dorms after graduations, or even walk them down the aisle when they get married? They're going to need *somebody* to do it, if Luca can't, and my bet is they'll look to you. How do you plan on telling them you can't do those things because you didn't want to work for it when you had the chance?"

Enric's gaze dropped from Mac, but not before he saw the flash of shame in the younger man's eyes. "I know that, but I'm busy, too. It's not as easy as just making the choice to come, I actually have to make the time to be here."

"We'll make the damn time. Your moment of wallowing is over, Enric. It's time to *work* for it. You want to complain and whine? You can do that when your muscles ache and your bones hurt from therapy. You won't be complaining because life is so unfair that you have the possibility of a second chance, but you're too involved in your self-pity to see it."

"I'm not—" Enric stopped mid-sentence at the sight of Mac's scowl, then quickly added, "This is unfair. You tricked me here."

"I'm sorry this happened, it *sucks*. But you're better than what you're being. And you know it, Enric."

"All right."

That was that.

Mac let Enric wheel himself to the front entrance, and go inside alone. He had to want it, after all. Mac couldn't do that for the guy. He had to do that himself.

Satisfied with his good deed for the day, Mac got back in his vehicle, and headed for the heart of the city for some work he had to do.

Or rather, a woman who didn't like to wait.

It seemed no matter the time of day, there was always some kind of activity inside The Dollhouse. Mac understood that a great deal of made men in the Pivetti Organization made use of the business for more … carnal reasons, despite their supposedly happy wives at home. While he didn't approve of another man's infidelity, it also wasn't Mac's place to comment on a man's personal tastes and choices so long as all parties were willing in whatever goings on happened behind the closed doors in The Dollhouse.

But for every man who walked into The Dollhouse with some sort of sex on his mind, another man would be waiting to chat once the business of pleasure was out of the way. Family business was better held at safe establishments, and thankfully, The Dollhouse had proven itself to be just that.

Even with the unfortunate shooting and subsequent attention it received from the officials before the boss was locked away.

Mac, on the other hand, was careful about just how much time he spent at The Dollhouse. He certainly didn't go there for pleasure—his wife was more than capable of handling his needs whenever and however he wanted them taken care of. And because it *was* Melina's business, there was no hiding the fact she was Mac's wife.

He had no intention of tampering the Pivetti men's desires to discuss or conduct business, especially in a place where Mac had eyes and ears listening. He figured that if he showed his face at The Dollhouse too much, other men might feel his presence was also being asserted into their business. That would not be good for him on the Capo side of things, or the side where he needed information about the men to make sure everything was running smoothly while the boss was away with no plans of that changing.

Again, eyes and ears.

So, Mac stayed away from the business as much as he possibly could. He only showed up on rare occasions, barely talked to anyone but his wife while he was there, and he didn't stay for long before leaving without so much as a goodbye to any man he might see on the main floor.

The plan had been working just fine for him.

Today was no exception to that rule as he entered The Dollhouse, his gaze sweeping the main floor and taking inventory of faces he recognized. No one too important, he noted, and certainly not anyone he had been having trouble with—Anthony, to be specific.

Mac quickly crossed the floor, accepting a tumbler of water from one of the servers as he headed for the back office where his wife usually was when she was working. Ever since their son had been born, work, schedules, and life was a carefully planned event for Mac and Melina. He was aware his wife struggled with the idea of working full-time and leaving her newborn son with either Mac's mother, or even Mac in the evenings, when the baby was so new. But at the same time, his wife was unwilling to hand more control of her business over to someone else so that she had more time to be with her boy.

Melina made it work—somehow. She did paperwork at home, and worked evenings when Mac was done for the day. She broke her days up between being home, or at The Dollhouse, and then back again.

She was tired. He knew she had to be. At the same time, Melina was too stubborn, and too hard of a worker to let any venture of hers fail.

Mac had all the respect for his wife in that regard.

He was not about to tell her that she couldn't do something when he, more than anyone else in their lives, knew exactly what Melina Morgan Maccari was capable of. So far, they had made this work, and that was exactly what he planned to continue to do as long as his wife wanted to do so as well.

Of course, he didn't think for a second that Melina would ever be the barefoot-homemaker type, but should there ever come a day when that was what she wanted, he'd make sure she had all of that and more, too.

Happy wife, happy life.

Mac had already learned that in his short marriage.

At the end of the hallway, Mac was surprised to find his wife's office door firmly closed. She knew he would be there to visit for the afternoon before he had to pick up Enric after the appointment, so he was confused why her office wasn't open as it usually would be. Melina only closed her door when she had someone inside, and didn't want the conversation being overheard.

Like when Mac was there.

He knocked three times on the door—twice lightly, once firmer. That way, Melina would know it was him, and not just anyone waiting on the other side of the door. It took another ten minutes before he heard the latch slide for the inside deadbolt.

Mac took a step back from the door, curious as to who would be so important to his wife that she wouldn't even allow him inside while she talked with them.

Relief settled through Mac as one of Melina's girls who worked at the club stepped out of the office, giving a quick assurance over her shoulder before passing him by in the hallway. She barely spared him a glance at all. Mac recognized the girl as one Melina considered a friend, of sorts, as she had been stuck with the girl as a bunkmate while in jail.

Erika, he believed was her name.

The relief he had felt was short-lived, as Mac was once again reminded that his wife had made him wait while she talked with Erika. Had it been a man inside, one of the many guards for the place, Melina would have let him inside in a heartbeat, especially if there was an issue to discuss about a girl or patron.

What had been so private with Erika that Melina didn't want Mac to hear it?

"Are you going to stand out there in the hallway all afternoon, or bring me the take-out you promised?" Melina called from inside the office.

Mac pushed his concerns aside for the moment, plastered on his signature smirk, and entered his wife's office. As usual, Melina sat behind her large desk, queen of the room like always. It made him smile—genuine and wide—to see how well she commanded her own space, and how damn good she looked doing so.

He held up the bag of take-out. "From your favorite place."

"Life saver," Melina replied, snatching the bag as soon as he was close enough to hand it over. "Thanks."

"Always welcome, doll."

Mac dropped a kiss to the top of his wife's head as she began emptying the cartons from the bag. His hand found the back of her neck to feel the heat of her body and softness of her skin. It was also a way for him to gage whatever internal stress she might be feeling, but not exactly showing, depending on how taut her muscles felt there.

She was smooth and relaxed under his touch.

Mac took the carton of chicken and noodles Melina offered, setting himself on the very edge of the desk as he dug into his food and she opened up her own. "Important meeting, or what?"

Melina glanced up, her plastic fork freezing in front of her opened lips. "Pardon?"

"Erika, right?"

She set her food aside. "What about her?"

"I know she's someone you consider a friend and all ..."

Melina's eyebrow arched high. "Say whatever it is, Mac."

Mac was too smart for that, especially where his wife was concerned. Nothing good would come from him spitting out his thoughts without any consideration to how she might take them, especially if the way he felt was the complete opposite to his wife's feelings regarding the girl.

"You know I have access to the books, right?" Mac asked. "*Both* sets of books, doll."

By both sets of books, Mac was referring to Melina's accounting that happened *before* the clean-up came. Books that showed specific girls, clients, and how much cash men were throwing at which woman when he spent his time with her. Mac knew exactly which girls brought in the most cash at The Dollhouse, and from which man that seemed to favor them.

Erika was no exception.

"Is there a point you're trying to make?" Melina asked calmly.

Well, Mac was taking that as a win. He hadn't seemed to piss his wife off yet, and that was one of his many priorities next to keeping her safe, of course.

"Erika brings in decent cash," Mac said.

"Yep."

Melina popped a bite of food into her mouth, saying nothing else.

"But it's all from one client, too."

"And?"

"That client is Anthony Corelli, doll."

Melina didn't blink a lash. "I'm aware."

"You're not going to make this easy on me, are you?"

A sensual smile curved his wife's lips at the corners. "Nope."

Mac sighed, putting his food aside and stepping down from the edge of the desk. Melina turned her chair to face him, and he bent down to put his hands on her bare knees while his eyes met hers. Face to face, there were no games between them, no jokes or misinterpreted words. He really needed his wife to hear him for this, and this was one of the only ways he could ensure that would be the case.

"Melina, that girl's only client is a man that has—at times—made it his mission to ruin me," Mac said, "and you're hiding behind closed doors with the chick."

Melina frowned. "Is that what you think?"

"No, not necessarily, but it could have that impression on certain people."

"People like Anthony?"

Mac shrugged. "Exactly."

"Maybe that's part of the point, Mac."

Well, he had not been expecting to hear that. "Go on."

"Erika isn't interested in picking up other clients besides Anthony because she doesn't *need* to. He keeps her well paid so that she is always at his beck and call, and only his. He likes that, and I think part of that reason is—"

"You," Mac interjected quietly.

"She's mentioned things—he talks about me, sometimes you. Obviously there are some similarities between Erika and I."

Mac tried really hard not to scoff, and failed like a *cafone*. "Skin color, but that's about it."

"Be nice."

"That's it, doll."

"Be that as it may, Mac, I think Anthony has a taste, and Erika fits that bill. He is her client, he keeps her paid, and she doesn't mind ... feeding into whatever it is he wants at the time. So, if I can use that to my—*our*—benefit, than I plan on doing exactly that."

Mac took in his wife's words slowly, and what they might mean. "And what are you planning with him and her, exactly?"

"Right now? Nothing. But should there come a time when that trust he has for her can be used to my benefit for something, then yes, you can bet your ass I plan on using it for anything I can."

"Doll ..."

"What?"

Mac sighed. "Don't go making games where there aren't any to be played."

Melina smiled in that way of hers again. "There's something I've learned about this life of ours."

"Do tell."

"Everyone is playing a game, even if you don't realize you're a piece on the board. This is no different. I just might be a step or two ahead of the rest."

"Be careful, Melina. I don't want you stepping into someone else's pile of shit."

"As long as Anthony is the one cleaning it off my boots, I don't give a damn."

Be that as it may ...

"You need to be careful who you trust," Mac said simply.

Melina nodded. "That, Mac, is one thing you don't need to worry about."

"But you *will* tell me if something important comes

up, or if shit turns sour in some way, right?"

"Always."

That was all Mac needed to know. While he still didn't feel one hundred percent okay with whatever plans Melina had going on where Erika and Anthony were concerned, he had to step back and trust his wife to do the right thing.

And hell, if she *did* stumble upon the kind of information that might do Mac some good while doing harm to Anthony at the same time, he wasn't about to complain. He simply didn't want to see his wife get hurt in some way over her ... scheming.

"Be careful," Mac said again as he retook his seat on the edge of the desk.

"Got it. Now you tell me, how did it go with Enric?"

"Easier than I expected."

"How much guilt did you put on his shoulders?"

Mac smirked. "A bit."

"He'll be grateful, Mac."

He knew that, too.

"But he's going to hate me on the way there," Mac muttered heavily.

"Probably."

It was not going to be an easy road.

It would be a road worth traveling, though.

That made all the difference.

"Before I forget," Melina said, gaining Mac's attention again. "Meet me at your mother's tonight for supper—bring Enric, too. We have plans to make."

"What now?"

He didn't mean to sound so whiney, but Jesus, they hadn't stopped since the baby was born.

"Marquise's christening."

Ah.

Yeah.

Mac couldn't say no to that. "Family first, doll."

Melina laughed. "God is a very close second."

Very close.

It would be a big day for them all, and they had some important choices to make regarding who would be involved in a special way. Mac had to admit, he was looking forward to it a little bit.

Christenings were … special in their lifestyle.

Almost, if not as important, as weddings and births, really.

Mac finished his meal quickly, knowing by the time he got back to the other side of the city, Enric would be just about done with his appointment. He didn't want to make the man wait, because as it was, Enric wouldn't be in a good mood once he got out of the physical therapy appointment. It was hard, exhausting work. Mac didn't need to pile on to Enric's troubles.

With a goodbye kiss to his wife, one that lingered long enough to make him wish time would speed up just enough for Melina to get her medical okay from the doctor to resume intimacy, Mac was heading out of The Dollhouse without a look back. He had noticed a couple of new faces in the main floor as he left, however, and he'd seen Erika sitting alone at the bar, nursing a cocktail of some kind.

Anthony hadn't been there at all, it seemed.

Mac wondered *why* Erika bothered to spend time at The Dollhouse when her client was not there. He knew Melina didn't require the girls to put in a set number of hours, and if Erika only really catered to Anthony, her presence wasn't needed at the business all the time.

He put the thoughts out of his head, deciding to worry about it another day. Erika was just a woman working for his wife, after all.

And what was good for Melina, would always be just fine for Mac.

CHAPTER SIX

If you wanted things done right, sometimes you had to do them yourself.

At least that was the motto Melina was currently subscribing to.

It wasn't that she didn't think she had fully capable people available to assist her with her current undertaking. It was just that she knew the importance of tonight's event, and she wanted everything to be perfect. Mac had expressed his appreciation that she cared about the men in his crew. Tonight would be a chance to show just how much.

For probably the hundredth time, Melina moved around The Dollhouse, checking things off the list she'd made earlier. Actually she'd moved past checking hours ago. Rechecking was more like it. She stopped and frowned when she noticed Mac sitting at the bar watching her with a smirk.

"Nice to see that one of us is acting like he doesn't have a care in the world," she said.

"And why would you think that, doll?"

"Because I'm running around here like a chicken with my head cut off, and you're all easy breezy."

Mac raised a brow. "Easy breezy? Hardly. I just know that my wife is fully capable of doing an amazing job at whatever she puts her mind to, so there is no reason to stress about tonight."

"Oh."

Mac moved from his seat and walked over to his wife. He tipped her chin up with his finger and offered her a full smile.

"You're the most confident woman I know, so tell me what about this night has you so rattled?"

"I wouldn't say I'm rattled. I just want to do this right. With everything going on, I think it's important that we all have a chance to decompress and enjoy some of the good in life. Besides that, I just want your guys to feel appreciated. Not that you don't do a good job of that on your own." Melina held up a hand in defense.

Mac put his arms around her waist. "You're doing something no other Capo's wife has even thought of doing. Your heart is in the right place and because of that tonight will be a success no matter what."

"Flatterer. I knew there was a reason I married you," Melina teased.

"The only reason?"

"Hardly."

Melina kissed Mac, her tongue slipping in his mouth in a kiss of love and appreciation. He returned her kiss with the same fiery fervor. Mac was a rare man and every day made her realize just how lucky she was to be married to him.

"The lovebirds at it again."

Melina eased apart from her husband and rolled her eyes as Erika walked in. "Don't hate. Appreciate."

Erika laughed as she came closer to her boss. "No hate here. Always happy to see you smiling."

"Good to hear. You look especially nice this evening."

"Always dress for the occasion, Boss Lady."

"I like that way of thinking. I'll see you in a few minutes, doll."

Melina nodded as her husband walked away before

turning back to Erika. "Well."

"Nothing yet. Just the usual complaints about not being respected and there needs to be change."

"Really?"

Erika nodded as she flicked away a stray strand of hair. "Yes. That man has a major chip on his shoulder."

"Thanks for the info. Look for your first bonus," Melina said.

"That wasn't much. Glad it helped. Excuse me while I check my makeup."

Momentarily left alone, Melina finished going through her check list before the club started to fill with people. The bartenders and wait staff appeared first, followed by the caterers and the DJ. Her girls came in next, and she was happy to see almost every girl that worked for her had volunteered to work tonight. If nothing else, Mac's men wouldn't be lacking for female company.

"Melina, the crew is ready to come in," Mac said appearing at her side.

Giving one last look to make sure everything was set up correctly, she took Mac's hand and joined him at the entrance to the club.

"Moment of truth."

"You know you don't have to do this. The party itself is enough."

She shook her head. "Nope. This is non-negotiable. Introduce me to everyone. I don't have to know what they do for you. I just want to know their names and thank them."

"Whatever my wife wants, she gets."

"I'm going to remind you of this conversation at a later date."

"I have no doubt of that," Mac said.

Before Melina could say anything else, the doors opened and one by one, the men started to file in. A good majority of them she didn't recognize, but she greeted them with the same enthusiasm of those she did know.

Every man was not only respectful, but seemed deeply humbled that she had gone out of her way for them. The appreciation in their eyes was one of the best gifts she could've ever received. Enric was the last of the men to arrive.

"Enric. So glad you could come," Melina said.

The young man rolled his wheelchair up to where she and Mac stood. His eyes shifted briefly to her husband before they went back to her.

"Thank you for inviting me."

"Always."

Melina leaned down and kissed his cheek. Enric had the good grace to blush before he addressed Mac.

"Skip."

"Enric. Enjoy yourself."

The young man nodded and wheeled away leaving Mac and Melina alone.

"Was that everyone?" Melina asked.

"Yes."

Melina released a breath. "Good. That was a lot of men to meet and greet."

"That meant a lot to them."

"I could tell it did. What was that between you and Enric?"

Mac put his hand against the small of her back and guided her back to where the party was in full swing.

"Nothing. I spoke some harsh truths to him, and he's still a little sore about it. He'll get over it eventually."

"Just how tough were you, Mac?"

"Enough. He has to shake this shit off. There are so many people that need him."

"I'm sure he will in his own time. Now how about you and I enjoy ourselves?"

Melina took Mac's hand and pulled him out onto the middle of the floor where a few of his crew and some of her girls were dancing to the slow grooves the DJ was playing. Melina slipped her arms around her husband and laid her head against his chest.

"Doll, I'm not sure I know this song."

"Why am I not surprised? I've got to introduce you to more soul and R&B music. This is *I Still Love You* by Next. It's one of my favorite songs, by the way."

"Is that so?"

"Yeah, it is."

The night seemed to pass in a kaleidoscope of music, laughs, and good food. *Fernando's,* the five star restaurant she'd hired to cater the event had outdone themselves in every way. Nearly two hours later, Melina had her share of stuffed mushrooms, prosciutto wrapped green beans and veal parmesan. Even Mac had admitted the food was almost as good as his mom's. Almost. Then he'd made her promise to never repeat what he'd said.

Of course, she'd promised before extracting a promise of her own from him later. The drinks continued to come, and the music continued to flow. Life was good. Each and every person at The Dollhouse had needed this. The escape from the harsh reality that any moment could be their last. A subtle reminder to live life to the absolute fullest in every way. Melina grabbed a flute of champagne from one of the servers and quickly downed it before pulling Mac back out onto the dance floor.

"You're not tired yet, doll?"

She shook her head. "No. It feels like I've cast my cares to the winds tonight, and I can just let loose."

"Maybe it's all that champagne talking," Mac teased her.

"Or maybe I'm just enjoying this time with my husband and counting down the days until we can be as close as humanly possible again."

Mac groaned. "You and me both. This is the worst kind of torture."

Melina laughed as Bruno Mars' *24K Magic* started to play. She and Mac danced together seamlessly as one. And then the music came to a loud and screeching halt.

"What the hell?" Melina said.

"Sorry to interrupt your little get together, but we need to speak with the owner of this establishment," a man's voice said on the loud speaker.

Melina looked over towards where the DJ booth was set up and noticed two men she hadn't seen before standing on either side of the DJ. Both were dark-haired. One older. One younger. With purposeful strides she made her way over, with Mac right behind her.

"I'm the owner, Melina Maccari. I'd like to know why you've come into my establishment uninvited and rudely interrupted this private party."

Both men exchanged glances before slipping their hands into their jacket pocket. Melina braced herself and cursed under her breath when she saw what they'd pulled out.

Badges.

Fuck.

"Detectives Meyer and Langley. We have a few questions for you, Mrs. Maccari."

Just like that, the night was ruined.

Melina didn't blame her guests for filing out as quickly as they could.

The stench of cop was in the air.

Beside her, Mac bristled while the detectives smirked as the club emptied. The assholes knew exactly what they had done.

"I'm sorry to inform you gentlemen, that coming here was a waste of your time. I have nothing to say to you."

The older mustached, Detective Meyer smiled showing tobacco stained teeth. "I think you might change your tune once you hear what we have to say."

"Unless you have a search or arrest warrant, I suggest that the two of you get the fuck out of my wife's establishment before I get our lawyer on the phone. I'm sure the police department would love another harassment suit."

Langley held up his hands. "No need for any of that, warrants included. We actually just came by as a courtesy to Mrs. Maccari."

Melina arched a brow. "Is that so? Public relations department hounding you guys now?"

"Hardly. We just thought you might like to know one of your employees has been picked up for heroin and cocaine possession," Meyer said.

Mac's hand slipped around her waist.

"I think you must be mistaken. All of my employees were here this evening, enjoying a party I threw for them."

"Hmm. Sure is a lot of employees for one place. If I didn't know any better, I'd say it looked like some low level mob figures were choosing their entertainment for a different kind of party if you catch my drift," Langley said.

"My wife has tried to be courteous by not having the two of you thrown out on your asses, but I'm not my wife. I suggest you leave now before I show you why the things they say about me may very well be true."

Detective Meyer's lip curled into a sneer. "Is that a threat, Maccari? We can haul your ass in right now for threatening a police officer. I'm sure the guys in booking will be happy to see you again."

Langley placed a hand on Meyer's shoulder and shook his head. Melina wasn't fooled in the least. They were playing the classic good cop/bad cop routine. Too bad for them it wouldn't work.

"Forgive my partner. Sometimes he gets a little too high strung. As I said this was just a courtesy to let you know, Brianna Carmichael is in lockup. She had half a brick of cocaine and ten ounces of heroin."

Detective Langley took out a picture and laid it on

top of the bar before turning back to his partner. "Let's go, partner."

Meyer leveled a hard glare at Mac before he reluctantly followed his partner out of the club. Melina's temple started to throb. This was not the shit she needed right now. She picked up the picture and cursed under her breath. The detectives weren't bullshitting. There was Brianna in her booking photo looking worse for wear.

"How the hell could this happen?" she asked.

Mac took the photograph from her hand and crumpled it into a ball.

"It doesn't matter how. What matters now is that it did and that creates yet another problem we don't need."

There was a hard edge to his voice.

"You think this is my fault?"

His hands found her shoulders. "Of course not. You can't control what someone does when they're not working for you, anymore than I can. I know how selective you are with the women you hire to work here."

She rubbed a hand over her face. "I did. I vetted all of them. I don't understand this. Brianna isn't some young stupid girl. She's a pro. A pro with two kids to support while she studies for her MBA. This isn't her."

Mac laid the balled up piece of paper on the bar and leaned against it, quiet for a moment.

"It's very likely then that she could have been setup as a way to get to you and me."

Melina considered the possibility. "That makes sense, but then the next question is who has the most to gain from taking us down. The cops? Or someone else in our world?"

"It could be either at this point. You and I seem to have a target on our backs no matter where we turn."

"Then we need to do something about it. I don't like feeling like a sitting duck, Mac."

"I know that. Neither do I, but right now it's best if we lay low. As far as Brianna goes, you know she can't work for you anymore."

Melina crossed her arms. "Yeah. Yeah. I know. Any association with her is bad for business all around. We don't need any more heat from the cops on us."

"Exactly."

Melina sighed. "When is this going to stop, Mac?"

He shrugged. "I don't know. All we can do now is remain vigilant and tread very carefully."

"Yeah. That seems to be our new reality these days. Guess I'd better get the cleanup crew here."

Melina walked towards her office to place the call and silently fumed. Was this what life would always be like married to Mac? Loud explosive moments of happiness, followed by uncertainty and distrust around every corner? She didn't like it. Melina was a straight shooter. The subterfuge and sneaking around annoyed the fuck out of her. If you had a problem with someone, address them head on. But that wasn't the way Cosa Nostra operated and as much as she disliked it, she was going to have to get used to it.

For better or worse.

When she'd said her vows, she'd meant every word of them. Melina was no shrinking violet. Times were tense and unpredictable now, but as long as she and Mac had each other, they could weather any storm. Even the ones they never knew were coming.

Ten weeks.

Melina couldn't believe it.

She stared at her son as the priest held him and liberally sprinkled water on Marquise's forehead. Biting her lip, she silently hoped that her son wouldn't cry. Next to her stood Mac, stoic and strong. Even so, she didn't miss the sheen covering his eyes as they watched their baby be christened.

On either side of them were Marquise's godparents, Enric and Victoria. It hadn't taken any convincing for Victoria to agree to be Marquise's godmother. She loved her nephew as if he were her own child. And Marquise was fond of his Aunt Tori as Victoria referred to herself. You could see it in the way he smiled whenever she was around and reached for her. Yes, they had a bond and choosing Victoria made sense.

Enric, on the other hand, had not been so amicable at first. In fact, the young man had argued that they should pick someone more deserving of such an honor. It had taken a gentle reminder from her that there was no one more honorable than the man who'd saved Marquise's life before he was even born. Enric had grown quiet and then he'd agreed. She glanced at him and saw him shifting his attention back and forth between Victoria and Marquise. It seemed something was still brewing between those two.

As the priest handed Marquise back to her, the church parishioners clapped. Another soul had been brought into the Catholic faith. It was a day to rejoice for all. Mac put his arm around her, kissing the top of her forehead as they returned to their seats. Cynthia waited on a pew and eagerly reached for her grandson. Marquise gurgled as he went to his grandmother, and Melina's heart melted a little inside. Mac held her hand as they sat through the rest of the service.

When it was over, Cynthia rushed off, explaining she had a few last minute things to pick up from the store. She would expect them over in an hour and a half for dinner. Though the two of them had looked forward to a quiet evening at home, they knew they could not refuse Cynthia's orders.

"I can't believe he's growing so fast," Melina said as they exited the church.

"Neither can I. Seems unreal sometimes."

"What does?"

"That we created something so perfect," Mac said.

"He is that. Aren't you, Marquise?"

Melina smiled at her son, and rubbed her thumb against one of his fluffy cheeks. Every time she looked at their child, she felt a fresh rush of love.

"So I managed to catch a glimpse of the little *principe* today."

Melina stopped walking and looked up. Anthony stood in front of them. His eyes glued to her son. She shifted Marquise so that he was now looking over her shoulder.

"Anthony, I'm surprised to see you here," Mac said.

"Sometimes you just get tired of the same old thing. I decided to try something different today. Glad I did, though."

"And why is that?" Melina asked.

"Because I got to see how well you and your son are doing. We're all family here, Melina."

"Hmm. That's news to me," Mac said.

"It's Sunday. A holy day. There's no need for hostility."

"Trust me. You would absolutely know if I was hostile, Anthony. I just find your sudden interest in my son a bit curious is all," Mac said.

"It's up to us to look to our futures in these uncertain times. Children make you do just that."

"Yes, well if you'll excuse us, Anthony. We have somewhere to be," Melina added.

"A pleasure as always, my dear."

Mac and Melina continued their descent down the stone steps of the church until they reached their waiting limousine. Once they were inside and Marquise was firmly strapped into his car seat, Melina turned to her husband.

"Him showing up on the day of Marquise's christening is no coincidence. The bastard is up to something."

"Yes, he is."

Melina swallowed hard as a fresh welling of terror swelled up in her throat. She kissed her son's cheek as he slept, blissfully unaware of the chaos going on around him.

"Do you think … he would hurt our son?" she whispered.

Mac didn't say anything. He simply looked at her with an empty expression. She understood perfectly, and it scared her to the depths of her soul.

CHAPTER SEVEN

"Five more," Victoria said.

Enric gritted his teeth, a sneer working its way over his roughened features. "Woman, you're enjoying this too much. I can see it written all over your face."

"Three, two, one," Mac's sister counted down, a sardonic smile curving her lips. "All done."

Enric let the tension bands go with a heavy exhale. Neither of the two had seen Mac enter the rehab clinic, so he chose to stay back and watch their interactions while he had the chance. Call it his intuition, but he was pretty damn sure that he was witnessing the beginning of something happening with those two.

What, exactly?

He wasn't quite sure.

But there was something about Victoria that prickled at Enric. And there was something about Enric that *really* rattled Victoria's chains.

That kind of shit could make waves.

Mac leaned against the wall, waiting to see what his sister or Enric might do next. In the rehab clinic, probably nothing inappropriate that might cost Victoria her job, but he still wondered … His mother had always told him that spying only led to trouble, but this was too good to pass up.

Victoria bent down, staring at Enric at eye-level.

"Every single time you get put on my rotation, you won't work your legs. Not on the weights, resistance, or even simple exercises."

"So what?" Enric asked.

"That routine is just as important—more so, Enric—than what you *will* do with me. You need to keep it up."

"Not with you, Vickie."

Victoria glanced up at the ceiling. "You're being ridiculous because of pride."

Mac couldn't help but notice how his sister didn't react negatively to a nickname she had previously despised.

"Let me keep what I've got, woman," Enric said.

"Don't you get it?" Victoria asked sharply. "You'll get a lot more than just pride from this, Enric."

Enric looked like he didn't believe a single word that was coming out of her mouth. "Prove it."

Mac almost smiled at the glimmer of determination in his sister's eye. Victoria was predictable in that way, and she certainly wasn't one to back down from a challenge. Maybe it was a Maccari thing—something bred into their DNA that made them too damn stubborn for their own good.

Enric had just gained someone else on his team, whether he wanted Victoria there or not.

And ... should something come of that, Mac wouldn't be surprised, either.

Waves, after all.

Mac waited as Victoria said her goodbyes to Enric and then headed towards the front station with a clipboard in hand. Another girl in scrubs came to ask Enric if he needed help getting cleaned up to leave, but he refused, opting to head towards the locker room on his own.

A good twenty minutes later, Enric rolled back out of the locker room with his bag in his lap, and Mac finally decided to make his presence known since he was the man's ride. Enric noticed him approaching immediately, and pushed his wheelchair in Mac's direction.

The young nurse from earlier approached with a file in hand, probably the usual signoff and paperwork for his doctor. Enric snatched the folder and said, "Thanks, now scram."

The nurse did, not saying a word as she went.

Apparently, his bad attitude must have been well-known amongst the nurses.

"Could you at least smile at them while you're acting like a spoiled fucker?" Mac asked. "I mean, you are going to be coming here for a while. Don't shit where you eat and all that."

Enric scoffed. "Little late for that."

Interesting.

Mac wasn't going to push it, though. Besides, he was going to be stuck in a vehicle with Enric for a couple of hours. No need to get the guy in an even worse mood.

"You done?" Mac asked.

"Yep."

"Great. Let's get out of here and hit the road."

Enric was already wheeling himself towards the exit doors before Mac had even finished speaking.

An hour and a half later, and the prison housing was finally in sight. Enric hadn't said a single word for the entire drive, instead opting to stare out the window. Mac didn't mind the silence, for the most part, but since their destination was close, it was time to talk.

"Let him worry a little over you today," Mac said. "Don't brush him off or make one of your usual snide comments if he asks after you."

Enric's gaze stayed firmly on the window. "He doesn't need to bother. Besides, he has far more important things to be worrying about, given his situation."

Mac sighed, shaking his head. "That's not how it works, man. Not for us."

"Us?"

"Fathers."

Enric stiffened a bit in his seat. "I get that, Mac, but

I've done just fine on my own for a long while. I don't see the need to change anything between Luca and me anytime soon. We've done perfectly well like we are. Especially now, given the outlook of his circumstance, there's not much point to me depending on a father who can't help me from his position."

Ah.

So that was it.

It wasn't that Enric didn't want to allow his father closer, but rather, wasn't willing to take the risk of being hurt if he did.

"You act like Luca abandoned you for all these years," Mac said, passing his companion a look. "We both know that isn't true. Whatever distance is between the both of you is not by Luca's hand, but your own. You made that choice."

"I'm aware."

"Enric."

Mac got nothing in response.

He sighed loudly.

"*Enric.*"

"What?" the younger man snapped.

"It's never too late to admit that you might need your dad, even if it's just to have him ask if you're *okay*," Mac murmured.

"I *am* okay, Mac."

"That doesn't mean you don't need him to ask, so then you know that *he* knows you'll be just fine regardless, and maybe then that'll help his worrying, too. Luca loves you, but only as much as you have allowed, Enric. Again, that was not by his choice."

Enric didn't respond.

Mac didn't really need him to.

Enric wheeled himself out of the doors, looking slightly happier than he had before he entered. Mac hoped that was a good sign that the visit between father and son had gone better than expected. But then again, sometimes it was hard to tell with Enric.

"James Maccari, you're up next," came the call from the guard behind the Plexiglas.

Luca was no longer allowed visitors in small groups, but now, only one-on-one.

Mac passed Enric by with a nod as the man collected his things from the designated bin.

"I'll be waiting outside," Enric said.

"No smoking in the vehicle," Mac warned.

Enric scowled. "Yeah, yeah."

"I'm serious. Melina would have a fit if she smelled it."

Enric knew the rules.

And how Melina could be.

"I got it, boss," Enric muttered.

Mac readied to turn and correct Enric's casual use of a title that was in no way designated to him. Skip was one thing—Mac was a Capo, after all. Boss, though? That was quite another thing.

He didn't get the chance to correct Enric, as the guard at the door impatiently waved him along, looking like he was two seconds away from sending Mac back the way he had come. Mac couldn't afford to miss the meeting with Luca because he had mouthed off to a pushy guard. Especially considering the meetings with the locked up boss were already far and few between, Luca rarely used the phone to make calls to his men, and Mac happened to be one of the few that Luca *did* call on.

Mac was shuffled down a hallway, through another set of metal doors, then came another longer corridor, before being checked and rechecked again. He had already given up his jacket, the contents of his pants pockets, and his cell phone at the visitation check-in. Still, further in, he was given a more thorough search, and had his shoes replaced with booties.

Three thousand dollar leather loafers replaced with three dollar paper booties.

It was fucking undignified.

"*Cazzo*," Mac swore, "be easy with the leather, *merda*."

The guard behind the table barely passed Mac a glance as he unceremoniously dumped the expensive shoes into a waiting gray bin. There was no gentleness involved in the actions at all.

The only thing Mac could do was shoot the guy with a look that voiced his inner irritation before he was shuffled along *again*.

Damn.

He was starting to feel like the prisoner.

If somebody brought out the cuffs, Mac was gone.

Mac missed the simplicity of the jail where Luca had first been housed while he waited out his hearings and inevitable trial. Visiting the Cosa Nostra Don back then had not been so difficult or exhausting. The change in venue was apparently due to Luca's high profile, and the very nature of his charges.

At one time, the justice system had been innocent until proven guilty. Yeah, right.

Luca had been denied many things since his arrest— from contact with people outside of his lawyer, to a proper bail. The dignity of justice was gone.

Mac no longer believed that guilt had to be proven in a made man's circumstance, only believed.

Luca was the very proof.

Unless, that was, there was something that Mac didn't know. Something about the entire thing with Luca that he was missing.

Who knew?

Soon, Mac found himself in a secure visitation room, sitting across the metal table from Luca while the man picked at his supper on a tray. The food on the tray didn't appear to be very appetizing, and at least one of the reddish-brown lumps was something Mac couldn't decipher.

Luca waved a plastic spoon over the lump, seemingly noticing Mac's stare. "Take a guess."

"Uh ... shit?"

The boss chuckled in his drab, gray prison uniform. "Close enough. They say it is meatloaf. I say my wife, and her absolute shitty ability to cook anything, could make a better meatloaf."

Mac's brow furrowed. "Should it be that soggy?"

"No."

Well, then.

Speaking of Neeya ...

"I heard Neeya finally closed the deal on the mansion with a buyer," Mac said.

Luca didn't bother to look up from his food as he answered. "*Sì*, the lawyer let me know the last time he was in. Eleven million—a bit less than what I paid for the estate, but it's a decent price given the current market."

"The lawyer let you know?"

"That's what I said."

"*Neeya* didn't think to call?"

Luca sighed. "Something on your mind?"

Apparently, Mac was not being as sly as he thought he was with his line of questioning.

"You don't seem bothered that she sold your home," Mac noted.

"Hers, not mine." Luca smiled thinly. "From the day we married, every single thing I ever owned or bought was put into her name. It's *all* hers, Mac. And as such, she can do with any of it whatever she wishes to do."

"But doesn't any of it feel like yours?" Mac asked, knowing that he was already toeing a very careful line. It was not his place to ask questions or to demand answers about another man's—never mind the *boss's*—wife or marriage. Luca would have every right to shut Mac down. Mac persisted before Luca could do just that. "The cars you collected over the years, your family heirlooms, the paintings of your father and grandfather? None of it feels like yours?"

Luca finally glanced up from his food. "There is only one thing in this world other than my surname and the legacy it holds that belongs only to me now. Neeya knows what that is—she has always known. I've never doubted that."

Mac wanted to ask exactly what that was, but checked his impulse, knowing that he had already pushed his luck and Luca's good graces more than enough. The man was in prison, sure, but he was still who he was.

A boss.

And that deserved respect.

Always.

"Enric is doing well," Luca said between bites. "Mentioned he gained himself a new therapist."

Luca shot Mac with a sly smile, adding, "You, I mean."

"Someone has to keep his whiney ass in line."

"As long as you don't push too hard."

Mac stilled in his seat, catching Luca's eye for a moment. He heard the warning in the man's tone, but even more importantly, he heard the request. Not from a boss to his capo, or even a man to a man.

No, a father to a father.

Mac heard it.

"Enric has plenty of others to push him where I won't," Mac assured.

Luca nodded. "Good. *Perfetto.*"

"Have you had any contact with Enzo?"

"Not since ..." Luca trailed off, as though he had to consider how long it had actually been since he had a discussion with his underboss. "A while."

As far as Mac knew, Enzo was still being housed in

the jail where Luca had first been staying. He didn't understand why the boss had been moved due to the nature of his charges and upcoming trial, yet the underboss facing the same issues, had not.

Unless …

"Do you think the Feds are working Enzo for information?" Mac asked.

Luca shrugged. "You would have to be the one to tell me that, Mac."

The boss had offered the reply so easily, as though he didn't truly care one way or the other, but Mac didn't believe that to be true. Loyalty was everything to Luca, and if the man had even the slightest inkling that someone was infecting Enzo to turn on his boss and old friend, then a life would be lost.

"And what news do you have for me?" Luca asked, effectively changing the subject before Mac could press the man for more details on Enzo.

"Anthony."

Luca scowled, chewing his bite of food with a bit more force than before. "Keep going."

"He *suggests* that he has contact with either you, or Enzo, and behaves accordingly."

"Is that so?"

"Does he?"

Luca tapped a single finger to his temple. "Not *me*."

But perhaps Enzo.

Mac got the man's unspoken words. "*You* would be the better of the two, given some of his … actions lately."

"Like what?"

Mac quickly went over some of Anthony Corelli's latest nonsense, and the way the rest of the Pivetti Capos and their men were reacting to the actions and such. "He's certainly gotten the idea stuck in his head that he is justified—if not *expected*—to take some kind of control while others are unable. We've discussed this before, Luca."

"I'm still not sure why Anthony is going that route."

"I think it's pretty obvious. He'd like to find himself in the boss's seat when you're unable to fill it."

It was the first time Mac had suggested the inevitable to Luca. That the man, no matter how good his lawyers were or what the unknown would bring them, would not be free. He would not be returning to his previous position as the head of the family. It was what it was, and they needed to face what it could mean.

Luca was the boss.

That meant, up until he no longer held that title, he made the calls as to who should follow him and why.

"What about that rat problem you were having?" Luca asked.

Another subject change?

Mac pushed back his irritation. "I'd like to think that's Anthony, too."

"Really?"

"I have my reasons, just no proof."

"Would a rat kill while being tangled with the officials in some way?" Luca asked.

"He's the only one that makes sense."

Luca nodded. "Well, we'll certainly have that figured out soon enough, won't we? And after it's all said and done, if you still have the problem, then you know Anthony *is* the one causing those issues."

"After what is said and done?" Mac asked.

The boss went back to his food like he hadn't said a thing. "Soon enough. Tell me about your wife, and that baby of yours."

Mac had no choice but to give into the boss's request, knowing questioning Luca would likely get him nowhere. Once the man made up his mind, or decided to do something, it was already done, essentially. He didn't feel the need to explain it or talk it out with someone else.

It was simply a wait and see situation.

Mac would wait and see what Luca had done.

Mac checked his watch for the fifth time, before glancing around the upscale restaurant to see if his guest had shown up yet. There was no one at the front, making him sigh.

Maybe he could be a little bit more patient, given the situation. After all, he had planned this night as a sort of surprise for his wife, with no prior notice so that she could prepare. It wouldn't be strange for Melina to have a minor freak out at the idea of suddenly arriving home to babysitters, her bags packed, and a new dress waiting on her bed. He hadn't given anyone permission to explain *what* to tell Melina, and she was given nothing to expect. The only thing his wife would have found was the dress, and a note saying she was expected elsewhere for the evening, and to dress and look accordingly.

It was time, Mac thought.

Time for his wife to get away. Time for her to have a break, even if it was only for one night. It was *definitely* time for Mac to spend some time loving and showing his wife just how much he appreciated her.

It had been too long for them.

Since Marquise had been born, too much had been pushed aside. Mac didn't blame his son for that, as that's what happened when babies came along. Things changed. Lives had to change accordingly. The old rules no longer applied.

He was simply going to work around that little issue.

New rules, Mac mused.

Too many times, he had *just* started something with his wife at home in their bed, only to have the cries of a hungry or wet baby interrupt his not-so-innocent intentions. He knew that Melina had gotten her all clear from the doctor, which meant she was good to have all the fun in the world with Mac.

As long as they could find the time.

Mac was no longer looking for time.

He was fucking *making* it.

Marquise would be perfectly fine for one night with his godfather and godmother. He wasn't even leaving his own house. He would sleep in his own crib, and wake up there in the morning. The only difference?

He would not be cock blocking his father.

Win.

Melina would have had her panicked moment when she arrived home, waffled a bit on leaving the baby, but once she realized there was no other option, she would follow along with Mac's game. He was sure of it.

"You look mighty pleased about something," came a voice from the side.

Mac smiled at the silky, familiar tone of his wife. He found Melina standing at the side of his table, and chuckled at his own distraction. He missed her coming into the restaurant, which was a shame. He had really wanted to watch her walk across the floor in the dress he bought her for the night—the black, tight, sequined number hugged Melina's curves beautifully, and fell three inches above her knees.

"Well, what is it that has you smiling over here all by your lonesome?" Melina asked.

"Just thinking about you, doll, and all the hell you must have given Victoria and Enric before you left."

Melina's gaze narrowed as she stared out the restaurant window. "Yes, well, I'm sure Marquise will be perfectly fine for one night. *Now.*"

Mac cocked a brow. "Now?"

"I may have made some threats."

"Melina."

"What?" His wife smirked, shrugging a single dainty shoulder like she didn't have a care in the world. "Momma

Bear doesn't play, Mac."

No, she certainly didn't.

"They're doing me a great favor by watching the baby tonight," Mac said.

Melina waited for him to stand, pull out her chair, and only then did she sit, allowing him to push her back into the table. "You sprung this on me with no warning. I have not left Marquise alone for a whole night once since he was born. Some attitude should have been—at the very least—expected."

Mac nodded, letting his fingers drift through the soft curls at the nape of his wife's neck. He loved it when she wore her hair down in curls. They always looked like silk, soft and shiny, and he couldn't help himself but to touch. Her warm caramel-toned skin felt the same under his fingertips, only he felt the blood rush to the surface of her neck, her pulse picking up slightly, as his fingers drifted over her throat.

Leaning down, Mac placed a lingering kiss to his wife's cheek. "Oh, I always expect the attitude, doll."

"You're working for something tonight, aren't you?"

Mac had no intention of hiding that. "All night, if possible."

Melina's grin turned a bit wicked as Mac took his seat across from her. "You didn't need to take me away for the evening to get a good fuck, Mac."

He shot her a look.

Melina smirked. "What?"

"Yes, I absolutely did. Tomorrow, I intend to be exhausted because of one thing, and it is *not* going to be because a baby was hungry or wet."

She didn't even try to argue with him.

A server moved towards their table, offering to open the bottle of wine Mac had waiting, and ready to take their order. It was only after the server had left, and his wife was nursing a glass of wine, did Mac speak again.

"If you have something specific you might like to do

tonight, now would be the time to speak up and say so, doll."

Melina pursed her painted red lips. "What did you have planned first?"

"A show after this, then a beautiful suite with a hot tub and a big ass bed."

"That sounds lovely, actually."

"I thought so," Mac mused, grinning. "But I figured I should ask *you* if there was something you might like to do otherwise."

Melina looked up, swirling the wine in her glass. "A drive, maybe."

"A drive?"

"When do we ever get to drive, just you and me, anymore?" she asked.

Never.

He was always gone somewhere.

She was always busy.

"A drive it is," Mac agreed.

Mac moved his chair closer to his wife as they waited for their food to be served. By the time the food did finally get to them, he might as well have had Melina sitting in his lap, but she didn't seem to mind. There, he could give her all the attention she had probably been missing lately.

"You didn't tell me about the trip to the prison yesterday," Melina said as she righted her napkin on her lap. "Or how it all went."

"No business tonight, doll."

"It's not business. It was a *visit*."

"It's always business," Mac said with a wink. "And we're not doing that tonight."

His tone brokered no room for argument. Melina handed a fork over to him, and smiled like a pleased kitten with her cream as her husband fed her.

Melina played with the shimmering jewels on her clutch as Mac signed them into the hotel, and waited for the room key to be handed over. The dinner had ended long before the show was supposed to start, and Mac decided to take his wife on that drive, which lead them out of the city. By the time they had got back, the show was already well beyond the beginning, but Melina hadn't minded. She convinced him to leave the show before it was even over.

"Thanks," Mac said as the room key was finally handed over. He placed his hand to his wife's lower back, and directed her towards the elevator. "Let's go, doll."

Mac swore he could feel the shivers of anticipation already beginning to race through Melina's body, even through her sequined dress. He didn't blame her—already, he was counting the steps left to the elevator, and then the floors between the bottom and their suite. Too many, he decided.

He was a bit impatient.

"Top floor," Mac said as they slid into the elevator.

He would run down to the car to get their bags after.

Melina hit the appropriate button, and the doors slid closed, leaving them alone in the elevator before another guest could slide in with them. "I'm starting to wonder what kept you from booking the suite for the whole weekend."

"Because I know my wife," Mac murmured, his hand sliding down from her back to her pert ass. He gave her backside a pat. His fingers slipped up under the hem of the dress, so he could slide the tips along her inner thighs. Smooth and warm skin met his fingertips, and he grinned sinfully as she shot him a look over her shoulder. "By tomorrow morning, you'll be happy and sweet, but also ready to go home. A phone call won't be enough. You'll have to see Marquise, touch him ..." Mac chuckled, adding, "Smell him, probably."

That was some weird mom shit he didn't understand, but on more than one occasion, he had caught his wife sniffing their son's head like it was some kind of drug.

Melina shrugged. "Probably."

"Exactly."

"Can't you at least wait until we get inside the suite?"

Mac's fingers traveled higher between her thighs under her dress, coming in contact with thin lace covering her damp center. Heat met his fingertips, and another one of those shivers raced through his wife as he stroked her over her panties. "No, not really."

"God, you are ..."

"Going crazy?" Mac offered.

"Something," she said.

The faintness in her tone had him laughing deeply under his breath, and he knew then that his stroking, as light and teasing as it was, was definitely doing something for her. If only he felt like giving the camera up above their heads a bit of a show, he bet he could get his wife looking all kinds of crazy for the security people.

Mac held back.

But only barely.

"Something crazy," Melina added when the elevator shifted a second before the door opened to their floor.

She tossed him a sly wink over her shoulder as she stepped out into the hall, snatching the keycard from his hand and not even bothering to wait for him to follow. Mac shook his head, and stuffed his hands into his pockets to resist the urge to grab hold of his wife and drag her back where he could get his hands back between her beautiful thighs.

A few more steps, he told himself. *Not long now.*

He could wait a few more steps.

Surely.

Mac was lying to himself.

Melina had only managed to stop in front of their room, and slid the keycard into the slot before Mac was dragging the zipper of her dress all the way down. He split the fabric open as his hand dove back between her thighs. All he could see was more skin, and the curve of her ass covered by lace. Her breathless laugh filled the quiet, dark hallway before she stumbled into the room, and he followed, kicking the door closed with a loud slam behind them.

Mac didn't waste a bit of time after that. He finally had his wife alone, *almost* naked, and there was a guarantee of no interruptions.

Hell yes.

"You *are* impatient," Melina teased.

Mac shut her taunting up with a hard kiss, using her momentary distraction to his benefit to yank her dress down over her shoulders and hips until it pooled at her feet. He'd been playing with her silky hair all night, but not the way he liked, not the way he really *wanted* to. He fisted those soft strands at the nape of her neck to keep her in place as he explored the sweet heat of her mouth, taking away all her breath and soaking her in as his other hand roved down over her body.

Pretty lace covered her breasts, and her skin heated under his touch. He dragged his hand lower until he could grab a handful of her ass, too. Mac brought his wife in closer, needing to taste more of her, wanting to touch more of her.

He always wanted more of her.

Mac dotted kisses along his wife's jaw, feeling her smile grow sinful under his lips. "There's a stand right behind you, doll, do me a favor and bend over it for a few minutes."

It wasn't even a request.

Melina's brow rose. "Isn't there a bed in here?"

"We'll get there."

Eventually, he held back from adding.

Mac fully intended on dragging this night out as long as he possibly could. It had been far too long since he had his wife, since he had loved her properly, and he didn't want to waste a single moment of it.

When Melina didn't react as quickly as Mac wanted her to, he was the one to turn her around, his hand snapping against the curve of her backside just hard enough to make her gasp the sweetest sound. Instinctively, his wife reached out for the stand, her fingers curling around the edges as her back curved under his touch running down her naked spine.

Mac's fingers tangled into the sides of her panties, and in a flash, he'd pulled the scrap of lace down her legs and out of his fucking way. The sliver of her pink sex peeking out at him, teasing him, was enough to bring him to his knees.

Quite *literally*.

The moment his mouth came in contact with his wife's pussy, Melina jerked forward, a loud cry bouncing off the room's walls and echoing back. Mac sent out a silent apology to any other guests on their floor that might be interrupted by his wife's loudness, but he couldn't feel it in himself to be too guilty.

After all, the only thing he could taste was the hot, heady tartness of his wife's arousal soaking his tongue as her hands slammed down onto the table, and she demanded more. The only thing he wanted to hear was her cries as they got a little bit more desperate, and she rode his face just the way she liked the best.

The smell of her, the taste of her ... that was heaven to Mac.

A sinful heaven, to be sure, but heaven all the same.

Mac fully intended to tease his wife over and over throughout the night, until she was pink-cheeked and flushed all over, both begging and ready to demand what she wanted, but right then, he just wanted to make her come. His hands slid down from her ass to her ankles, and his fingers wrapped tight as his tongue found that *sweet* spot that made his wife shake.

Melina stiffened above him, her back curving harder, and her legs trembling under his hold as more of her juices flooded his tongue and she came.

Hot, loud, and hard.

Fuck, yeah.

Way too long.

Mac was standing before Melina had even finished. His hands dragged up the backs of her legs and thighs to soak in her heat and shivering. Her quick breaths, broken up by bouts of breathless laughter, had him smiling.

"And *now* you can get in bed," Mac whispered in her ear. "But—"

"Keep the shoes on."

She knew him so well.

"You got it, doll."

Mac barely gave the hotel room a once over as he followed close behind Melina to the sectioned off bedroom, private from the main rooms. He probably should have stopped to appreciate the expensive settings, waiting trays, and champagne set out for them to enjoy. He had other things on his mind.

Like the sway of his wife's ass.

And her legs in those heels.

Damn.

"Back or knees?" Melina asked over her shoulder.

"Back," Mac answered. "We'll get to the other bits later."

Melina only shook her head, but did as he said, falling to her back on the bed a second before he was standing at the bottom, shedding his clothes piece by piece. It was only after he was completely naked and had a condom slid down the length of his erection—one baby was enough for now—did he finally climb in between the open invitation of his wife's thighs.

Melina sighed sweetly as Mac's cock filled her full. Her pretty lips fell open in a perfect O shape as her head tilted back into the many pillows. It was like a tight, wet, warm velvet had suddenly wrapped his dick and wasn't planning on letting go anytime soon. Mac was damn near lost in that sensation.

Another flex of his hips, and he found himself even deeper.

Melina tensed. "Easy."

Mac ran the tips of his fingers over the slope of her nose and cheekbones, careful, sweet touches as he felt her inner muscles flex around his cock. "I will."

Even sex couldn't quite be the same after a baby, he knew. As much as he wanted to fuck his wife as hard and as fast as he could possibly manage to, he simply couldn't do that. It *had* been too long, and she needed to be loved accordingly.

"This," Mac said, his fingertips gliding over her bottom lip.

"Hmm?"

Airless and soft, her words came out like a caress.

Mac kissed Melina's bottom lip. "This here," he said again, repeating the motion. "All your shapes and curves. I love them."

Melina smiled, her legs wrapping tight around him, the heels of her pumps digging into the backs of his thighs. A shift of her hips, and he was pulling out again, sinking back inside her wet sex slower than before.

He didn't mind slow for now.

He felt so much more when he took the time to enjoy it.

Her russet eyes watched him, pupils blown and bliss so evident. "So is this going to be a new thing—this taking me away for a night?"

"Yes. Definitely *yes*."

Melina stretched and yawned against Mac's side, shimmying in closer to his body at the same time. Morning light spilled in through the window, highlighting the curves of his wife's body as he traced them for the hundredth time with his hands.

"You were right," she murmured, the exhaustion yet happiness thick in her tone.

"I usually am, but indulge me this time. About what?"

"I don't want to leave, but I have the strangest urge to go home and sniff the baby's head."

Mac snorted, entirely amused at the admission. "He smells like lotion and milk, Melina."

Or depending on the time of day or when he fed, Marquise could have a whole bunch of unpleasant smells, too.

"And me," she mumbled. "He smells like me and mine."

His brow furrowed as he took in those words, unsure of how to reply. "Like your things, or …?"

"No, like my baby. He smells like *mine*."

"Oh."

Melina smiled against his pec. "It's a mom thing."

"We can get going, doll."

"Okay."

"Go have a shower and I'll get some breakfast up here. We'll eat before we go."

Melina dragged herself out of the bed, both looking as though she wanted to leave, and like she might crawl right back under the sheets with him. As she disappeared into the attached bath, she called over her shoulder, "But call and check on the baby."

"He's fine. I'm sure."

"Call!"

Mac was already reaching for the phone. It rang twice before someone picked up at his home. The angry wails of Marquise echoed in the background.

"*Ciao*," Mac said into the phone.

"I think he likes his milk straight from the boob," Victoria muttered in the other end.

Mac did his best not to laugh, and failed miserably. Marquise wasn't even breastfed now. "So he's basically good, then?"

"Here, talk to your equally annoying *friend*," his sister grumbled.

Two seconds later, Enric was on the phone, sounding slightly happier than Victoria. "I think Marquise has just figured out that his mom actually isn't home this morning. He was fine through the night taking a bottle, but today he's looking for her."

"Makes sense," Mac said. "We're going to eat and then we'll head home right after."

"Great." A beat of silence passed before Enric asked, "Did you get a call this morning?"

"I turned the cell off last night—I only gave the room phone number to you and Vic."

"Huh. You might want to check your phone."

"Why?" Mac asked. "What happened?"

Something *always* happened.

He wanted *one* night with his wife.

Mac was not asking for a lot.

"It's Enzo," Enric said.

"What about him?"

"Guess they found him dead in his cell this morning during roll call. They haven't called it or made an official announcement yet, but the guy's a staunch Catholic, so …"

"He didn't kill himself."

"No good made man would, Mac."

Had Luca just made his move?

113

CHAPTER EIGHT

When Melina emerged from the luxurious two person stone shower it was as if the hot water had washed away her worries.

At least some of them.

On the other hand, perhaps it was the spectacular loving her husband gifted her with last night and early this morning. She hadn't intended for them to go so long without being intimate. After all, Mac was a man and he had needs. Just as she did. Those needs had been satisfied in every possible way and were directly responsible for the good mood she was in.

Though she and Mac had desperately needed an evening away, Melina would be glad to get back home to their son. There was no doubt in her mind that Marquise had noticed her absence by now. Throwing her hair up in a ponytail and squeezing into a black jumpsuit, Melina didn't bother with makeup.

Leaving the bathroom she found their bags packed and the bedroom empty. A delicious aroma reached her nose, and Melina followed the scent to the dining area where she found a large breakfast spread on the table. Heat lifted from the food, and she couldn't help how her mouth started to water.

She started to sit down at the glass table trying to decide what she was going to eat first. That's when it dawned on her she still hadn't laid eyes on her husband.

"Mac?"

Melina made her way into the living room and that's where she found him. His back was to her as he looked out of the window, down at the scene below him. With one hand pressed against the glass and the other in his pocket, he looked calm. At ease. At least he would to someone who didn't know him like she did. The energy coming from him screamed trouble.

"Mac?" she called again.

He turned around and smiled at her lackadaisically. "Why aren't you eating?"

"Why aren't you?"

"I was waiting for you, doll." He came towards her.

"I'm here now, so let's eat."

She offered her hand, and he took it to follow her back into the dining area. He was quiet as he pulled out the chair for her, allowing her to sit down. Melina unfolded her napkin and put it in her lap as Mac took his own seat.

"Our son misses you," he finally said.

"I bet he does. He's not used to me being away this long." She took a bite of the French toast she'd put on her plate.

"Vic assumes he prefers the boob to the bottle or something, and he hasn't even breastfed since he was brand new."

Melina put her napkin to her mouth in an effort not to spit out the food she'd been chewing on. Laughter bubbled up hard in her throat.

"That sounds like something your sister would say."

"You know Vic."

Melina poured herself a glass of orange juice and took a sip before she spoke again.

"Yeah, I know Vic. I also know you, so what happened?"

"Doll, what are you talking about?"

She waved a finger at him. "Nope. Don't even try it.

You looked like a man on top of the world before I went to take my shower. Now it looks like the weight of the world is on your shoulders again. Something happened so don't waste your breath lying to me."

Melina cut another piece of the cinnamon flavored French toast as she waited for her husband to speak. Mac scowled as he helped himself to pancakes and eggs. A few minutes later he finally spoke.

"There's been a death."

Melina nodded. "Okay. Whose?"

Mac's eyes were steely. "Enzo."

She put her fork down. The breakfast she'd been enjoying so much, suddenly tasted like sand in her mouth.

"How? Why?"

"That is what has to be figured out."

"It seems that every time we turn around death is breathing down on us."

"It happens in times of upheaval and uncertainty."

Melina took a sip of the cold, tart sweet orange juice as she considered what her husband said. He was right, but that still didn't make up for the obvious. They had no idea what to expect next.

"This isn't going to be resolved anytime soon," she said. It wasn't a question.

"No. It isn't."

"Then the question remains. Who has the most to gain with the boss imprisoned, and his next in command dead?"

"Me," Mac said with no inflection in his voice.

Melina rolled her eyes. "Those that don't know you might say that. Those that do, know better."

"I really don't want to spoil our day talking about this, doll."

"No use in pretending it didn't happen either, Mac. But okay."

They finished the rest of their breakfast in silence and when it came time to leave, Mac gave a hefty tip to the man at the front desk for the excellent service they'd received. As she buckled her seat belt, Mac hopped into the driver's side and started the car.

It was amazing how one phone call really could change everything. For less than a day they had been able to put the problems with the Pivetti Organization on the backburner and simply be a husband and wife enjoying a night away from their growing infant. Now they would return to high alert and suspecting the motives of every person around them. That kind of deceit and distrust was toxic to the soul and for the first time Melina wondered if she was truly strong enough to withstand the new storm that she knew was brewing.

"Mama missed her baby so much. Yes, she did."

Melina held Marquise up in front of her and kissed his nose. The smile on his face hit her straight in the heart. It was love, light, and heaven all wrapped in one. He reached for her, and she pulled him into her arms, fondling his curls as she breathed in his soft, baby scent.

"Doll, you act like we were gone a week or something," Mac teased.

"Shut it, Maccari."

Sitting beside her on the couch, Victoria laughed. "I guess she told you, buddy."

Mac shook his head. "Don't encourage her, Vic. You two always gang up on me when you get together."

"What can I say? It's what sisters do," Victoria said.

"God bless you, Skip," Enric said.

Melina watched as Victoria's eyes narrowed on the bodyguard. "Just when I was beginning to like you."

Enric folded his arms. "You still like me."

"Whatever," Victoria huffed.

Mac muttered something under his breath before he came over and took Marquise from Melina. A wide smile curved his face as their son grabbed Mac's thumb and put it in his mouth. Melina couldn't help laughing as Marquise sucked noisily.

"I missed you too, little guy. I heard you were giving Aunt Vic and Uncle Enric a fit this morning."

Marquise seemed to frown at his father's words.

"Okay. Maybe my information was wrong," Mac said.

Marquise released Mac's thumb and cooed at his father. The sight of them together was everything to Melina. The sheer bliss on her husband's face every time he held the angel they'd created. Yes. Moments like this were worth any battles they had yet to face.

"We'd better get going, Skip," Enric said in a quiet tone.

Mac frowned at the young man, a subtle droop in his shoulders as he gave Marquise back to Melina.

"I'll be back soon, doll."

He kissed her hard, before pressing a soft kiss on the top of Marquise's head. A few minutes later, she and Victoria were alone. Her son nestled into her arms, pressing his face into her chest. Soon he was asleep.

"So … wanna talk about it?" Victoria asked.

"About what?"

"Whatever is bothering you, I guess? Both you and my brother are trying to hide it, but you're both tense as hell."

"No point in crying over things you can't change, Victoria. Besides, why don't we talk about you and Enric?"

Her sister-in-law rolled her eyes. "What's to talk about? Just when I think he's not so insufferable, he opens his mouth and ruins my delusion."

"You should be used to cocky Italians by now."

"Yeah, right. Enric is a special breed of cocky."

"Yes. A special breed. Don't overlook that."

Victoria folded her arms. "Meaning what? I hope

you're not saying what I think you are."

"Yes, I am. There's something between you and Enric. I for one would like to see it play out. I think secretly you do, too."

"You're playing matchmaker now? Jesus. This is where I make my exit."

Melina smirked as Victoria kissed Marquise's cheek and got to her feet.

"We all deserve a little happiness in this messed up world we live in." Melina got to her feet to walk Victoria out.

"I think being married to my brother is making you soft, Melina. What happened to the hellcat I first met?"

"She's still here. I just save her for special occasions."

"I hear you. Give me a ring next time you want to hang out or have me babysit. Baby sugar works magic on your mood, let me tell you."

"It sure does. I'll call you soon."

The two women said their goodbyes, and Melina relocked the door behind Victoria. Marquise was still sound asleep in her arms. Smiling to herself, she carried her son into her bedroom and laid him gently down in the middle of her and Mac's bed. There was no real reason Marquise couldn't have been put in his crib, except she wanted to watch him sleep. She'd only been away from him a single night, but the depths of which she'd missed her baby surprised even her. Would it always be like this? A bond so strong that you hated to be away from them if you didn't have to.

Melina touched one of Marquise's soft curls. He was growing so fast. Every day it seemed he was reaching some new milestone. She knew there would never be a day when something about her son didn't fascinate her. All that mattered was making sure that there would be more days ahead for him. For all of them. Victoria had been too perceptive for her own good, but there were just some things that she couldn't talk about.

Enzo's death was one of them.

Though the man had held a grudge against Mac, she hadn't felt about him one way or another. That didn't make his death any less shocking. The Pivetti Organization was crumbling rapidly. Luca was one of the few good men left standing and with a very real prison sentence looming in front of him. He was the last domino that needed to fall before a complete takeover happened.

The jackals were already waiting to pick over the scraps.

Speaking of jackals, easing herself carefully from the bed so as not to wake up her son, Melina left the room and went back into the living room. Locating her purse, she reached inside and removed her cellphone, quickly dialing a now familiar number. She was almost ready to end the call, when the other line was finally picked up.

"Hey, I was just thinking about you."

"Really? And why is that?" Melina asked.

"Let's just say a particular someone is saying some very interesting things," Erika said.

"You mean your good friend, Anthony."

"Of course. Who else?"

Melina held the phone tight to her ear. "Tell me what you know."

"We spent some time together a few days ago, and he told me change was in the air. Naturally, I didn't pay much attention to that because it was such a broad statement. But then he said it wouldn't matter when a king falls because a new ruler is already in place."

Melina chewed her lip for a moment. She knew exactly what Anthony was referring to, but she decided to play along a little further. "That's still a little cryptic."

"Yeah, it is. But then he said that there was only room for fresh blood now, and those that think they're untouchable are about to find out that they're not," Erika said.

"It sounds to me like Anthony wants to hear himself

speak and pump himself up a little bit in the process. No doubt he's trying to impress you." She wandered back into the bedroom where Marquise was still sleeping soundly.

"He definitely does that, but I think there's more to it this time. Anthony said if I stick with him a little longer, it will be well worth my while."

Melina was silent a moment as she digested what Erika had just told her. Anthony Corelli was an interesting individual.

An individual about to make a move.

A big one.

She could only imagine what it could be.

"I guess all we can do is keep our eyes open and see if Anthony's bark leads to bites."

Erika laughed. "That's an interesting way of putting things."

"Indeed. I'll be in touch. Keep up the good work."

"Will do, Boss Lady."

Melina ended the call and put her phone on the nightstand before she crawled back into bed, and rested next to her son.

A coup was in the making, and Anthony was leading it.

She wasn't surprised. Not in the least. Anthony was one of those men that was never satisfied with what he had. He always had to be greedy, reaching for more, determined to destroy anyone in his path that threatened his self-involved plans. He was like a shark swimming towards bleeding prey.

That made him dangerous.

A war was coming.

God help them all.

Mac had been unusually tight lipped in the days since they'd returned from their evening out. She'd tried several times to bring him out of it. Nothing seemed to be working. Even when he spent time with Marquise, the smiles he gave their son didn't quite reach his eyes. It was as if Mac was there but he wasn't. She knew it hadn't helped matters that she'd shared the latest Erika had garnered from Anthony.

She had her proof when Mac nearly punched a hole through the wall of their bedroom. He had no idea that she'd seen him. Something was very wrong.

Her husband, who usually was one of the most collected men she'd ever met, had lost his cool. It was a defining moment to her.

A moment she didn't want a repeat of.

She sat beside him now as their limousine pulled up to the church. They were attending another funeral.

Enzo's.

Regardless of the animosity between Mac and Enzo, her husband had still given the man the respect he was entitled to as underboss. Despite the fact that Mac had to kill Enzo's son for the betrayal that lead to a whole host of other problems, he was still putting his own feelings aside to show respect one last time. It was one of the qualities she both admired and loved about her husband. It was also one of the qualities that could quietly infuriate her.

"Mac?"

"Yeah."

She faced him and took his hand. "I need you to do something for me."

His expression was blank. "What?"

"I need you to remember that Marquise and I love you, no matter what."

Mac frowned. "I know that."

"Then act like it." Her tone was steely, more than she intended.

"Everything I do is for you and our son. You know

that."

"I know. Just don't forget that all we really need is you in the process."

"And what is that supposed to mean, Melina?"

"It means I have no idea what kind of stress you're under, or the depths of the danger you're protecting us from, but stop taking that stress out on me and your son."

She offered him a tight smile before she exited the limousine. Melina didn't like fighting with Mac. They were a team, facing whatever the world decided to throw at them. They couldn't have division between them. But sometimes the hard truths needed to be said. She'd barely taken a breath before Mac was at her side, taking a hold of her arm.

"You and Marquise are everything to me." His voice was even but his jaw was tight.

"I know."

"Then I admit to being at a loss."

Melina caught her husband's eye and for the first time the words she'd said to him gave her pause. Weariness and sadness colored his face. Things had to end and soon for all their sakes. In the meantime, he needed her to do what she did best ... be his partner. Uncaring of anyone that might see them, she leaned close and kissed Mac. He didn't hesitate to return the kiss and the force of it rocked her to her core.

Passion.

Excitement.

Love.

It was exactly what both of them needed.

It always would be.

When Mac finally pulled away, the hint of a smile played on his face. "Thank you."

"For what?" she asked.

"For explaining things as only you could. I understand now."

"Then my work is done."

"Mine is only just beginning, doll."

Feeling a lightness that she hadn't in days, Melina allowed Mac to help her up the stairs that would lead them inside the massive church. A throng of people passed them, some nodding politely at her husband. Others seemed to do their best to avoid his gaze. Saying the atmosphere was tense was an understatement. As they took their seats, Melina steeled herself. Sitting directly across from them was Anthony Corelli. He made no effort to hide his interest in their arrival.

"Looks like my biggest fan is here," Melina whispered.

"Vultures love to circle at times like this."

"King Buzzard over there could look a little less obvious."

"King Buzzard?" Mac tried to smother his laughter.

"Well, it *fits*."

Before Mac could say anything else the service began. They held hands as the priest conducted the service. Melina could only wonder how many of these they would have to sit through. How many more families would be destroyed for the sake of greed and power? Melina blinked back tears when Enzo's widow approached his coffin at the middle of the service.

The priest stopped momentarily, distracted, and concerned. Though Madeline had said her goodbyes already, it was as if she was a woman possessed now. There weren't words adequate enough to describe the look of sorrow on her face. To lose her only son and then her husband. It was a grief that no one should ever have to experience. The service continued, and Madeline continued to stand in front of Enzo's coffin.

And then grief won.

A cascade of tears poured down her cheeks as her sobs filled the church. The priest stopped, ready to comfort her, but was quickly waved away by none other than Neeya Pivetti. Melina watched curiously as Neeya went to Madeline, and helped the grieving woman back to her seat. Melina exchanged a glance with her husband. Mac seemed as surprised as she was to see the Pivetti Don's wife today.

Soon the eulogy was over, and Enzo's coffin was closed for the final time as pallbearers carried him from the church. Still crying, Madeline rose to follow behind her husband's coffin. Her cheeks were still tearstained, but there was a hardness in her eyes. A hollowness. After today, Madeline would never be the same. Melina's heart broke all over again. She squeezed Mac's hand tight.

"Are you all right?" he asked.

She shook her head. "No. Not by a long shot."

"This won't be us. Whatever it takes. Whatever I have to do, I won't let our life be destroyed."

"No one can predict the future, Mac, but I have absolute faith in you."

"And that means everything, doll."

Slowly the church started to clear, and Mac and Melina followed the departing crowd. Once outside, she glanced around the thinning crowd and spotted Neeya walking down the steps, and towards the sidewalk where cars waited to take the mourners away from the church.

"Neeya," Melina yelled.

The woman continued on as if she hadn't heard Melina.

"We should get going," Mac said.

"Yeah, we should."

Feeling a bit miffed, Melina watched as Neeya was helped into the back of a white limousine. The chauffeur closed the door for her, and a minute later the car was driving away. Mac and Melina had just reached their own waiting vehicle when a fireball erupted. Before Melina could react, Mac was pushing her inside the car.

"Stay down, doll."

Melina didn't dare move as car alarms went off.

Soon, screams filled the air and a thick, smoky odor

filled her senses.

No. It couldn't be.

Ignoring her husband's instruction, Melina lifted her head and looked out the back passenger window.

Blood rushed in her ears.

She refused to believe what she was seeing.

Flames engulfed a white limousine.

A white limousine that had only departed moments ago.

A white limousine carrying Neeya Pivetti.

CHAPTER NINE

The screams were deafening, but it was nothing compared to the noise level of the blast. Tires squealed, and Mac saw a black car speed out of the parking lot, followed shortly after by several others—people wanting to get away. Most were scrambling like rats, crouched low against vehicles or scattering on all fours, rushing to their waiting vehicles.

Mac reached for his wife to keep her right where she was. He didn't want her moving an inch, just in case the limo wasn't the only car with a planted bomb waiting to blow. An enforcer was always placed at his vehicle to watch it, so he wasn't worried about theirs blowing the hell up.

"Mac," he heard Melina say.

So faint.

So unsure.

Mac couldn't move, let alone respond to Melina. He was frozen in place, stuck watching the flames engulfing the now unmoving limo, and the black plume of smoke rising higher towards the sky. A part of his brain understood what he was seeing, but another part couldn't process what it all meant.

Or maybe he didn't want to process it.

Oh, he surely understood the bomb the very second it happened. The blast damn near pushed him to the ground, but now, it was almost like his mind was trying to backtrack and *forget*.

No, maybe not forget.

Refuse.

Refuse what he saw.

Refuse what just happened.

Refuse what it would mean.

A made man's wife had been in that limo. The *boss's* wife. *Luca's* wife.

"Neeya," Melina mumbled from inside the vehicle.

Mac wondered if his wife could read his thoughts, though he knew how stupid that was. Melina was simply voicing her own shock and pain to a frightening reality. Her friend—one of the few his wife actually had in this dangerous life of theirs—had been inside that limo. A bomb of that magnitude was not survivable.

His thoughts flew back to his boss instantly in that moment.

Luca.

How would he tell Luca?

"Ma!"

"Mother!"

"*Ma!*"

Mac was brought back to reality with a bang. And by the horrified, agonized shouts of three young women bursting through the dispersing crowd.

Beautiful girls who looked like both their mother and father. Respected daughters of a Cosa Nostra boss and his wife.

Rose.

Hope.

Lora.

Pivetti girls. Pivetti daughters.

Twenty-two.

Twenty.

Eighteen years young.

They had still lived at home with their parents. The oldest two attended college while the youngest had recently graduated from a private high school.

Frantic.

Terrified.

Lost.

Each one of the Pivetti girls took on those expressions. They were pulled back—fighting and screaming the whole way—by family before they could get any closer to the danger of the burning limo.

To their mother …

"My God," Melina whispered.

"I didn't see the girls earlier," Mac managed to say.

Melina didn't reply.

Mac searched through the faces in the crowd, although he wasn't entirely sure what he was looking for. Or *who* he was looking for.

His vision blurred.

The people became fuzzy.

They needed to leave.

Now.

So much had happened because of one action. So much more would happen because of it, too. But all of that was just too much for Mac to consider and deal with in those moments.

Mac had other things to worry about.

Like his own damn wife, who was very much alive.

Mac intended to keep her that way, too.

"Time to go, doll."

Melina didn't fight him as he pulled her away.

Mac wasn't even sure that he had properly parked his car before he had cut the engine. He couldn't find it in himself to care, either, as he headed towards the cement and barbed wire protected building. He had far more important things on his mind.

He had only taken his wife home, waited long enough to make sure she was settled in with their son, and then he hit the road. He had to get to the boss. The boss had to *know*.

Mac had tried to call into the prison, stating it was an emergency. But he had refused to give any details of the emergency, so he wasn't promised a call back from Luca. He'd even tried getting ahold of the boss's new lawyer, but the offices were closed, and no one was replying to the afterhours messaging line.

So … Mac panicked.

Knowing the prison visiting hours, he jumped in his vehicle and decided to just go the fuck over there himself. If it were him—had it been his wife in that limo—Mac would want to be told by someone he knew, respected, and trusted.

Luca didn't need to see it on a news program.

He shouldn't be told by a passing guard.

That was just goddamn undignified.

Mac made it inside the prison in record time. He weaved through the people in the entrance, cutting through the line waiting to get through the first—and easiest—security check. He ignored the annoyed "hey's" as he slipped into the front of the line and was waved through the metal detector by a guard.

Less than three minutes later, he was cutting through another line—this one to check in, sign in, and request a visit if possible.

He could tell just by the amount of visiting people that he would likely have to wait. It was clearly a busy day for the prison. That only made him more anxious as he stepped up to the window, and a clipboard was passed through.

Mac jotted down his name and details, as well as Luca's, the reason for his visit, and so forth. Then, he pushed the clipboard back through to the gum-snapping, waiting woman.

"Please have a seat," the woman said, waving towards a waiting area filled with people. There weren't even any seats left to sit in. *Fuck.* "Someone will call your name to bring you through another round of security checks before your visitation."

Mac sighed. "It's kind of an emergency."

Understatement.

The woman glanced down at the form Mac had filled out. "You only stated "Emergency" on the Reason for Visitation line of the form. According to the rest of your information, you are neither the inmate's lawyer, nor doctor, so I can't request a faster check-in. Sorry."

Mac had every mind to stand there and argue with the woman, but he knew that wouldn't help. This was her job—she was only doing it according to the prison policy. And if he did let his mouth fly, he might find himself escorted out without even having seen Luca at all.

He didn't want that.

"Sure, no problem," Mac told the woman, offering her a smile that was entirely false.

Mac rested against one of the walls in the waiting area, since there weren't any chairs to take. He surveyed the faces of the waiting people, just to make sure there were none he recognized. In the far right corner of the room, a television played the expected weather forecast for next week.

He kept watching TV, hoping he wouldn't see anything—or very little—about the car bombing. It would, of course, be front page news, but it was unlikely that the media would get details for another few days.

Kids ran around the waiting area. Some colored at a small plastic table in corner. The waiting people chatted, like a dull roar in the background of Mac's mind. He wasn't really hearing any of it at all. He was too focused on the news program.

The broadcast did show a brief flash of the event,

anchor's stating they would have more details soon. One suspected dead, they noted, but no names yet from police. Roads were closed due to officials' presence, dangers, and cleanup.

The small snippet didn't even name who the funeral had been for.

Mac let out a small sigh of relief.

He wasn't sure how long he waited there, resting against the wall. An hour, but more like two. Long enough that when he finally heard his name being called, the guard had to call it louder the second time just to break Mac from his daze. With stiff limbs, Mac walked forward.

The guard looked down at the clipboard in his hands and said, "Sorry, but the inmate you requested to visit is no longer taking guests today, so you'll have to come back on another day."

Mac's fists clenched into balls at his sides. "Sure, but this is kind of important."

"Can't help it, man. I'm just doing what I'm told."

"Luca Pivetti's wife was killed today, and I would really like to be the one to let him know, before he finds out from the fucking news or some stranger."

Again, the guard looked down at his papers. "I take it, the inmate is already aware, given the guard noted he was unwilling to have a visitor due to receiving some bad news that was upsetting. Like I said, nothing I can do, man."

Mac's stomach fell. "Shit."

He wanted to ask *how* Luca knew, but figured this guy likely wouldn't know.

"Besides, we only allow inmates one visit per day unless there are special circumstances. The inmate has already had his one visit today."

What?

"Who?" Mac asked.

The guard shrugged. "Not allowed to give those details out."

This was getting Mac nowhere. He thanked the

guard—for fucking nothing—and headed back out to his car. Mac had just dialed his wife's number and put the phone to his ear when he looked out the window. A familiar face was walking across the parking lot.

What were the odds?

And *why*?

"Hello?" he heard Melina ask on the other end of the call.

"Anthony."

"What?"

"Anthony is at the prison," Mac told his wife. "He was here to tell Luca about Neeya."

"Why would Anthony be there?" Mac paced the length of his living room, needing space and movement while he ranted away. "Why would the boss even allow that man to *speak* in his presence?"

"Mac," Melina started to say.

"He's a fucking snake! Anthony is a snake, and Luca knows it."

"Mac."

His wife's tone came out firmer the second time, but Mac was too lost in his own head to heed the warning. He kept venting and pacing, still trying to figure out what in the hell he had missed in this whole thing.

All the while, his wife sat on the couch, feeding their son. She kept one eye on Mac the whole time.

For all its guts and glory, Cosa Nostra was, at its heart, nothing more than a game of sorts between unworthy men, and the honorable ones. Mac liked to think that men who played the game by the rules—men like himself—were given an advantage of sorts. That advantage usually came in the form of trust from other made men. A sort of respect that led credence and support to his position and even slightly lessened the target on his back.

And then there were the men like Anthony.

The unworthy ones.

Liars.

Cheats.

Sneaks.

Fucking *snakes*.

Men who played the game by their own rules, even to the detriment of everyone else around them. A man who would probably fuck over his own mother, if he thought it would somehow get him higher in the family.

Mac had learned over the years—the majority of those being spent on the sidelines as a solider of Cosa Nostra—that the unworthy men eventually ran their course. Karma, of sorts. *What goes around, comes around.* Those men always got what they deserved.

Except …

Mac blew out a hard breath, and scrubbed a hand down his smooth-shaven jaw.

Anthony had not met his karma, yet. His shitty moves and untrustworthy nature had yet to come back around and bite the man in the ass like it should have done ages ago. Maybe it was Mac that was being impatient, but at the moment, he couldn't exactly afford to be much else.

Especially now.

The one thing Mac *definitely* wouldn't do?

Not for Anthony, or any made man?

It was simple.

He would never sacrifice his own honor to expose their lack of it.

There had to be another way …

"Mac."

Finally, Melina's tone had turned annoyed enough for Mac to really take notice. He turned to face his wife, only to find her standing a couple of feet away, with her hands planted firmly on her hips. A frown marred her pretty lips.

Where was their son?

Hadn't she just been feeding him?

"What did you do with the baby?" he asked.

"I put him in his crib for his nap," Melina said slowly, as though she were talking to a small child and not a grown man. "He had his bottle and fell asleep in my arms. I thought your going-ons might wake him up if I kept him out here."

Fuck.

Had he been going on for that long, lost to his own thoughts?

Mac felt like he was losing his damn mind.

"Sorry, doll," he muttered.

"You're overthinking your problem—you do that too much, Mac."

"Anthony is not a simple problem. The boss had a conversation with him, and after everything that's happened, it's not simple."

"So get rid of him," Melina said like it was the most obvious thing in the world. "That is an easy enough solution."

"On the surface, sure. To say it, absolutely. To actually do it, though? No, it's not that simple. Maybe for someone else, but not for me. Cosa Nostra has rules for a reason. Made men follow the code for the oath they spoke for a reason."

"What about someone who isn't made? What about a woman?"

"Doll."

"What about me?" she asked.

Mac held back his immediate rising urge to shut down that idea. And he only did that for Melina's benefit—no need to go pissing off the Queen of his household. He had enough problems without adding that one to it, as well.

"There are some aspects of my affairs that I would rather you … not touch," Mac said, choosing each word carefully.

"I have a woman at The Dollhouse whom Anthony calls on several times a week. He wouldn't even know what hit him. And neither would anyone else, for that matter. We could just get rid of him after it was done like nothing even happened. Simple, clean, and there goes all your problems."

Mac had to admit, Melina's suggestion *was* appealing to the side of him that just wanted Anthony gone. The other part of him—the honorable part—knew he couldn't agree because it was, at its core, wrong.

He glanced up at the ceiling, again being careful with his words. "People would still look to me, doll. I'm the only one with any kind of serious, public beef with that idiot right now."

"Assumption and proof are two very different things," Melina pointed out.

"Then why does assumption—not proof—kill men like me more often than not?"

Melina didn't respond.

Mac figured his point was made.

Melina frowned. "What if *this* was Anthony's point?"

"Pardon?"

"Making people look to you," she clarified.

Mac still didn't understand.

Melina rolled her eyes, saying, "Yesterday, the funeral and the bomb—*Neeya*. Being the first to see Luca. Making it appear like now *you* have to say to others that the boss wouldn't accept a visitation from you. Giving people a reason to think that maybe Luca has cause not to trust you—like people should look to you, Mac. What if all of *that* was Anthony's point?"

Mac fell silent.

Melina nodded at his reaction. "Yeah, sometimes, I think you just need someone else to say things for you to actually hear them."

"You make a good point."

"So, what are we going to do about it, Mac?"

Mac didn't even bother to question the "we" part of his wife's statement. He had come to find that sometimes, Melina was the only person on his side. More than sometimes. Or so it seemed. It wasn't a bad thing, really.

Far from it.

A man only needed one person on his side to get anything done. The *right* person.

His moll.

"We wait and see," Mac said as Melina continued to stare at him expectantly. "We wait and see what Anthony does now, and we go from there."

"You have heard the old saying about striking while the iron is hot, right?"

"Patience, doll."

"It's not virtuous when your life is on the line," she said with a huff.

Mac could only chuckle at that. "Maybe, but I don't think I'm the only man with his life on the line right now."

Mac slipped into the warehouse for his usual weekly meet with his crew. He had a dozen and one other things to worry about, and his guys could handle themselves if needed. He called the meeting anyway.

If there was one thing Mac had learned about being a good Capo, it was that his crew came first. They *had* to come first. Their problems with other people, issues on the streets, or even complaints about him—he needed to hear them. They wanted a Capo that gave enough of a shit to actually listen when they had something to say. That was the kind of behavior that led to a damn good Capo and crew combo.

And because of that, his guys trusted him.

Plus, routine was not always a bad thing where foot

soldiers were concerned. Those men rarely spent their time in meetings with people above them in ranking. They didn't have to be at certain places at specific times all throughout the week like Mac did, and they had no real structure to their days. They could do whatever they wanted, and be wherever they wanted, so long as they were making money while they did so.

But once a week, he demanded they be at his warehouse.

They always came.

On time.

He was damn proud of his crew.

The loud laughter and chatter of twenty young men quieted as Mac walked across the warehouse floor. He surveyed the faces of his guys—a habit he had developed—to get a sense of what their meeting would entail. No one in particular stood out, and given the week they already had, that wasn't a bad thing.

Well, all except Enric.

The young man sat off in the corner alone, looking entirely lost to his own thoughts in his wheelchair. Mac specifically wanted to have a chat with Enric about Neeya, the upcoming funeral, his sisters, the boss ... and more.

There was a lot to discuss.

Enric had been staying quiet, so Mac hadn't been able to get a decent conversation in with the guy. Now was the time, apparently.

Mac didn't plan on having the conversation in front of the other guys, though.

"Hey, Skip."

"We were starting to wonder if you were gonna show."

Mac waved off the greetings of his guys. "We're going to make this fast today. Unless anyone has any issues they need me to hear immediately, then I would like to make a few things clear for the upcoming days and send you on your way."

A few guys shook their heads. Some verbalized their agreements. None seemed to need or want to talk about anything that was an issue for them.

Mac was grateful.

"*Perfetto.* Then let's get this over with, so we can all be doing what we would rather be doing."

Mac took a seat on the waiting stool in front of his half-circle of guys. It was something the men had always sat out for him in preparation of their meetings. Mac gave Enric another look from the side, noted the guy was still lost to his head, and sighed.

"Clearly, we've had a rough week, especially with the one funeral, and the boss's wife in the limo. Now, more than ever, I need you all to be careful. In all things, with all people. Keep your noses clean, your heads down, and be respectful, even when you think no one is listening. Stick to your own business, but be *mindful* of the business around you at the same time. Until we know more about the bombing, the boss, and all of that shit, keep a low profile, but keep your eyes wide open. Got it?"

More nods.

More confirmations.

That grateful feeling swelled in Mac again. He knew that most Capos did not have crews like his, with guys that behaved appropriately and respected their Caporegime's position. Other Capos constantly struggled with insubordinate men and rebellious nonsense, often leading them to use violent means to keep their crew in line.

Not him.

Not his crew.

Mac spoke. They obeyed.

Mac clapped his hands and stepped off the stool. "Head out, and remember what I said."

The guys didn't need to be told twice. All of them headed for the warehouse entrance, except for Enric. It was only after the final guy had left that Enric finally turned his gaze on Mac.

A tired sadness waited there in Enric's eyes. A heavy weight rested on his shoulders. All the questions Mac had wanted to ask bled away, and so did his ability to find the right words to comfort the young man.

"How's your sisters?" Mac asked after a few seconds of stretched silence.

Enric shrugged. "Lost?"

That was probably as good a word as any, Mac supposed.

"Your father?"

"You tell me," Enric mumbled, looking down at his hands in his lap.

"I would, but—"

"He's not seeing you, either."

Mac shook his head. "No, but I did hear that his lawyer got a viewing with a judge about allowing him out for the day of Neeya's funeral. Shackled and with escorts, apparently. But it's something."

"So I was told."

"You want to grab some grub?" Mac asked. "You've got a physical therapy appointment today, too, right?"

Enric didn't answer, instead saying, "She never made me feel out of place—Neeya, I mean. I came from another woman, before her, but she had no reason to accept me if she didn't want to being his wife and all. I was the bastard son, nothing more. But she still tried. And even when I wouldn't get close to Dad or her, she still kept trying for the girls' sakes. I just never felt …"

"Comfortable," Mac said, filling in the obvious blank.

"I'm wondering if that was a mistake, I guess."

"It's better not to dwell on things you can't change, Enric, and work on what you have right now, and where you want to go."

The young man nodded. "Sure."

"Easier said than done, I know."

Regret weighed heavily on everyone. It didn't matter how broad the shoulders, that weight was an impossible one to carry without some sort of injury.

"Food sounds good," Enric said after a quiet moment. "I'll probably have to miss the appointment, though. Lora has some sort of thing today, and she asked me to be there."

Mac waved his cellphone high. "Good thing is, we happen to have one of your therapists on speed dial—I'm sure Victoria won't mind coming over to your place later to get something done."

"*I* would mind," Enric muttered. "It's bad enough having her at the clinic. She tries to kill me, I swear."

"She does not. She wants you to walk, like the rest of us do, so she pushes you because you can take it, and she knows it. Lock the pride down for a bit. There are more important things to worry about, Enric."

"Whatever you say."

Mac was going to respond, but his buzzing phone stopped him. He checked the screen only to see a messaging scrolling across from his wife. Direct, concerned words.

Anthony is at The Dollhouse with lots of men. Not for my kind of business. It looks like a meeting. Get here now.

Mac swore severely.

What was that fucker up to now?

He gave Enric an apologetic look and a shrug. "Food is going to have to wait. We have a situation to deal with."

Enric didn't even ask what was going on. He simply followed behind Mac like the good solider he was, even in his state.

CHAPTER TEN

There was boldness.

And then there was blatant disrespect.

Anthony Corelli was exhibiting the latter.

Anthony coming into The Dollhouse on his own wasn't a surprise. After all, he had a thing for Erika. But Anthony hadn't done that. In fact, Erika was nowhere in sight and wasn't scheduled to even be in this particular day. No. Anthony had done this purposely. With narrowed eyes, she watched as Anthony sat at the table holding court like he was some kind of king. A cigar in one hand, a glass of cognac in the other, he was the picture of a man without a care in the world.

Everything in her itched to go over, and give him a piece of her mind, but at this point Melina knew it would do no good. Anthony was here for a reason—to disrespect her husband. She knew there was bad blood between the two men that predated her relationship with Mac, but this stunt had only reinforced just how bad the blood really was. If Anthony had come to her place of business with a few men that worked for him, she wouldn't have liked it. However, she was a savvy businesswoman, and as long as the money was green she would take it.

But this was something else.

These were other Capos.

Capos who had been appointed by Luca Pivetti.

Capos who now seemed to be following the lead of Anthony Corelli.

The jackals had already started to circle, and the prey wasn't even dead.

As Melina watched the men laughing and joking as if all was right in their world, she thought about Luca Pivetti. There had never been any love lost between her and the Pivetti Don. In fact, there had been a time when she thought the man wouldn't be satisfied until she was permanently out of the picture. But times and situations had changed. Luca Pivetti's life would never be the same. It was a shame that the formidable man who was now grieving his wife and the potential forever loss of his freedom probably had no idea he was already being betrayed. While there was a lot Melina would never know about the rules of *la famiglia,* she did know impatience and disrespect when she saw it.

Melina glanced at the Cartier watch on her wrist. She'd texted her husband ten minutes ago. She had no idea where Mac's day had taken him, but she hoped that he would be walking through the doors soon to set Anthony straight. Moving behind the bar, Melina quickly made herself a glass of rum and Coke. Taking two large sips, she set the glass down as her thoughts became more dangerous.

It would be easy to kill a man like Anthony.

Maybe easy wasn't the right word.

She wouldn't shed a tear if the bastard was dead that was for certain.

In fact, Melina was sure that the Pivetti Organization, as well as she and her husband, would all be better off, but there were rules that had to be followed. The murder of a made man had to be properly sanctioned. To do so without an approved order would equal the killer's own death sentence. Anthony was safe for now.

At least from her.

No. She wouldn't kill him, despite the fact that he'd

sought to undermine her husband every chance he had. Despite the fact that he'd all but threatened their son. No, she couldn't kill him right now.

But that didn't stop her desire from wanting to.

Speak of the Devil.

Melina took another sip of her drink. The velvety feeling of the rum coating her throat as Anthony rose from his seat. With a predator's smile, he stubbed out his cigar before he came towards where she stood behind the bar.

"Melina, always a pleasure to see you."

"I'm sure it is for you. Sorry, I can't say the same."

He placed a hand over his heart. "You never miss a chance to cut me down, do you?"

"You make yourself an easy target."

"Or perhaps there's more to it than that," Anthony alluded.

Melina took another sip of her rum and Coke before she smirked. "And what would that be?"

"I think as much as you pretend to detest me that isn't really the case at all."

Melina laughed. "Your ego is way out of control so let me debase you of this foolish notion. I wouldn't be with you if you were the last man on the planet. I'd rather die alone."

Anthony bristled, his brows knitting together. "You never know how you'll react when faced with certain choices, my dear."

"In this case I do."

"Such a strong woman. I'm sure James Jr. doesn't even realize just how lucky he is."

Melina fought the urge to grit her teeth. "Mac knows exactly how lucky he is. Anything else is a bullshit insinuation."

Anthony smiled. "Forgive me, *bella*. It was not my intention to upset you with my presence."

"Then how about you and your buddies remove yourselves and everything will be wonderful."

"This is a public establishment is it not?" Anthony asked.

Melina opened her mouth to answer, but stopped when her husband rounded the corner. Her eyes slid to Mac's face, and she didn't miss the icy flames burning in his eyes. He didn't even acknowledge the other men sitting at the tables. His gaze was reserved for Anthony and Anthony alone.

"Of course, it is," Mac said smoothly.

Anthony shifted so that he could face Mac, a smirk on his face. "Ah, Mac. Nice of you to drop in."

"Somehow I doubt that's true."

"Well maybe not entirely true. After all you did just interrupt a delightful conversation I was having with your stunning wife."

Melina's gaze moved between Anthony, her husband, and the other Capos sitting at the tables watching the confrontation. Things could go south at any moment. Anthony was deliberately goading Mac any way he could.

"I'm sure Melina wouldn't be of the same opinion, but that's neither here nor there. I'm more curious as to why you're calling public meetings these days."

As if you're in charge.

Mac's unspoken words hung in the air between the two men.

"Public meetings? Oh, Mac, my boy. I think paranoia is starting to set in a bit. There's no meeting. Just a few good friends and businessmen patronizing an up and coming establishment. No doubt you and Melina are grateful for the business."

Mac's eyes narrowed and a tic moved in his jaw. Melina didn't know how Mac was keeping his cool. Anthony was obviously out for blood and using every slick comment he could to piss Mac off.

"Even a blind man can see when a joker tries to set himself up as a king and blind I'm not, Anthony. I know Melina appreciates the invitation you sent to the other

Capos to meet at her establishment. However, unless you gentlemen are interested in spending money on the other services The Dollhouse has to offer, might I suggest a change in venue."

"It seems things have happened that you aren't privy to. With age comes experience, however, I think we've caused your wife enough stress this evening. Until we meet again."

Anthony smirked before he walked away unhurriedly back to where the other men sat. Melina and her husband watched in silence as he said something to them. One by one, they all stood and put their jackets on before they rose and took their leave. A few of them left wads of money on the tables. Others did not and only barely nodded at Mac. Anthony was the last to leave.

"I really wish I could put a bullet between his eyes," Melina finally said.

"Me, too, doll."

Melina came from around the built in bar to stand in front of her husband. She took his face in her hands. "You got here pretty fast."

"I drove like hell."

"Why? Surely you couldn't have thought I was in danger."

Mac's eyes held hers. "Not really. Anthony is inappropriately fond of you, but you never know what crosses a mind like his. It doesn't take a genius to know the best way to hurt me is through you and our son."

"I think I can safely say that Anthony is not interested in alienating me. In fact, he's under some misrepresented belief that he intrigues me somehow."

Mac's eyes narrowed until she barely could see their color. "On what fucking planet?"

Melina slid her hands down her husband's neck and to his broad shoulders. "The planet in his mind. When I assured him I'd rather die alone than be with him, he warned me that you never knew what decisions you'd make when situations arose. I think I understand what he was saying pretty loud and clear, Mac."

"So do I. He plans to set himself up as the new Don, and once he gets me out of the way it's open season on you."

Mac's nostrils flared and beneath her hands his body tensed as he stared off into space. Anthony had all but declared war. He wanted to destroy everything that she held dear to satisfy his own selfish lusts and greed.

"I meant what I said, Mac. I'd rather die than belong to Anthony."

"You dying will never be an option. Not ever."

Mac focused his gaze on her. One of his hands came up to cup her face in his hand.

"Good, because I have a lot more living to do."

"I'm going to stop him, doll. I swear it. No one is going to take you from me."

"There's no way I would ever willingly go. There's not a man alive who could ever take your place," she told him.

Mac smiled for the first time in a long time. "Good to know. Now why don't you and I head home?"

"Absolutely. Just let me tell the staff I'm leaving."

Melina gave Mac a quick kiss on the cheek before she stepped away to go talk to the skeletal staff on duty today. She'd made it down the hallway when she stopped and looked back. Her husband ran a tired hand across his face. The level of stress he was under was evident. He needed a chance to take his mind off things, and she had the perfect distraction in mind.

Melina stood over Marquise's crib watching him as he slept. The slow rise and fall of his chest. The way he wiggled his nose in his sleep. She could watch him sleep all night, but she wouldn't tonight. There was someone else who needed her undivided attention. Leaning down she pressed a final kiss on her son's temple before she went and quickly showered and dressed.

Staring at herself in the mirror, Melina smiled. She looked damned good. Exactly what the doctor ordered. Adding the pair of black spiked heels that her husband loved to her outfit, Melina went in search of Mac. She was surprised to find him in their rarely used solarium that overlooked the pool. Mac leaned against the tempered glass door with his back to her.

He was still, deathly so, but you couldn't miss the sloop in his shoulders. The way his head was bent forward as if the weight of the world was on him. She wanted to take that weight from him as much as she could. At least tonight. Walking over to him she looped her arms around his waist and leaned against him. She inhaled his scent and they were silent, just the two of them in their own world.

"I can't remember the last time we've had a moment to just be still," Mac finally said.

"Neither can I. Feels nice, doesn't it?"

"I didn't understand just how much I needed it until now," Mac confessed.

"Are you finally admitting you're not invincible?" Melina teased.

"Most definitely. I'm man enough to admit that I am not infallible."

"And that is one of the things that makes you such an amazing man. Not being afraid to admit that sometimes things get beyond your control. But no matter what you just keep moving forward."

"Motivational speaking, doll? I know some people who will pay good money for a message like that."

Melina thumped her husband. "I heard sarcasm."

Mac straightened and Melina loosened her arms around him, stepping away as he turned around to face her.

"Never."

His eyes roved over her, as understanding dawned on him.

"Positive about that?" she asked.

He nodded, reaching out a hand to touch her hip.

"Then why don't you let me give you another kind of motivation?"

Melina pushed him until his back was leaning against the glass.

"What did you have in mind?" Mac asked.

"Why don't you let me take care of everything?" She pressed her hand against his chest as she leaned close to him.

"Whatever my doll wants."

"Smart man."

Melina's hands found his shoulders as their lips met. She kissed him, slow and unhurried. Her mouth opened, allowing his tongue to touch hers. Melina moaned as he kissed her deeper. Her breasts rubbed against him, nipples pebbling through the lace of her lingerie. One strong arm came to settle around her waist as they kissed.

"You are so fucking sexy," Mac whispered.

"So are you," she said between kisses.

Mac's lips traveled from her mouth to nip at the lobe of her ear, and she dug her nails into his shoulders. A pulsating ache was starting between her thighs. It was always like this.

Every touch.

Every kiss.

A pleasure she would never get tired of.

Melina bit her lip as Mac sucked on the lobe of her ear. She was rapidly losing the little control she had. If she wanted this evening to go the way she'd planned, she had to reign herself in. As his hot tongue traced the shell of her ear, Melina reached for his belt and quickly undid it before moving to the top button of his slacks. With one firm tug, his pants pooled around his ankles, leaving Mac in just his black boxer-briefs. The swell of his desire for her radiated hot against her hand, and she touched him through the material.

"Bad girl," Mac said.

"You have no idea."

Mac leaned against the glass door, staring at Melina as her hand delved inside his boxer-briefs. When her hand closed around him, he groaned. Fiery and steel all wrapped in one. With her free hand she pulled his boxers down until his thick length was exposed. For a moment, she just stared at the masculine part of him that never failed to excite her. Even now, she could feel the moisture gathering between her thighs.

"You keep looking at my cock like that, doll, and we're going to have a real problem."

Melina laughed. "Is that so?" She stroked him slowly from base to tip. "Sounds like I'll have to do something about that then."

In one fluid motion, Melina dropped to her knees and took Mac in her mouth.

"Fuck."

Her tongue teased the tip of his cock, tasting the pre-cum that had gathered there.

Salty.

Tart.

Uniquely Mac.

Her pussy clenched in response as her mouth moved up and down the long length of him. Gently her teeth scraped over him as she sucked him hard. He filled her mouth completely as she relaxed allowing him to hit the back of her throat.

"Look at me, doll."

Melina kept up her ministrations, but she refused to meet his eyes. She couldn't. She knew what would happen if she did. Her thighs trembled as the heady desire to please her husband raced through her body.

"Look at me while you suck my cock."

The need in his voice tugged at her. She moaned around him as she slide up his thick shaft to suck the head of his cock. Her tongue teased his slit, and then she finally met his gaze. If she hadn't already been on her knees, they likely would've buckled at the force of desire in his eyes.

Hot.

Hungry.

Need.

"That's it, doll. Just like that."

Melina cupped his balls as she increased her tempo. Her eyes watered as her head bobbed up and down. Mac groaned a strangled sound, and he swelled inside her mouth. She positioned him towards the back of her throat, sucked hard and then he was filling her mouth with the essence that was uniquely Mac. His eyes closed momentarily as he growled his release, before he was grabbing her under the arms and jerking her up from the floor.

Without a word he placed a searing kiss on her lips that stole her breath and nearly made her buckle. Melina didn't fight as her husband turned her so that she was leaning against the glass. She gasped when her lace panties were ripped from her body. The cool air touched her ass, before Mac's hand did. His smack to her ass stung in the most pleasant way.

"Do it again," she whispered.

Mac obliged just as two fingers sunk inside her.

"So fucking wet," Mac growled.

Any response she might have made was cut off when her husband's cock replaced his fingers. Melina's breath hissed in her throat at the fullness she felt. Hot, thick and wonderful, Mac's cock slid in and out of her slippery wetness driving deeper and deeper with each powerful stroke. His arm held tight around her waist forcing her back against him. She met him thrust for thrust, sending hot tugs of pleasure straight to her pussy.

"Harder."

Mac's fingers dug into her hip as he drove harder, faster and deeper than he had before. His breath was ragged on her neck with every pound of his flesh into hers. Her pussy trembled. Her body ached as a dam of bliss exploded between her thighs.

"Yes! Fuck yes," she cried out.

Rivets of pleasure ran through her body from head to toe as her clit continued to throb in the aftermath of her pleasure. Above her, Mac nipped her ear as he found his own release, spilling inside her. Then they were silent, the only sounds in the room were of their heavy breathing as they struggled to catch their breath.

"You're … going to be … the death of me, doll."

Melina laughed. "I can't think of a better way to go."

Releasing his grip from around her waist, Mac turned her to face him as he hastily pulled up and secured his pants. A moment later, he had her in his arms.

"Round two in the bedroom?" Mac asked.

"Absolutely. I've got more surprises."

"Lucky me."

The two of them laughed as they set off towards their bedroom, and Melina was pleased that her evening plans were turning out to be a complete success.

Something soft touched her cheek. Melina groaned, opening one eye to find her husband watching her with a predatory gaze.

"Why are you awake so early?" she asked.

Mac smiled, rubbing his thumb down her cheek. "It's ten in the morning, doll."

"What?" Melina opened both eyes and rolled to face her husband. "Why did you let me sleep so long?"

"I figured after last night you could use the rest."

"Spoken like a man really full of himself."

"If I remember correctly, only one of us was full of something last night and it wasn't me."

Reaching beneath the covers, Mac tweaked her nipple as he wrapped his arm around her pulling her even closer.

"All right you got me. My brain is too foggy for a comeback right now but don't get used to it." Melina rested her head on Mac's chest as his arms encircled her.

"I wouldn't dream of it, doll."

They rested, entwined together listening to the sounds of each other's deep, even breathing. Moments like this were rare. Precious and rare. Melina ran her hands up and down her husband's back. Then a thought came to her mind.

"Marquise?"

"I gave him a bottle two hours ago while you were still sleeping. He's still asleep in his bed."

"You're such a good father."

"And you're a good mother."

A good mother.

A good mother like Neeya Pivetti.

Melina swallowed around the lump in her throat. It had only been a few days since the untimely death of the woman she'd considered a friend and more. Tears formed in her eyes and she blinked quickly in a futile attempt to stop them from falling. She knew the exact moment her tears touched Mac's skin.

"Doll, talk to me."

She cleared her throat as she took a moment to collect her thoughts.

"I was thinking about Neeya. This is the first chance I've had to process the fact that she's gone," she finally said.

"I know you two were close."

Melina rearranged herself so that she could look her husband in the eyes.

"She went out of her way to make me feel welcome. She didn't have to do that or anything else she did for that matter. I don't use the term friend lightly, but that's what Neeya was to me. A friend."

"The boss's wife was an amazing woman. The only person that could go toe to toe with Luca and come out the winner. Neeya was a formidable woman."

Melina nodded. "Yes, she was. I think I wouldn't be half the wife I am now if it weren't for learning from her example. There are so many fine lines to walk, but she navigated them all with unmatched poise."

"That she did. I can't even begin to imagine how Luca is dealing with this right now."

"Or their daughters."

The girls.

Rose, Hope, and Lora.

Their mother was dead, and their father was behind bars likely facing a lifetime of imprisonment leaving them to deal with everything on their own. They may have been legally adults, but nothing in the world could prepare you for losing a parent. She knew that firsthand.

"Would you mind looking after Marquise for a little while?" she asked.

"Of course not. We'll have some father and son bonding time. You going to be okay?" Mac cupped her face in his hand.

"Yeah, eventually. I just want to go and check on the girls. Offer my support. Let them know I'm there if they need me."

"I know that will mean a lot to them. You're an exceptional woman, doll."

Melina smiled at her husband before she threw back the covers. "I'm not exceptional. I just understand what they're going through."

"It's more than that."

"Maybe. You're sure you'll be all right with the baby?"

"Are you insinuating I can't handle my son on my own?" Mac pinched her hip.

"Hardly. I just want to be sure you're up to it in case I'm gone longer than I expect, that's all."

"Take all the time you need, doll. Us boys will be fine." Mac leaned close and kissed her on the mouth hard. "Now get going."

"Yes, sir."

Melina rolled out of bed and headed towards the bathroom. She'd barely made it inside, when she heard Marquise's cries.

"I got him," Mac yelled out.

"Okay."

Melina turned on the shower, grabbed a washcloth and stepped under the hot jets. As the water flowed over her body, she made a mental note to plan another special evening for her husband. He really was a remarkable man.

Twenty minutes later, Melina was showered and dressed. She'd pulled her hair into a simple ponytail and chosen distressed blue jeans and an off the shoulder black top, paired with spiked black boots. She added small black diamond studs in her ears and tinted gloss before she left the bedroom in search of her husband and son. She found Mac and Marquise in the living room. Mac held their son as he appeared to be watching TV with wild fascination.

"What are you two so interested in?"

"Not us. Your son is apparently fascinated by *The National Geographic Channel.*"

"Is that so?"

Melina stepped closer and turned her attention to the television where a narrator explained two male lions were fighting each other for mating rights and territory. She watched a few minutes more with her attention moving between her son and the television. Finally she spoke again.

"The beginning of brilliance starts now."

"On that we can agree. I have a car waiting for you

downstairs," Mac said.

The last thing Melina felt like doing was sitting in the back of a limousine.

"It's not a limousine, doll."

She offered him a grateful smile. "Thank you."

Melina kissed Mac long and leisurely before she turned to her son who had momentarily turned his attention from the television and was staring at her with wide eyes.

"You be good for your daddy, okay? But don't have too much fun without me."

Marquise cooed in response, smiling at her. She placed a soft kiss on his forehead and then exited the house. Outside awaited a black Hummer, and standing next to it was a man she couldn't recall seeing.

"Good morning, ma'am."

"Good morning. I don't believe we've met."

He extended his hand. "Leonardo. Pleasure to meet you, Mrs. Maccari."

They shook hands before Leonardo opened the back right passenger side door and helped her inside. Two minutes later they were pulling out of her driveway and heading towards the home where the Pivetti daughters now lived.

It was still surreal to Melina that she would never again visit the Pivetti mansion.

That she would never again hear Neeya's voice.

Or see the quiet way the regal woman took over a room.

Or be able to seek the older woman for advice.

No.

Those days were gone, and they could never return.

Releasing a breath, she wiped away a tear that spilled down her cheek. No. Neeya was gone, and it wasn't just the loss of the woman as a friend that pained her, bringing her to tears. It wasn't just her loss as a mentor and wise confidant. No. It was something else. Something she hadn't been able to admit out loud yet, even to her husband.

Losing Neeya had been like the loss of another mother.

Melina's own mother had died when she was barely eight years old. There had been no one there to guide her through life and experience the milestones every young girl dreamed of. Neeya had filled that void.

A steady guide through the world of the mafia and all its clear and hidden dangers.

A warm figure who'd given her a priceless gift at her wedding and a spectacular baby shower when she was pregnant.

A woman who welcomed her with open arms and gave her something she had been missing for a long time … a mother's love.

Yes.

Neeya Pivetti had filled a void in Melina's life and now her death had created yet another.

But she didn't have time to give life to her own pain. There were others hurting worse than she was. Three girls who needed someone they could turn to. Melina only hoped that she could be that person. She was drawn from her own thoughts as the Hummer slowed to a stop in front of a stately but small home. Standing outside in front of the small white columns holding up the half porch were armed guards.

With Neeya selling off her assets before she'd passed, she and the girls had moved, but Melina hadn't been expecting a place like this. It was understated, with nothing that drew attention to it. Very different from the opulence that had been the Pivetti mansion. But maybe that was the point. Leonardo came around and opened the door for her. She thanked him, and he nodded as he helped her down and walked with her to the front door. Melina didn't recognize any of the men, and they offered no smiles.

"I'm Melina Maccari, here to see Rose, Hope, and

Lora."

"Any weapons, ma'am?" one of the guards asked.

Melina thrust her purse into the hand of the man and then spread her arms. "Do you need to frisk me, too?"

One of the other guards, a bald man with thick muscles, nudged the one holding her purse.

"No, ma'am. Forgive him. He's new. The last thing we want is problems with Mr. Maccari," the bald man said.

"Thank you," Melina said.

The man gave her back her purse and opened the door for her. Leonardo trailed behind her. They stepped into a small atrium. The walls were eggshell in color, but bare. Melina took a few steps further down the hall.

"Hello?" she called out.

A few moments later, a young woman appeared in the hallway. Slender with bronze skin, high cheekbones and silky black hair hanging gracefully down her back she was the picture of elegance … just like her mother. Even clad in a simple white blouse and black slacks, she moved as if she owned the room.

"Rose."

"Melina, what an unexpected surprise." The barest hint of a smile crossed her face.

"I hope I'm not intruding. I wanted to check on you and your sisters."

"It's never an intrusion. Let's talk in the living room," Rose said.

Melina followed the young woman down the hallway and soon they were in a mid-sized living room. Again the décor was simple. White couches, glass tables, and a small ottoman. Rose took a seat, and Melina sat next to her, putting her purse down on the floor next to her.

"Where are your sisters?"

"Hope is upstairs finishing a paper for her Anthropology class. She insists on not falling behind in her studies. Lora is spending some time with friends. I really do appreciate you taking the time to come here today. We haven't had many visitors."

Melina raised a brow. "That I don't understand."

Rose offered her a smile that didn't reach her dark eyes. "It seems these days we're not high on the list of importance."

Melina reached for the younger woman's hand. "That will never be true."

"Oh I'm afraid it is. You see one thing I inherited from my mother is being practical. My father will likely never see the outside of a prison cell again which leaves his power all but non-existent. The jackals are already at the door ready to tear him apart. That leaves my sisters and me temporarily forgotten until whoever takes over decides how to use us to serve their purpose."

There was no venom behind Rose's words, just a simple practicality. Even Melina couldn't deny the truth that the young Pivetti woman had spoken. These were uncertain times for all of them, but especially for the three *principessas*. It was only a matter of time before they would have to face even more uncertainty ahead of them.

"You have inherited your mother's wisdom, Rose. But count me among those who are concerned for your well-being. I know the pain of losing a mother and no matter your age it is never an easy thing to accept."

Rose nodded. "No, it is not, especially when her death was unwarranted. But I don't have the luxury of grieving. I have to be strong for my sisters."

"Rose, everyone deserves a chance to grieve. You are entitled to it. Take it."

"Perhaps, once the funeral is over."

"How are Hope and Lora holding up?"

"Hope is unfailingly stable. No matter what storm is going on around us, she holds it together. Lora is volatile. Angry one minute. Sad the next. Dad not allowing us to visit him is not helping matters."

"I can imagine he doesn't want you to see him upset. I also imagine that he's also keeping you away for his own protection. Lora, being the youngest and closest to your father, it's easy to see why she is a storm of emotions but you're doing the most important thing … being there for her."

Rose withdrew her hand from Melina's and quickly wiped a tear from her eye before she stood up.

"I can see why my mother always spoke so highly of you. She thought of you like another daughter."

Melina swallowed the lump in her throat and blinked back her own tears. "That means the world to me."

Before Rose could say anything else, a man's voice boomed through the house.

"Girls?"

Melina didn't recognize the voice, or the tall man that walked casually into the living room. Clad in a gray expensive Italian cut suit, his eyes were dark and piercing. His black hair was thick and full with only some slight gray at his temples, giving him an even more debonair appearance. His skin was a deep shade of olive as if he'd spent a great deal of time in the sun.

"Grandfather, what are you doing here?"

Rose flew into his arms, and the man offered her a small smile as he hugged the girl close to him. Melina stood up and grabbed her purse, preparing to leave and give them some privacy.

"Did you think I wouldn't be here?"

Rose leaned back to look at the man. "Truthfully I know how busy you are in South Africa and everywhere else you go, I wasn't sure."

Her grandfather nodded with a tight pinched smile. "Then I haven't done a very good job being a grandfather have I?"

Rose opened her mouth to say something, but he placed a finger against her lips. "Please, Rose, introduce me to your friend."

The young woman stepped out of her grandfather's embrace and turned halfway towards Melina.

"Grandfather, this is Melina Maccari, a good friend of Mom's. Melina, this is my grandfather, Massimo Dinunzio."

Massimo extended his hand. "A pleasure to meet a friend of my daughter's despite the circumstances."

They exchanged handshakes, and Melina was unnerved beneath the man's gaze. He stared as if he could see straight to her soul.

"Likewise," she said, honestly unsure if she truly meant it.

When Massimo released her hand, Melina turned to Rose. "If you or your sisters need anything or just want to talk, don't hesitate to call me."

"We will, Melina, and thanks again for coming by."

The two women hugged before Melina left the room to where Leonardo stood waiting in the atrium.

"I'm ready," she told him.

"Yes, ma'am."

He opened the door for her, and Melina departed the house glad that she'd come. In the darkest hours, everyone needed someone to be there for them. The arrival of Neeya's father and her own visit, both would go a long way towards showing the Pivetti *principessas* that they were not alone.

CHAPTER
ELEVEN

Funerals were not usually events that Mac liked to attend. But who did, really? This particular funeral was not quite the same.

He had more reasons than he could count for why he needed to pay his respects to Neeya Pivetti.

Mac opened the back door to the town car, and offered his hand to his wife. Melina still wouldn't ride in the back of a limo after everything, not that Mac blamed her. She stood at her full height by his side. Her hand smoothed down the black Versace dress she wore, while her other tipped the wide brim of her sun hat down just enough to hide her face from the people who turned to look at them from the gallery.

He could still see her face, though.

And it kind of broke his heart.

"You okay?" he asked.

Melina nodded. "It's harder than I thought it would be, that's all."

"What is?"

He didn't know what she would say.

Melina didn't fail to surprise him. "You say goodbye, and it's final after this. I've had very few people in my life who I would rather not say goodbye to. Neeya is one of them."

Mac supposed his wife's large brim hat made a lot

more sense, in the grand scheme of things. Or rather, he better understood why she was wearing it. Melina was—always—strong, resilient, in control, and detached even in her highest emotions. She had learned to be those things, and today, perhaps she was struggling in those departments.

"It's meant to be a short ceremony, doll. We will be out of here before you know it, and back in the privacy of our home."

Where she could do whatever she needed without people watching her. Cry, grieve, or be sad and quiet. Whatever.

"I wish that helped," she murmured sadly.

So did Mac.

"Come on, Melina."

She took his arm, and tucked her hand into the crook of his elbow as they walked towards the crowd gathering on the steps of the church. As far as Mac knew, because rumors traveled through the grapevine of made men, Neeya's father had taken care of the funeral arrangements. There was word the man had also visited with Luca, too, but Mac hadn't been able to confirm that was true, or get a meeting with Massimo to ask.

The man likely *was* busy.

Mac let it drop, though he also wanted to speak with Luca, or someone who had spoken with the boss. Especially after seeing Anthony at the prison. Massimo, however, did not answer to Mac, or any other made man, for that matter. He couldn't demand the man's presence and expect a result that would be in his favor.

Neither Mac, nor Melina, bothered to stop and speak with some of the familiar people on the church steps. He kept his wife close, and directed her through the parting crowd, before they entered the church. Hints of vanilla and incense clung to the air, and a sea of black clothing moved all around them.

Mac wasn't paying much attention to any of that, as

his attention was snagged by his stiffening wife, and the way her gaze darted to the very front of the church. A shined, black casket sat high on the altar, closed up tight, with a large arrangement of lilies, roses, and gardenias covering nearly the entire top.

The style of the flower arrangement matched the ones connecting shimmering tulle between each pew.

Mac reached for one of the arrangements, curious why someone would want such delicate, pretty arrangements for something like a funeral.

A voice from behind stopped him.

"Careful with those," a male voice said, "they're not meant to be played with before it's time."

Mac turned to find an unfamiliar face watching him and Melina. Still, he had heard enough about the man, and Melina described him well enough, for Mac to know he was staring at Neeya's father—Massimo.

With a deep olive complexion to speak of his Italian ancestry, standing just an inch taller than Mac, and dressed in all black, Massimo smiled.

"It's *Mac*, Mac Maccari, correct?" Massimo asked

"Or James, depending on who's trying to piss me off that day," Mac replied.

Massimo's stony features cracked with a smile. "I was told your friends call you Mac."

"Which friends are those?"

"The only ones that should matter."

Touché.

Mac nodded to the bushels of flower arrangements on each pew. "I was thinking those seem more appropriate for a wedding than a funeral."

"Neeya's favorite flowers," Massimo supplied, "and it's a time to celebrate my daughter, not grieve."

"Good point. I hadn't thought of it that way."

"Most don't. Society would rather us mourn our dead. We should celebrate the joy they brought into our lives, before we send them off with a smile. We've been taught it's not appropriate to be happy in times like these, only sadness and solemnness will do. I won't have that for my Neeya."

"How are the girls?" Melina asked, stepping into the conversation for the first time.

Massimo's gaze swung to her instantly. "Better, thank you for asking. We were lucky enough to get them a private sitting with their father before the funeral, so that's why they aren't here just yet." He glanced down at his watch, adding, "They'll be coming anytime, now."

"And how is Luca?" Mac dared to ask.

"Like his daughters, I suppose."

"Better, then?"

Massimo shrugged. "Better than he was."

"So you have spoken with him," Mac stated.

The man's dark eyes lit up with some unknown emotion, mixed with a touch of mirth. As fast as Mac had seen it appear, it was gone. As though it had never been there to begin with.

"It was nice to meet you, *Mac*." Massimo nodded at Melina. "And you, Melina. Very nice to see you again. Please, though, leave the arrangements alone, lest we start something earlier than we intend to."

Mac had *no* idea what the man was talking about. Massimo didn't intend to explain it, apparently. He walked away before Mac could even bother to ask.

"He's a bit strange, isn't he?" Melina asked.

Mac looked at the flowers again, curious and bothered at the same time. "Strange is one way to put it."

"There *are* a lot of flowers, though."

Mac agreed.

The things were everywhere.

In pots, on the ends of every pew, damn near covering the altar, and strung in garland along the stained glass window sills.

Everywhere.

Yet, all he could smell were the vanilla and incense.

Were they fake flowers?

What did it even matter?

"We have to find a seat," Melina told him.

Mac let his wife find them a pew, and put the flowers and the strange feeling he had, out of his mind.

For the moment.

Once they were seated, Mac carefully looked around to find faces he recognized. Their pew was only two behind the very front, where Enric sat in the inner aisle, likely waiting for his half-sisters to join him. Towards the back, Mac found several Capos, and one in particular that made his irritation swell when he found the man was looking at him, too.

Anthony.

The bastard.

Mac greatly disliked the image of Anthony sitting surrounded by made men, as though he had created a wall to protect himself with. It bothered Mac more than those same made men had, for whatever reason, chosen to align themselves, even if only visibly, with Anthony.

Especially at Neeya's funeral.

For now, Mac would have to let it go.

But he wasn't leaving it that way for long.

"They do look better," Melina said, drawing Mac from his thoughts.

"Hmm, doll?"

His wife gestured subtly towards the three girls making their way towards the front of the church. Mac hadn't even noticed the Pivetti *principessas'* entrance. They only nodded and said quiet hellos as they passed, but never stopped to actually greet anyone. Mac had to agree with his wife's assessment, though, as the girls *did* look to be in better emotional states than they had the last time he saw them.

Perhaps their grandfather's presence brought along with it some kind of magic to make them smile through the hell this day was sure to be.

Mac didn't know.

It was only the rattle of chains that made Mac look away from the girls, and back towards the entrance of the church. Shackles, actually.

Luca Pivetti had been allowed to dress for the day, apparently, but that was about as far as they let him go. He was shackled around his ankles, his wrists, and the chains looped around his waist under his suit jacket. Two guards escorted him down the aisle; their hands, one on Luca, one on their weapons, were steady and ready. Although Luca didn't seem to pay anyone a bit of attention, as all eyes turned on him with each step he took.

In fact, he didn't look away from his wife's casket.

Mac couldn't bring back a single time when he had seen his boss look as dead as he did in those moments.

So gone.

Lost.

A deafening pain that left him numb.

It was shocking.

And Mac understood *completely*.

He couldn't empathize, of course, but he understood *why*.

Mac relaxed slightly when Melina's hand touched his shoulder, and pressed lightly. It was as though she was silently telling him he was okay, she was okay, and *they* were okay. Like she could read his mind.

Luca was escorted by his guards to the front of the church, and it was only then that the man finally spoke, and his stony façade cracked. He said something to the one guard, gesturing towards the casket with opened hands, but not quite loud enough for those around him to hear what he was asking for. The two guards looked between one another, spoke quickly and quietly, then finally nodded.

"Thank you," Luca said, although Mac barely heard the words.

Mac finally understood what Luca had asked for as

the man stepped towards his wife's casket, and the guards stayed behind. He swore every eye in the church was on Luca while the boss approached the black casket with outstretched hands, still chained in shackles.

And maybe that was the point, Mac thought.

Maybe Luca was the best possible distraction.

Because no one except for Mac seemed to notice Massimo heading towards the entrance of the church, and pulling a small, black item from his inner jacket pocket at the same time. It was too far away for Mac to discern what exactly the item was, but he couldn't miss the unmistakable action of Massimo pushing down on it with his thumb, as though he were pressing a button.

Mac finally understood why there had been so many goddamn flowers, then, and exactly how strategically the bushels had been placed throughout the church. Each bushel linking between the pews exploded in color, sending out plumes of smoke and a powdery substance of neon colors.

And the *sound*.

The sound that accompanied the exploding bushels came off like a screeching war cry.

The noise, mixed with the explosions of color, smoke, and flying petals, sent the attendees flying to the floor. Some were likely too scared to move, worried that this was another bomb incident. Others probably reacted out of instinct alone to get the fuck out of the way of whatever was happening.

It was fucking pandemonium above their heads as Mac stared upward.

Plumes of colored smoke, a catacomb of noise, and the shouts of frightened people.

Distractions, he knew.

But he couldn't *see* through the goddamn smoke to know for sure what was happening.

"Mac," Melina said, her fingernails cutting into his arm through his jacket, "what is fucking happening?"

He didn't know how to answer her.

Through the colored smoke, and the suddenly moving people, Mac was sure he saw Neeya's casket toppled over. Its top looked to be open, and white satin had spilled out, stained by colored powder from whatever had been stuffed inside those bushels of flower arrangements.

Except ...

There was no body.

It was empty.

Luca wasn't standing there anymore, either.

The guards—

Mac couldn't see the damn guards standing just a few feet away like they had been only moments before, but that was because the two men were now lying face down in the aisle, with bullet holes in the backs of their heads.

What is happening?

Just as the smoke began to clear, the sounds started to die down, and the colored powder seemed to be falling and settling, *more* bushels popped off on the opposite sides of the pews, sending people scattering in a different direction. Mac turned his head just in time to see several flower arrangements by the entrance explode as well, swallowing running guests in color and clouds of smoke they likely couldn't see their way to get through.

Holy shit.

"This way," Mac heard a familiar voice say. "Hurry up, now. Move."

"What in the hell did you do?" Mac asked, barely able to see a foot in front of his face. The church was ruined, likely.

Massimo laughed in the smoke. "Only giving them a proper send off, as I should."

Melina coughed, and then tucked her face into Mac's jacket as they tried to stay as close to Massimo as was possible. The man moved through the mess like he knew exactly where he was going, as though he had walked it a hundred times before this day in preparation for this moment.

And perhaps he had done just that.

Mac wouldn't be surprised.

"Here we are," Massimo said, "deep breaths once you're in the fresh air. Don't question the driver in the car, and try to be nice. It's a bit of a drive."

"What?" Mac asked.

Massimo answered nothing, simply shoved Mac, which sent Melina with him, out a side exit door of the church.

A black car was waiting.

A man stood there with a door opened for them.

Melina sucked in a huge gulp of air, and Mac did the same, needing to cleanse his throat and lungs of that awful powder.

"Get in," the driver said, offering nothing else.

Melina looked to Mac, and he shrugged.

What else could he do?

Friends, Massimo had said. Mac's *friends* called him one thing only. It was only a friend who could have told that to the man, and made sure it was important enough for him to repeat.

Don't question the driver.

"Get in, doll," Mac said.

Mac climbed in behind his wife without a single look back.

"My dress is ruined," Melina muttered.

She tried again—a futile effort—to wipe the bright colored powder from her black dress, and sighed when it did nothing to help. His suit was ruined, too, but he couldn't find it in himself to give a shit at the moment. He had more important things to consider.

"That's the first thing you're considering right now?" Mac asked, chuckling.

His wife shrugged. "I have to think about something, don't I?"

"The three black cars we're suddenly driving with aren't one of them?"

Melina glanced out the windows, taking note of the vehicles Mac mentioned. "What is happening?"

Mac kept asking himself that, as well.

"I have no idea, doll."

"Also, I lost my hat."

Mac pressed his lips together in an effort to hide his amusement at Melina's pout. "I will get you a new one."

"I liked that one, though."

"And you'll like the new one, too."

Melina stared out the window again. "How long have we been driving?"

"Thirty minutes."

"Did you see the guards on the ground?" she asked quietly.

Mac passed a look at the driver, who had not once even looked back at them during the drive. "I did. *And* how Luca was gone."

"So, that whole show ..."

"Was clearly planned," he supplied.

"I'm not sure Neeya would appreciate her funeral being used as an escape plan for her—"

"I'm not sure that was a funeral at all," Mac interrupted, remembering something else he had seen through the smoke and distractions. "But what do I know?"

"Pardon?" Melina turned to him with confusion written heavily across her beautiful face. Mac didn't want to explain what he had seen—or rather, what was missing—inside a toppled over casket. He didn't want to tell her something, give her that hope, and then take it away. "What does that mean, Mac?"

He pulled his wife closer in the back seat, pressed a kiss to the top of her head, and watched the black cars move slightly closer to theirs all the way around. "Let's just wait and see, doll. I think something big just happened, and someone clearly intends to let us in on the secret, considering what's going on now."

"Except we don't *know* what's going on."

"Shit, it can't be any worse than everything else we've already dealt with."

Melina laughed, pressed a quick kiss to his lips, and settled back against the seat. "Massimo said it would be a bit of a drive, didn't he?"

"Apparently."

"You should call your mom for Marquise. Let her know we might be late."

Mac was already pulling out his cell phone before his wife could finish her sentence.

The helicopter sat waiting and ready, in the middle of what appeared to be a private airstrip that had little life, and likely hadn't been used in a long while. The chopper's blades circled fast, and Mac could see a pilot waiting inside as their car came to a stop a good fifty feet away.

It wasn't the strange place that took Mac's attention. Nor the helicopter, or the other vehicles stopping alongside theirs.

No, it was the woman standing just outside the chopper. The flowy skirt of her red dress blew wildly in the wind of the chopper's blades; her straightened, jet black hair billowed out behind her.

Yet, she stood still.

Like a statue.

Waiting.

Entirely unmoved.

Mac blinked a few times, just to make sure what he was seeing was actually real. Each time, the woman still stood there, frozen as stone, and surveying the cars. Her hands folded together over her middle, as calm as ever in her posture, yet her gaze was where Mac found the truth.

Wild and worried.

Melina sucked in a quiet breath; her hand on Mac's thigh tightened to an almost painful point as she too realized *who* she was looking at. "Neeya."

Very much alive.

Very real.

"You will have a few moments," the driver said, his first words to them since the church, "and then I will return you to your own vehicle where you left it."

Mac opened his mouth to ask the man a question— several, maybe. Like who in the fuck was he, who had hired him for this, what was happening, and *why*. So many questions.

Massimo's request clung heavily in the back of Mac's mind.

Mac questioned nothing.

"Thank you," Mac said.

"You may exit the vehicle," the driver said.

Damn near at the same time the driver said those words, Mac saw the back doors open to the three other vehicles that had been with theirs the entire drive. From one, Massimo stepped out. From another, the three Pivetti daughters. From the final car, Luca stepped out, still shackled and like everyone else, a mess of powdered color but with a smile on his face.

Mac grabbed the car door to push it open, but hesitated when Melina didn't follow him immediately. "Doll?"

A hesitance stared back at him from his wife. Something else lingered in her eyes, too. Something he hadn't expected—betrayal, maybe.

Mac knew exactly why.

Melina had allowed herself to grieve for Neeya. She had been affected by someone she let close to her heart. Only now, it seemed those feelings had been for nothing.

"Ask her why," Mac urged. "You'll never know whatever it is you're wondering about unless you ask her, Melina."

"She could have told me, Mac."

"Maybe she couldn't. Maybe this was all a big what if. What if everything single thing went right and it worked? You don't know any different."

"Unless I ask," Melina whispered.

Mac nodded. "Yeah, doll. But we're here, right, so someone asked for that. Luca, her … someone asked for us; that means something."

They stepped out of the car just as the shackles keeping Luca contained were snapped off with massive bolt cutters. The man who had removed the chains tossed the tool back into his car, then disappeared out of sight without as much as a word after Luca thanked him.

Luca passed a look to Mac, then to Massimo, and quickly to his daughters. His gaze lingered far longer on his wife still waiting by the running chopper. The noise was loud, but Mac still heard the quickly spoken words between the boss and his father-in-law.

"Go ahead," Massimo said, "you can thank me in a minute; I think she's missed you a great deal. She's never asked me for anything, after all, except for you, Luca. Then *and* now."

Luca gave a short nod. "Me, too."

Mac kept Melina close as Luca passed by his three daughters, though he gave each one a quick kiss. Neeya met her husband half way across the old, cracked tarmac. The way Luca hugged his wife, picked her up until her feet didn't touch the ground, and held her there was enough to make Mac look away.

Privacy, he thought.

Every man needed it in moments like those.

"I don't think I need to ask anything," Melina said quietly.

"Why not, doll?"

"Some things are just bigger than me, Mac. This is probably one of those things. I don't think it needs to be made about me, you know?"

Yeah, he did.

"Who got the guards?" Mac asked when Massimo's gaze drifted in their direction.

The old man cracked a smile. "Someone sly enough to not be caught, I suppose."

"That tells me nothing."

"Like father, like son, Mac."

Mac stiffened. "Enric?"

Massimo tipped a hand high as if to wave off any concerns Mac was thinking to say, but he still thought and felt them nonetheless. Enric had, for a long time, led Mac to believe he was in the same position as his Capo where Luca was concerned. Unable to see his father. Disallowed visits. Refused calls.

How much of it had been lies?

How many people all around them had been lying for this?

Melina tugged on Mac's suit jacket, drawing his attention to her again. He swore she could read his mind just by looking at him, and she repeated her earlier sentiment again in a new way. "It's not about us, Mac. It's about something bigger than us."

Luca was still hugging his wife.

Neeya's feet still hadn't touched the ground.

Mac remembered those words Luca had told him about his wife many months ago. *There is only one thing in this world other than my surname and the legacy it holds that belongs only to me now. Neeya knows what that is—she has always known. I've never doubted that.*

175

Mac realized, Luca had been talking about Neeya.

And maybe—just *maybe*—Mac could empathize with that. Because had it been his wife, had a second chance dangled in front of them when everything else seemed hopeless ... fucking hell, Mac hoped Melina would take it for them because he would take it for her.

No matter the cost.

"I want to ask how this was done," Melina said, shaking her head.

Massimo laughed. "Don't bother. I won't give an answer."

"Why isn't Enric here, too?" Mac asked. "We're here to say goodbye, right? I got that much. Everyone else is here—his daughters, us, and you. We're going to say goodbye, so why isn't Enric here to do the same?"

"The wheelchair made it a bit difficult, and Enric chose not to risk it. I pressed, the young man made his choice. Besides, he had a job to do, and he wanted to do that well. He's a lot like his father in that way. Sometimes, at the detriment of one thing, you perfect another. He knew that meant he would make sacrifices elsewhere."

Well, then ...

"All right," Mac said, his attention going back to the two people now approaching them.

"Massimo," Luca called out above the sound of the chopper blades, "I don't know how to thank you for all of this."

The older man tipped his hand in that dismissive way again. "No need to bother, Luca. Anything for my Neeya. We agreed on that long ago, didn't we?"

"We did."

Mac and Melina stayed back while Luca and Neeya chatted with their daughters and Massimo. He figured the private conversation wouldn't be appropriate for them to listen in on, anyway, and the chopper's spinning blades helped to muffle the conversation.

It wasn't long before Luca's gaze turned on Mac, and

the man came closer.

"Melina, could we chat?" Neeya asked.

Mac wasn't surprised that his wife stepped away from him without hesitating.

"Boss," Mac said when Luca stopped in front of him.

"Not anymore," Luca replied with a smile.

A *kind* smile.

Mac didn't think he had ever seen that from Luca before.

"Someone's gotta be the boss," Mac joked, "and for all purposes, it's—"

"Not going to be me," Luca interjected. "Not after today."

"I didn't realize I was important enough to get a meet with you before you head ... where is it you're going, anyway?"

Luca lifted one shoulder. "I don't know yet. Those weren't a part of my requests. Probably somewhere warm. Somewhere with lots of sand. Neeya loves that kind of place. She's been the Pivetti Queen for two decades—steadfast and always at my side. It's time for her to relax, so I don't give a shit where we go as long as she's happy about it."

Mac cleared his throat. "And your girls?"

Luca cracked another smile. "Just like their mother, but with enough of me to color them up. They're smarter and stronger than anyone has ever given them credit for. They'll be fine, and we'll meet up again someday. Neeya won't stay away forever. They have Enric to look out for them. Their grandfather to fall back on should they need him ... and you, too."

"Of course, b—"

"Not anymore," Luca repeated firmly. "And unless you don't care who you give that title to, I suggest you quickly figure out how to get the rest of the family to call you by that name, Mac."

He froze on the spot. "I—"

"Some bosses are born, Mac, but far more are made. It's a position you tend to learn better once you're in it."

"Funny, I seem to have a man who has gained far more allies in the family than me lately."

Luca tipped his head sideways a bit. "Anthony."

It wasn't even a question.

"Why did he go to the prison the day we thought Neeya was killed? Why did you let him in to see you, but not me?"

"Snakes are predictable," Luca said simply, "in the way they will slither to the closest warm thing if they believe it will benefit them to do so. See, that's why we tend to step on the snakes before we see them. Men rarely realize that they've been struck by a snake until it's too late."

"You didn't answer my question, Luca."

"Anthony is a snake. He thought I was an opportunity. Given the situation, I allowed him to think we were on the same page. I couldn't very well explain to him that my wife *wasn't* actually dead if I wanted to continue on with my plans, could I?"

"You still could have seen me."

"You're not thinking beyond that moment, Mac. Consider those you think are allied with him are currently in a state of panic. When all that smoke and dust clears, a boss will be gone, a dead wife will have risen, and Anthony will have no answers. A man who *should* know—yet he won't. Someone will, now, but he won't."

"He's been working on your seat since you went into lockup."

"And you're the only one who saw it happening," Luca said with a grin, "so make sure your ass sits down in my seat long before his does. Do you understand?"

"Yeah, I got it."

"Sound a little more sure, Mac."

"It's been a big day to take in."

"Tomorrow, it'll be over," Luca assured.

MADAME MOLL

Mac wasn't so sure about that.
For Luca, yes.
For him?
It felt like the world was waiting.
What the fuck was he supposed to do?
Wink and wave at it?

CHAPTER TWELVE

A heavy, cloying grief had become a part of Melina's life since the moment she'd learned of Neeya's death.

That grief was now lifted and replaced with a myriad of emotions she wasn't ready to deal with yet, especially saying goodbye again.

"You look exceptional ... for a dead woman," Melina said.

Neeya Pivetti lifted a well-manicured eyebrow. "You're angry with me."

Melina shook her head. "No. I was, but only for a minute. Some things don't require an explanation."

"You finally understand the most important lesson of all. Life without love is meaningless."

Neeya's gaze left Melina and fell on Luca. A subtle sheen of tears shined in the woman's eyes.

"Yes, it is," Melina agreed.

The older woman came closer and touched Melina's face. "In the short time we have known each other, I have come to love and care for you as if you were a daughter of my own."

"That means more to me than you know."

Melina swallowed the lump in her throat, blinking away the tears forming in her own eyes.

Neeya opened her mouth to speak but closed it and nodded at someone off in the distance.

"Our time is short, but I must ask a favor of you, Melina. Something I dare not trust anyone else with."

"Name it," Melina managed around the lump in her throat.

"Look after my daughters while I'm gone."

A tear slipped down Neeya's cheek as her mask of refined elegance finally slipped.

A mother's worry.

A mother's naked fear.

Melina knew the feelings all too well. They'd become a part of her existence from the moment she'd become pregnant with her own child. She couldn't imagine the depths of Neeya's own emotions as she prepared to face a new life … without her daughters.

"Of course. Whatever they need."

Neeya's hand dropped away as she placed a soft kiss on Melina's cheek. "Thank you."

"No thanks necessary. You'd do the same for me."

"Indeed I would.

Melina sighed. "Well, I guess this is goodbye."

Neeya shook her head. "Not goodbye. Just an I'll see you later and now that I know I have you looking out for my girls I can rest a little easier."

The older woman held out her arms, and Melina went into them hugging the Pivetti Queen hard. She didn't fight as tears flowed down her cheeks.

"Be safe, Neeya, wherever your journey takes you."

The two women moved apart, each wiping away their tears that had fallen.

"The same to you, my dear. Just remember that the strongest piece on the board is always the Queen. Your time is now."

Understanding dawned on Melina. "Are you saying what I think you are?"

"You're a smart woman. I never speak unless I have something worth saying."

Neeya patted Melina on the shoulder and gestured

towards the helicopter. She understood immediately. The time for saying goodbyes was over. Each step seemed heavier than the last as the two women joined their husbands and the Pivetti daughters. Luca Pivetti's eyes lit up as his wife came to his side. Wrapping his arm around her, the weary man placed a kiss atop her forehead before beckoning his girls to come closer.

Melina felt like an outsider as she watched the family exchange hugs and kisses. Tears misted in her eyes. The love the Pivettis had for their family was in the air. It dripped from their pores like a fine sweat, glistening and evident. The separation they would all be forced to endure was unjust, but maybe somehow, some way they would all be together again someday.

"It's time." Massimo's voice cut over the sound of the helicopters blades.

Melina reached for her husband's hand, sliding hers easily into his.

"It's going to be all right, doll." His lips brushed against her ear.

She turned to him and noted the emotion swimming in his own eyes. This was affecting him too. It would to anyone that had a heart.

"I hope so," she said.

Massimo came forward and put his arms around his granddaughters. "Time to go, girls."

The three young women nodded, and Melina bit her lip as she watched them hug and kiss their parents one final time before they were ushered into a waiting car by their grandfather. The two couples watched in silence as the girls were driven away. When they faced each other again, Melina noted the fresh tears going down Neeya's cheeks.

"And now I too must take my leave," Massimo said as he came to stand beside his son-in-law.

Luca held out his hand. "Thank you again … for everything."

The two men shook.

"Take care of her. If not you'll answer to me," Massimo warned.

A tic moved in Luca's jaw, but the man wisely nodded. Massimo Dinunzio was a man you didn't want to cross, even if you were a once formidable crime boss. Even now Luca was still wise enough to know that.

"Daddy," Neeya said. A hint of a smile played on her face as she held out her arms to hug her father. The two embraced briefly before Massimo patted his daughter's cheek and turned to Mac and Melina.

"Best of luck to the both of you. A shit storm's coming."

His piece said, Massimo got into the car that had brought him and was speedily driven away.

"Make me proud, Melina," Neeya said.

"Always."

Neeya reached for Melina's hand briefly before letting go and turning to her husband.

"Ready?"

"I've never been more ready," Luca said.

He nodded briefly towards Mac before he took Neeya's hand and helped her into the helicopter. Taking a seat beside her, Luca closed the door and the blades began to twirl even faster. Mac pulled Melina back away from the force of the winds made by the blades as the helicopter rose into the air and sped off into the evening sky.

"Let's go home, doll."

Melina allowed Mac to lead her to the remaining car and opened the door for her. She climbed inside. When her husband joined her, she took Mac's face in her hands and kissed him. He returned her kiss with equal enthusiasm before he stopped.

"Why did you stop?" Melina asked.

"Because I'm not inclined to give our driver a free show." Mac reached for her hand and brought it to his mouth, pressing a kiss to it.

"Good point." Melina was silent for a moment before she spoke again. "We have a lot to discuss."

"Yeah, we do, but for now let's just enjoy the ride."

"Yes. Let's."

The world they knew was on the verge of changing forever, but how that change would be brought about was best discussed elsewhere. For now, she would enjoy the comfort of her husband's arms as they silently contemplated the new future ahead of them.

Melina awoke reaching for her husband, but found the space beside her empty. After finally returning home yesterday evening, they'd spent a quiet few hours with their son before going to bed. They'd fallen asleep, wrapped in each other's arms. Mac hadn't said much yesterday, and she hadn't pushed for anything. Sometimes a person just needed to be alone with their thoughts. But the time for silence was over.

Getting out of bed, Melina pulled on her robe, brushed her teeth and left through the bedroom in search of her husband. It didn't take her long to find him. She leaned against the doorway frame. Mac leaned over Marquise's crib watching their son as he slept, but there was a tenseness in his body. Unease curled all around him.

"Good morning, doll."

Mac stretched to his full height and faced her. Shirtless, with a pair of pajama pants that hung low on his hips, the sight of her husband never failed to leave her a little bit breathless. And a whole lot grateful. She crossed the short distance to where he stood and placed her hands on his shoulders.

"Every morning with you is."

Mac raised a brow. "What did I do to deserve you

stroking my ego so early this morning?"

He kissed the tip of her nose and then twice on the lips. Melina smiled at him, momentarily lost in the hazel of his eyes.

"Nothing particular. I just felt like stroking your ego since you got out of bed before I could stroke something else this morning."

"The day is still young," Mac teased.

"Indeed it is, but there are some things we need to talk about first." Her hands dropped from his shoulders.

"I know."

"Let's not have this conversation in front of little ears," she said.

Mac nodded, taking her hand and leading her from their son's nursery and into the kitchen. They sat down at the kitchen table, and the air between them was momentarily strained. Her husband's eyes took on a hard glint.

"A lot happened yesterday."

"Yeah, it did," Melina said.

"When we walked into that funeral, the last thing I expected was what happened. Or what has the potential to happen now. But what I'm most concerned with is how everything will affect my family."

"What happens to either of your families is ultimately up to you."

"I know."

"I think somewhere in the back of your mind, you knew that when Luca went in this time he wasn't coming out. I also believe you knew what would happen, but what I didn't know was that you were ready to completely accept his blessing."

Mac leaned back and crossed his arms across his chest. "How do you know he gave me his blessing?"

"Because one thing Luca Pivetti is not is a fool. He may no longer be in a position to run the organization he built, but there is no way he wants everything he worked for to go to shit. It doesn't take a genius to know you are the only option for the continued survival of *la famiglia*."

Her husband ran a hand over his face. "For so long I've been trying to navigate my own path. To find my way out of the shadow that James' name cast over me."

"And you've done that your own way, but that doesn't stop now. It can't stop if either of your families are to survive. You know the kind of threat we face. I'm tired of waiting for the other shoe to drop, Mac. Something has to be done."

Mac pushed away from the table and stood up. Melina watched silently as he moved about the kitchen fixing a pot of coffee before he finally sat back down.

"And it will be, but taking care of this kind of problem is not just black and white. There are certain things that just can't be done on a whim."

"A made man is one that can't be arbitrarily killed. The consequences for an unsanctioned hit by someone connected would be dire, I suppose."

"Yes, they would."

"You can't kill him, but that doesn't mean there isn't someone else who can."

The coffee pot stopped, and Melina quickly moved to pour her and Mac a cup each. He remained quiet as she added one creamer and sugar to his and Cinnabon creamer to her own cup. She bit her lip as the unsaid words she hadn't voiced hung in the air between them. Her husband was a smart man, but she knew that even he had his limits.

"What if I'm not comfortable with what you're suggesting?"

Melina placed his cup of coffee in front of him on the table, before she sat back down with her own cup. Taking a long swallow of the sweet and creamy, hot drink, she took a moment to choose her words.

"We have no choice."

"There's always a choice, Melina."

"Not this time. The longer he has to gather men

closer to him, the more danger there is for us and our son. There is a threat that needs to be eliminated, and I am in the prime position to do it."

Mac took three long hard swallows of his coffee, before he set the mug back down on the table and pushed it away.

"I know that when you married me you were aware of what becoming a part of this lifestyle entailed. That there would be danger and sometimes we would have to get dirty, but blood on your hands was something I never wanted. Especially the blood of a snake like Anthony."

"I appreciate all of that, but it doesn't change our current situation. There are some things that need to be done, and sometimes the only person to do those things is a woman."

"I don't like it, doll."

"You don't have to. You just have to agree to it."

Melina finished her cup of coffee and waited, watching her husband. The war of emotions ranged across his face. Her husband loved her, valued, and respected her. He was also fully aware of what she was capable of, and that was where his indecision lay. To allow his wife to get her hands bloody or remain at a stalemate with a target on his back. There was only one option.

"Okay."

One simple word.

So much said without being spoken.

So many undercutting emotions.

"All right."

She stood, taking their coffee mugs from the table to wash them in the sink. Releasing a breath, she turned on the water at the sink and began washing the two cups. It was time to put things right. To protect her family. To cut the head off a snake once and for all. Melina was under no illusions about what she had to do and the aftermath that would follow.

"We'll make it through this."

Mac's arms wrapped around her and she leaned back against him, savoring in the warmth of his embrace. As long as they had each other, there was no threat they couldn't face. No challenge they couldn't handle.

"You look good enough to eat, doll."

Melina did a slow twirl in front of the mirror as her husband came to stand behind her.

"I'll make time for you to do that later," Melina teased.

"If you want, I can make time right now."

Mac's hands slid around her waist and up to cup her breasts through the red silk that covered them. His thumbs rubbed slow circles over her nipples, and Melina arched her back against him.

"I should've known you'd try and play dirty."

"Never that, doll. I'm only offering to give you what you asked for."

Regretfully, Melina moved his hands away and faced him. "If we weren't already running late, I'd take you up on your offer, but I for one am looking forward to opening night at Rosemarie's."

"Then we'd better get going."

Melina nodded, turning back to the mirror to tuck a stray strand of hair behind her ear. Tonight her hair was tousled in soft curls that fell down her back. A pair of black diamond studs sparkled at her ears. The red silk dress she wore ended at mid-thigh and hugged her every curve. Mac hadn't been able to keep his eyes off her ever since she'd donned the designer gown. She supposed the deep cut that showcased her cleavage didn't hurt things either.

"If you keep admiring yourself in the mirror, doll, I'm

going to change my mind."

"Okay. Okay. I'm ready."

Melina allowed her husband to lead her from their bedroom and into the living room. The sound of baby giggles drew them even quicker. They found Victoria and Enric tickling Marquise whose face was stretched wide with laughter. For a moment, she and Mac just stood there watching the scene unfold in front of them. The joy on their son's face as he played with his aunt and his father's subordinate was wide and clear. Melina didn't miss the long looks Enric and Victoria cast at each other when the other wasn't looking. Something was brewing between them, and it had been for a while. She only hoped when the storm finally hit, the young man and woman would be prepared for the winds that would follow.

"You two are in for a long night," Mac said breaking the silence.

"Meaning what?" Victoria challenged.

"Meaning Marquise is normally in his crib by now and yet you two have him up playing. It's going to be a while before he sleeps."

"I don't mind," Enric said.

"Me, neither."

Mac laughed. "The both of you will soon learn."

"Weren't you supposed to be gone fifteen minutes ago?" Victoria prodded as Marquise lay in her arms smiling.

"We get the hint," Melina said.

Quickly she and Mac kissed their son goodbye and hurried out the front door. Mac opened the back door of the car and helped her inside. When their car was pulling out of the driveway, Mac shook his head.

"What is it?" Melina asked.

"I'm going to have to have a talk with Enric."

"About?"

"My sister."

"What is there to talk about? They like each other,

even if they're not ready to admit it. They'll come to each other in their own time. The last thing Victoria needs is you sticking your nose in her business."

"She's my sister. She will always be my damn business."

"Careful, Mac. You're about to start sounding like a patriarchal jackass."

Mac looked at her, eyes glittering in the dark. "That's a new one, doll."

Melina shrugged. "Just calling it how I see it."

"I take it you see Enric and Vic as a good match."

She took her husband's hand in hers. "They remind me of us," she said quietly.

"In what way?"

"Well I didn't particularly like you much when we first met either although it was obvious you were pretty crazy about me."

Tracing the curve of her cheek, Mac kissed her softly on the lips. "No argument there."

"Yes, and somehow we found our way to one another when the time was right."

"Yeah, we did." Mac sighed. "Fine. I'll butt out when it comes to Vic and Enric."

"Good. I'm sure they both will appreciate it."

It wasn't long before they arrived at Rosemarie's. The old fashioned Italian style eatery was celebrating its grand opening tonight. Mac had explained that Raphael Arogosa came from an old Italian family and had grown up in the same neighborhood as Mac. He was one of the few boys in the neighborhood that hadn't become a part of organized crime in some way.

Instead the man had gone to culinary school and decided to open a restaurant in honor of his late grandmother. Her husband had been more than happy to help finance the endeavor with no strings attached. There was a line of people wrapped around the red brick building as their car cruised to a stop at the front entrance.

"Standing room only," Melina said.

"Good thing we're on the short list then."

The town car came to a stop, and Mac helped her from the vehicle. All eyes were on them as they walked up to the front of the line where two burly men were watching the doors and doing their best to keep the eager crowd in line.

"Maccari," Mac said.

One of the men grabbed the heavy brass door handles and held the door open for them.

"Thank you," Melina said.

"Welcome, ma'am."

They entered the building, and the soft strands of Italian opera played over loud speakers. Pictures of historic places in Italy lined either side of the wall. The smells of garlic and freshly baked bread filled the air.

"My mouth is starting to water," Melina said.

"Cynthia wouldn't be happy to hear you say that," Mac teased.

"What? I can't be excited about tasting anyone else's food but your mother's?"

"No."

"Asshole." She smiled.

Mac pinched her arm as they walked up to the distressed brown podium. A bubbly hostess directed a solitary man to a table near the front. When the blonde saw Mac, her eyes immediately took on a predatory gaze. Melina fought down the urge to slap the woman across her smiling face.

"Table for two," Mac said.

"Welcome to Rosemarie's. What's the name?"

"Mr. and *Mrs*. Maccari," Melina said pointedly.

"Down, tiger," Mac whispered in her ear before pressing a kiss to her cheek.

"Mac."

They turned towards the sound of the voice. A dark-haired man, with a slim build and shining green eyes came towards them wearing a red buttoned up shirt and black pants.

"Raphael."

Mac released her hand and turned to greet the man with a handshake and hug.

"I'm so glad you could make it. I assume this is your lovely wife, Melina."

"You'd be right. This is my queen. Melina, meet Raphael, one of the best chiefs on the east coast."

Melina smiled, extending her hand. "Pleasure to meet you Raphael. If Mac praises your cooking, then it must be good."

"Let's hope I live up to his expectations. There's a table set up for the two of you. Whatever you want is on the house," Raphael said.

"I appreciate that very much."

"It's just a little token of my appreciation for everything you've done."

"No need to thank me. You deserve this, and your grandmother would be proud."

"Thank you. Let me escort the two of you to your table," Raphael said.

Mac tucked Melina's arm through his as they followed Raphael to their table, situated near the center of the room. The textured earth tone walls and dark wood gave the place a homely feel. The dark red table runners that covered the cherry wood tables reminded Melina of marinara sauce and further reminded her of just how hungry she was.

As Raphael stopped at their table, Melina noted that they could see everyone around them. Mac pulled out a chair for Melina. He stiffened looking past her into the distance. She followed his gaze and saw Anthony Corelli at a table on the other side of the room surrounded by several men. Spotting Melina, he smiled and raised a glass of red wine in the air.

"How long has he been here?" Mac asked Raphael.

The strain was evident in his voice.

"Long enough for me to be ready for him to get the hell out. He's been acting like some goddamn king holding court all night."

"Have a seat, doll," Mac said gentling his voice.

Melina did as her husband asked.

"Thanks again, Raphael."

"You're welcome. I'll send a waiter right over."

Mac nodded before taking his seat across the table from her, where he was able to keep an eye on Anthony.

"The bastard doesn't know when to quit, does he?" Mac said.

"He's only doing this to provoke you."

"I know, but here of all places. Fucking here. This was deliberate. He knew I'd be here to support Raphael."

"He wants you to make a scene in an effort to bolster his own image. Let the interloper pretend to be a king. You and I both know who the real king is, so we are going to enjoy our night out just like we intended. Nothing has changed."

"You've learned this game well."

"Indeed I have, and first thing in the morning I'm going to make a phone call that is going to put us one step closer to having a problem taken care of once and for all."

Melina perused the menu that was left on their table as a waiter came over to get their drink and appetizer orders. She chose fried lasagna bites and left the wine selection up to the waiter. Mac went for fried calamari. When the waiter left, Melina did her best to engage Mac in conversation, but his attention was divided between her and whatever Anthony was doing across the room.

"All right, now I'm starting to feel a little pissed off," she said. Melina tapped his shin with the edge of her heel.

Mac reached for her hand across the table. "I'm sorry, but if you could see what I see right now." A muscle in his jaw tensed.

"Perhaps I should."

Discretely moving her chair so that she was now sitting on Mac's left hand side, it took less than a minute before she could see what had her husband still so riled up. Corelli held out his hand and Melina watched disbelievingly as two men greeted Anthony by kissing the ring on his hand.

"This almost leaves me speechless. Almost," Melina said.

"I've never seen a power play like this before. Luca not publicly naming a successor has this whole organization in an uproar."

"Think of it this way, Mac. In some ways, Luca did you a favor. By not publicly throwing his weight behind you, he gave you the opportunity to create your own legacy. To show that you don't need anyone to give you anything. That you are perfectly able to prove your capability on your own terms."

"Have I told you how much I love how your mind works?" Mac offered her a smile.

Melina shook her head. "No. Not lately."

She laughed as their waiter returned with a bottle of wine, their appetizers, and a bowl of fresh garlic knots.

"Well let me rectify that. I love your mind and everything else about you," Mac said.

"That's better."

Melina shared a quick kiss with her husband before they put in their orders for the main course, Eggplant Parmesan for Mac and Chicken Marsala for her. Popping a lasagna bite in her mouth, Melina moaned.

"This is divine."

"Glad you like it, doll. Try some of my calamari."

Melina allowed Mac to feed her. The calamari was perfectly cooked and tender enough to melt in her mouth.

"From the rapturous expression on your face, I'd say the calamari is a hit, too," Mac said.

"And you would be right."

His gaze momentarily strayed from her to Anthony's

corner again, and she put a lasagna bite in his mouth to refocus his attention.

"No more of that tonight, Mac. Appearances are everything."

Mac nodded, refocusing his attention. Melina hated the way Anthony was getting to her husband. Mac was usually calm and collected on even his worst days, but somehow Corelli seemed to have gotten under his skin in a way no one else ever had. It wasn't what he needed and certainly was not a good start for a future boss. Anthony was like a fly, annoying and always buzzing around. An irritant. But like with flies, all it took was one good swat to finally get rid of the irritant permanently. Anthony's swat was coming sooner than he realized.

"Are you sure about this? It's not too late to back out," Mac said.

Melina shook her head. "It's all going to be fine. You have to trust me to get this done."

"I do."

"Then everything else will work itself out," Melina assured her nervous husband.

Mac took both of her hands in his and brought them to his lips, pressing soft kisses on them.

"A man is supposed to protect his family."

"That's exactly what you're doing in a circumvent way."

"Yeah, I guess you're right, doll."

"Of course, I am. A woman is always right." Melina winked at him to lighten the tension in the room.

"I'm slowly learning that."

"Learn it a little bit faster then," she teased before becoming serious. "Is everything ready?"

Mac nodded. "Yeah. Downstairs in the car."

"All right, then I'd better be going. I need to get there first."

Turning, Melina headed out of their bedroom and down the hallway.

"You don't want to see Marquise before you go?"

She stopped momentarily and shook her head before she kept walking. "No. I'll see him when I get back."

She would have loved nothing more than to hold her son.

To kiss his cheeks and inhale his scent.

But that would only make her soft and right now she needed to be harder than she'd ever been before. There was no room for softness now.

Melina remained silent as Mac followed her out of the house to where an indistinctive black sedan with dark tinted windows waited for her. Not even an emblem to identify the make and model of the car was evident.

"Everything you need is inside," Mac said.

"Thanks."

"Do we need to go over things one more time?"

She faced her husband. "No. I'm good."

Mac swallowed hard. "Come back to me."

It was half order, half question. For a split second, Melina considered abandoning the whole thing. The half concealed fear on Mac's face was enough to undo even the firmest of resolves, but she couldn't give in to her emotions. There was too much at stake. Instead she smiled and wrapped her arms around him holding him close.

"Always."

Their lips met in a kiss that was full of all the things they were momentarily incapable of saying.

A forever love.

A fearsome passion.

A hope for a future beyond their dreams.

All the reasons why quitting now was not an option.

Melina stepped away from Mac. "I'd better go."

"Yeah."

She didn't miss the gruffness in his voice as he opened the driver's side door for her. Soon it would all be over, and their lives could get back to normal. Their new normal anyway. Sliding into the car, Melina turned the key that was already in the ignition and started the vehicle.

"I'll be back soon. Okay."

"I love you, doll."

"I love you too, Mac."

Closing the door, Melina quickly put on her seatbelt and pulled away from the house. She glanced in the rearview mirror, watching her husband become smaller and smaller in the distance. She hated to see the internal struggle Mac was having with himself, especially when it was unwarranted. But after tonight it would all be over. Melina was sure of it.

Her drive to The Dollhouse seemed to be shorter than usual. In no time at all, she was parking the sedan in an alley two blocks away. The small handbag she carried was a heavy weight against her shoulder. A reminder. Melina watched her surroundings as she made it closer to the rear entrance and let herself in. It hadn't been hard to convince her employees to take a day off. She closed and locked the back door behind her before turning on the lights and doing a quick walk through the place.

Melina unlocked the front door before going behind the bar to pour herself a drink. The rum and Coke was soothing as it went down her throat. She glanced at the clock on the wall. It wouldn't be long now. Downing the rest of the drink, Melina washed the glass and put it away before heading to the last room on the right. The one Erika usually frequented. Stepping side, she turned on the light and deposited her bag on the plush queen sized bed as she sat in the lounge chair next to it. The only bed she had an interest in being in was her own.

Minutes ticked by and she wondered for the first time if perhaps things might not go the way she wanted. Then she heard footsteps, and the door opened. Anthony Corelli stood in the doorway.

"Melina, what an unexpected surprise."

Anthony entered the room, removing his jacket.

"I'm sure it is."

"Did something happen with Erika?" he asked. His eyes roved over her.

"She had a family emergency."

"And she couldn't have called?" he pressed.

"Actually I asked her not to. I wanted to see you." Honey dripped from her voice.

Anthony sat down on the bed. "Hell must have frozen over. Why would you want to see me, Melina?"

Melina crossed her legs and smiled at Anthony. "Because we have something to discuss. Something important."

"Dare I hope you've finally come to your senses and realized that it's time to switch to the winning side?"

"And you're the winning side?"

Anthony moved closer to where she sat, leaning close enough to stroke the outside of her thigh. "A war is coming, Melina, and I will be the winner. I'd hate for you to be caught in the fallout, especially when you have a much more attractive option."

"And that would be aligning myself with you?" she pressed.

"I'm thinking something more permanent ... like marriage."

The man had no shame. No shame at all.

"I'm already married."

"You'll be a lovely widow, Melina, and then an even more beautiful wife."

His hand rose higher on her leg, toying with the hem of her skirt.

"What about my son? How does he figure into your plans?"

"He's half yours and young enough to not remember

his father. Marquise is in no danger from me, especially if you agree to give me a child of our own. I'll need a boy off you."

She had to give it to him. Anthony had everything figured out. In his mind, he could have whatever he wanted and that included her. To a man like him, her husband was only a bump in the short road to his rise to the top. It was obvious from the cool, predatory manner in which he watched her that he expected no pushback. From her. From anyone.

"You seem to have this all figured out."

"A man with ambition always makes time to think his plans through."

"Is that so?" she asked.

"Yes."

Catching his hand, Melina removed it from her thigh and stood up.

"Well there is one thing you didn't consider."

"And what's that, dear?"

"Just how much I love my husband."

In one fluid motion, Melina reached between her thighs and unsnapped the black Ruger 380 and aimed it at Anthony's head.

"You bitch!"

Before he could move, Melina squeezed the trigger. She watched dispassionately as Anthony fell back on the bed, dead. A bullet between the eyes signaled the end of a man that had never deserved to lead. A man who had discussed murdering her husband like someone discussed the weather. Inconsequential. She was glad he was dead. Opening up the bag that lay on the bed beside his dead body, Melina fished out the burner phone and pressed one.

"It's done," Melina said.

"We're on our way."

She ended the call and threw the phone on top of the bag. Anthony's blood continued to seep into the bedding but it didn't matter. Soon this room would be cleaned and scrubbed as if nothing had ever happened. And Anthony … Anthony Corelli was just another piece of trash lying in the gutter. His reign was over.

CHAPTER THIRTEEN

Mac held the back door to The Dollhouse open, and allowed the two men he had brought along for the cleanup to enter ahead of him. He was unaccustomed to seeing The Dollhouse as quiet and inactive as it currently was. Usually, Melina always had a girl or two on the floor, someone behind the bar, and patrons milling about.

He almost wondered why Anthony wouldn't have noticed those things himself, and questioned it. Then again, when a man had a goal and purpose, his attention tended to focus in on only those things.

Like pussy.

Melina sat at the bar nursing a red martini. Mac nodded for the two men to head towards the back and begin their cleanup without him. Once they were gone from his sight, he headed for his wife.

Mac came up beside Melina, and slid onto a barstool. "Needed a drink?"

Her russet gaze turned on him, and she smiled. "I figured I had earned at least one."

Sure she did.

Mac had worried—just a bit—about this plan of his wife's. If only because he had been raised to believe that women should not dirty their hands in the business of *famiglia*. They should not concern themselves with the business between men. He wasn't so stupid to think that was the way it *should* be, though.

He was quite aware, and had been for a long time, that Melina was not like other women, or other made men's wives. She was unique to her, and to *him*. She was more than capable of getting her hands into a pot, and stirring it. She was fully able to get a job done that a man could not do, and more so, because she *was* a woman.

His woman.

What man wouldn't be proud of that?

"Do you want to talk?" Mac asked.

Melina lifted a single shoulder. "About what?"

"Anything. Tonight. Anthony. How you're feeling. Any of it, doll."

"Like most men, he thought with his cock and not his head. Something he had wanted for a long time was dangling in front of him, and he couldn't refuse it, even if he should have known better. His loss was our gain, Mac. There's nothing more to say, really."

Well, he just wanted to make sure.

Mac leaned over and kissed his wife on her temple. "Do you want to wait and head home with me?"

"I'd like to go home and hold my son. Soon, preferably"

He understood that feeling all too well.

"Call me if you need me home sooner, all right?" he asked.

Melina nodded. "Okay."

Mac slid off the stool, ready to get to work and be rid of Anthony once and for all. He turned on his heel to head for the back hallway when Melina grabbed his wrist. She tugged, turning him back around and pulling him in for a hard kiss that froze him in place and made all the worries in his mind drift away.

God, he loved his wife.

Her lips brushed over his, soft yet insistent. Her tongue stuck against his mouth, demanding and teasing.

"I love you, Mac," she whispered against his lips.

Mac kissed her twice, one right after the other, on her smiling mouth. "Love you, doll."

"Can we have a break after this is all over? Just us, and Marquise, I mean. Maybe go somewhere, and do something. Without business and people? *Something?*"

"That sounds ..."

"What?"

"Perfect, doll." Mac grinned, and stroked his wife's cheekbone with his thumb. "I will figure something out for us to relax, and have a break."

It wouldn't be easy. Especially not considering if he was going to take over the family, his first order of business could not be to run off with his wife and *have a break*. But fuck all that noise because he would do it for his wife. Or he would figure something out for her.

Anything to make Melina happy.

Melina downed the rest of the red martini, and set it to the bar top. "I'm going to head home."

"How many of those things did you drink?"

She shot him a look. "Just the one, Mac. Don't worry about that."

He patted her on the backside with a smirk as she headed for the door. "Drive safe, doll."

Melina waved a hand over her shoulder, and then she was gone out the door. Mac made sure to lock the door behind her, which left him and his men only the back exit to use. That was fine, though, because all that was back there was their cars and a dumpster.

Mac found his guys wrapping up Anthony's corpse in clear plastic overtop a blue tarp. The two enforcers worked silently, rolling the man's body until nothing was visible, and never saying a thing to one another.

"The bed and rug needs to go," Mac said, noting the bloodstains.

"Will do, boss," said Ross, the taller of the two.

Teddy nodded at the wall. "Bit of blood spray there, too. We'll get it all, no worries."

Mac sighed, and folded his dress sleeves up to the elbows. "I'll get the bleach, then."

"Here, boss." Teddy held out his hand, and offered an item to Mac.

He plucked it from the enforcer's hand.

Anthony's signet ring.

"I would rather eat shit than wear this," Mac said, more to himself than the men.

"Yeah, but at least if you have it, then the *famiglia* men will know there's only one way you got it, boss."

"Truth."

Mac slid the ring down his finger. He'd destroy it the first chance he could. The snake had finally lost his head, and would not be coming back from this one.

"Let's get this done fast, but clean," Mac said. "I've got better places to be tonight."

His enforcers agreed.

Mac went in search of bleach.

Mac slid the French toast onto a plate, and added it to the serving tray. He made his wife's coffee just the way she liked, and added it with the rest of the breakfast. Scooping up the tray, he headed for the upstairs, making sure to check on Marquise as he passed the baby's nursery.

Marquise, fed and changed, had already fallen back asleep. Likely until ten or later.

The kid liked to sleep.

Mac closed the baby's door, and headed down the hallway to the master bedroom. Melina still slept contently under a pile of blankets. She didn't stir as Mac came in, set the tray on his side of the bed, and began untangling the blankets from his wife's sleeping form.

She, like their son, enjoyed sleep.

Maybe too much.

"Doll, wake up," Mac murmured.

Melina rolled over, grumbling under her breath.

Mac wasn't giving up that easy.

"Melina," he said, tugging the last sheet off his wife's body, "wake up."

"It's too early, Mac, go away."

"First, it's eight. That's not early."

Melina *psht'd* under her breath, never turning back to look at him. "The baby hasn't made a sound, so it is not eight in the morning. If you're looking for an early morning lay, you might as well go rub one out in the shower because I am not getting up."

Mac glanced up at the ceiling, determined to keep his laughter in. "Marquise *did* get up. I fed him with the extra bottles you had prepped in the fridge, and laid him back down once he was changed. He's out like a light again— gets it from his mother."

"Liar."

He grabbed the clock on the bedside table, and put it in front of his wife's face, ignoring how the cord pulled against the stand and almost knocked off Melina's book. "See, I am not lying."

"Ugh."

"So, you don't want the coffee, French toast, and strawberries, huh?"

Melina sighed. "I guess."

"Keep acting like you're not preening inside."

"That's right—you keep letting me act like that, Mac." His wife turned over, peering up at him with an amused gaze. "Are you going to feed me, too?"

"If you want me to."

"Might as well," she mused.

Once Melina had propped herself up against pillows, Mac joined her in the bed. She sipped on steaming coffee, while he cut pieces of French toast for her to eat from the fork he held out.

"I am, though," she said, half yawning. "Tired, I mean."

"Mentally tired is just another form of exhaustion, doll."

Melina hummed an agreement under her breath.

"Also, you take this being spoiled thing far too seriously," Mac added, offering his wife another bite.

Melina took it with a sexy grin. "Someone makes it easy for me to do, Mac."

He chuckled. "Point taken."

Melina was halfway through her breakfast before she spoke again. "What's going to happen now?"

Mac shrugged. "We'll stay quiet for a few days, let Anthony's people figure out he's gone missing, let them make their loops for a bit on where he could be, and then I'll call a meet. The rest is history."

"That's it?"

"That's it, doll. Threats tend to work well on men who have little interest in the effort it would take to take over a family, never mind *run* one. They only need a boss to answer to. I will be the one to give them that."

Melina dragged her fingers through her hair, and then piled it high on top of her head to set in a messy bun. "And Anthony's body is ...?"

In the bottom of a river, inside a deep freezer that had been filled with cement. It was never coming back up, and good luck to the fucker who found the deep freezer and wanted to pull it up from the water.

"Gone," Mac said.

"Mac."

"Gone, doll. That's all you need to know. You did your job, and I did mine."

Melina pursed her lips. "I waited up for you last night."

"You made a bit of a mess. We made sure that room was perfect before leaving."

"Sorry about that," she said.

Mac laughed. "I've seen worse. You finished?"

"One last drink of this, and yes."

Melina tossed back what was left of her coffee, and then Mac made the tray full of empty dishes disappear outside of their bedroom door. His wife was stretching like a little kitten against the pillows as he came to stand by her side of the bed.

"Do you want to sleep a bit more? I'll look after the little *principe*."

Melina winked up at him. "After, sure."

Mac didn't even get the chance to reply to what his wife was suggesting. She snagged his wrists in her grasp, and tugged him back into bed with her. Her lips met his as her thighs widened to let him fit their bodies together, while their tongues warred.

Their kiss was always so familiar to him, now. All teeth, and tongues, and lips. He couldn't get enough of the taste of her, and he'd happily die from simply forgetting to breathe. Her mouth was his drug—a sweet poison that made him high. A sin he could never quit.

Mac edged Melina's boy shorts down her thighs, and let her kick the underwear off as he pushed her camisole up high enough to expose her breasts. Her nipples hardened under his roving thumbs as she shoved his sleep pants down. Never once did his wife's lips leave his, and it damn near killed him to pull away.

But he had something else to taste.

Something that was just as sweet and sinful as her mouth.

Melina arched off the bed as Mac kissed down her stomach, only stopping at her navel to flick his tongue against her skin. He set her legs over his shoulder, heard her sharp intake of air, and then he buried his face between her thighs.

Tart.

Hot.

Heavenly.

Melina's soft pussy tasted like bliss on his tongue. He covered her sex with his mouth, let his tongue burrow into her clenching slit, and lapped up her arousal. Her heels dug into his shoulders when he sucked hard on her clit before letting his tongue flick fast against the throbbing nub.

"Jesus," Melina whined, "don't stop, Mac."

He certainly wouldn't.

Not until he got what he wanted.

Her shaking, coming all over his tongue, and ready to be fucked.

Mac felt his wife's orgasm coming on fast—in the tremor rocking her hands that had tangled into his hair, how her legs tightened to keep him in place, and in her tone as it turned higher in pitch. Desperate, even. Her hips rocked into his mouth, wanting more, and her taste became sweeter on his tongue.

"There," Melina breathed. "*God, Mac.*"

As she began to cry her way through the orgasm, Mac slid up Melina's body, caught her parted lips in a kiss, and fit his cock between her thighs. Already clenching and wet from her orgasm, she was damn tight as he thrust in. Every fucking inch of her held him strong, taking his breath away for those first few brief seconds.

He couldn't stand to stay still; every muscle in his body demanded he *move*.

Melina's fingernails raked stinging lines down his back as he fucked her, and he could still feel the aftershocks of her orgasm squeezing his length with every flex of his hips. One of his hands cupped her throat, and his thumb stroked her lips. His other hand tangled into her hair while her legs locked around him, and she met him thrust for thrust.

There was something crazy about his wife when he fucked her.

Something especially beautiful.

Something ...

Mac rolled over to his back, and took Melina with

him. She never broke stride on top of him; their familiar rhythm came so easy for her. She knew where to pick up where he left off. She rode him wild, so crazy. All dark waves of hair falling over her shoulders and dark eyes locked on him. Her one hand flatted to his midsection, while her other dipped between her thighs to tease her clit.

Her bottom lip caught under her teeth, and he *knew*.

"Gonna come again for me, doll?" he asked.

"Gonna make me, Mac?"

Fuck yes.

They did have all morning, after all.

Mac slid the gold cufflinks into the sleeves of his suit jacket. Behind him, Enric sat in his chair, staring down at the screen of his phone.

"You could skip this meet, if you wanted," Mac said.

Enric didn't even bother to look up. "And what, miss seeing the man who will take over my father's position? I don't think so—I need to be there."

"You know, we never did talk about the fact you didn't tell me Luca's plans."

"Why would I?"

"Because I'm loyal to you, Enric."

Enric smirked. "Yes, and look at where *my* loyalty has gotten you, Mac."

Mac's gaze met Enric's in the mirror. "Point taken."

"Actually, should I be using *boss* now, or …?"

"Not like this; not when it's just us," Mac said.

"All right."

"Something came in the mail today, by the way."

"Oh, what?" Enric asked.

Mac held up a signet ring—the second he could add to his collection. "Your father's ring."

Enric didn't look surprised. "I would like to have that when you're done with it."

"Of course."

Mac would need his own to be made now, anyway.

"I walked yesterday," Enric murmured.

Mac stilled. "What?"

"Like twenty steps?" Enric shrugged. "I felt like I was going to die, and I slept from the time I got home until this morning because it took that much out of me. But …"

"You walked," Mac said, his smile growing.

"Yeah. Victoria should have just worn an 'I told you so' sign. She was fucking smug about it all."

"She cares a great deal about you."

Mac held back from asking questions about the two's relationship, but only because he promised Melina that he wouldn't.

"And I think you care a great deal about her," Mac added.

He couldn't help himself.

Enric chuckled low. "Doesn't matter. She won't let me take her out, anyway."

Mac frowned. "Why the hell not?"

Certainly not because of Enric's current state, Mac knew. His sister was not the type to let a disability affect her feelings about a person, romantically or not.

"Getting romantically involved with a patient would cost her a lot," Enric said quietly.

Shit.

Mac hadn't even considered that.

"You're not always going to be a patient, Enric," Mac pointed out.

"Yeah, but by then, things might be—"

Mac's ringing phone stopped Enric from finishing his sentence. He gave the young man a look to say they weren't finished with their conversation as he picked up the call.

"Yeah, Mac here," he said.

"The Dollhouse just got raided, boss," came a familiar voice. The enforcer let out a hard breath, adding, "Your wife is being cornered by cops, and it's not looking good."

Mac cursed. "I'll be there in thirty."

He hung up the phone, and grabbed the handful of items on his dresser to shove in his pocket. Keys, his wallet, and whatever else.

"We have to go," Mac said to Enric.

"What's happened now?"

"Raid on The Dollhouse. Our meet with the men will have to wait."

Enric scowled, and wheeled himself out of the bedroom behind Mac. "Jesus, why can't I have one good day before it all goes to shit, huh?"

Yeah, Mac often asked himself that question, too.

CHAPTER FOURTEEN

Life had returned to normal. At least, whatever the new normal was for Melina and her family. Her last encounter with Anthony was just a dark memory she had no wish to dwell on. What was done was done. Mac had assured her that the pall Anthony had cast over their lives was no more. The only thing that mattered now was ushering in the new transition of leadership that had to take place.

Melina wasn't foolish enough to think that everyone would welcome Mac with open arms as the new boss. There was bound to be discontent among some, but whether that discontent would fester into something more only time would tell. Pushing such thoughts away, Melina left her office and headed to the bar at the front of The Dollhouse. Though it was only midday, business was in full swing. Only a few of the private rooms remained empty. With a practiced hand, Melina fixed a glass of rum and Coke.

She'd only taken a few sips of the heady drink when the wall behind the bar shook. Two bottles of top shelf liquor fell crashing to the floor, and Melina moved quickly in case anything else were to fall.

"What the hell?"

Melina turned just in time to see men and women in full police gear surround the bar.

"Melina Maccari, you are under arrest on charges of

prostitution, and conspiracy."

She barely had time to process what she'd just heard, when Melina was roughly dragged from behind the bar and handcuffed. The cuffs bit into her wrists, but she refused to give them the satisfaction of knowing that she hurt. Instead she focused her attention on the one who'd read the so-called charges against her.

"I'll be sure to send a bill for the liquor you destroyed to your department."

"If I were you, I'd be more concerned about the prison cell that awaits you."

Melina knew that he was trying to rile her, but she refused to rise to his bait.

"We also have a warrant to search the premises, Mrs. Maccari."

She swallowed hard as more men poured down the hallway towards her girls and the patrons they were with.

"There is no need for this disruption of my business."

"We're well aware of just what kind of business you run, Mrs. Maccari," the bald, brown-eyed cop in charge said.

"You know it's a legitimate one with all the proper permits despite these absurd charges that say otherwise," Melina shot back.

"We'll see about that," the lead cop said before he followed the rest of his men down the hallway, leaving Melina alone with the female officer that had handcuffed her.

There was nothing Melina could do to stop them. Her heart had skipped a little when she noticed a few of the officers carrying metal cases. This was no fool's errand. They expected to find something. Melina bit the inside of her lip as some of her girls were herded in front of her trying their best to shield their nakedness.

"You could have let them cover up," Melina said sharply.

A few more officers appeared, pushing in front of

them several men that were frequent visitors.

"I'll have all of your badges for this," one of the men yelled.

"I'd like to see that."

Melina's hands clenched into fists behind her back. It was one thing to be arrested, but to be humiliated was another thing altogether. She would not forget this day. The way the women looked to her with fear in their eyes. The burning anger behind the eyes of her patrons. The laughter of the cops as they antagonized the men and women in front of them.

"What now, Sergeant Masters?" the officer holding Melina asked.

"Have everyone brought to the station. The women on charges of prostitution, and the men on charges of solicitation."

The orders came from the bald man who'd spoken to Melina earlier with such disrespect. As the women and men were marched out against their will, Melina steeled herself to be lead out behind them. She was surprised when Sergeant Masters came to stand in front of her, with a shit eating grin on his face.

"Mrs. Maccari, it appears that my officers have found something quite extraordinary here," he said.

"There's no doubt you're eager to tell me."

"Indeed. I admit I thought it strange that all of the rooms here have beds save one."

"Sometimes furniture does need to be replaced," Melina said.

"No doubt here you are required to replace furniture often, but there is more than that. It appears as if someone has cleaned the entire room."

"Now it's a crime to keep a clean establishment?"

Sergeant Masters laughed. "It is when such a thorough cleaning is used in an effort to hide evidence. I admit even I was amazed to see how the room lit up. The luminol made the room light up like the Fourth of July. I didn't expect to see bleach all the way to the ceiling."

He watched her now intently, as if searching for some break in her character. Some weakness. She refused to give him any. "Is that all?"

Masters smirked. "You're a tough cookie. I'll give you that, but every cookie crumbles one way or another."

Melina smiled. "Not this one."

"We'll see about that. Irwin get her out of here."

"Gladly, boss."

Swallowing down the trepidation that slowly started to seep into her bones. She was being arrested. Again. From past experience, Melina knew that she could survive inside. She'd done it once before. But this time was different. This time wasn't just some petty misdemeanor charge facing her. No. The conspiracy charge had all but proven that. The cops were after something much more substantial. Melina could only pray that bleached down or not, the last room on the right would not lead to the life she'd worked so hard for, crashing down around her.

The ache seeped into Melina's bones.

She steeled herself so that her teeth wouldn't chatter. This was deliberate.

A classic cop tactic to make her as uncomfortable as possible before they questioned her.

Yes. She'd been through this before.

Melina barely looked up as the doors to the interrogation room opened. She recognized one of the men. Detective Parks. This time he was with the female cop who had arrested her earlier. The woman had changed out of her blue uniform and now wore a dark gray pant suit. Her sandy blonde hair had been pulled back in a tight bun at the nape of her neck. Her unfriendly eyes found

Melina's own.

"Mrs. Maccari, imagine seeing you again … so soon," Parks said.

"Through no desire of my own, I assure you."

"Good thing then that fate has brought you here once again. You've already met Officer Irwin."

Detective Parks leaned against the corner of the table while Irwin took a seat directly across from Melina. She smirked at her.

"You know it's really a shame," Irwin said.

"What is?" Melina played along.

"That you would choose to be a martyr for an organization that cares nothing for you or your sacrifice."

Melina shifted in her seat. "Can we please get on with whatever this is? I grow tired of present company."

"By all means. I can admit to being most eager to see you behind bars again," Parks said.

"Anthony Corelli."

Melina's eyes focused on Irwin. She lifted a defiant brow. "Am I supposed to know him?"

"Since he is a frequent patron of the whorehouse you run, I'd think you know him very well."

So, that was what this was all about.

Anthony.

The bastard was dead but yet he'd come back to haunt her once again.

"I run a legitimate and very successful business, but I can't be expected to know the name of every single patron that frequents my establishment."

"Let us refresh your memory," Parks said. He opened a manila folder and spread out an array of glossy colored photos that were date and time stamped. They were all of one person … Anthony.

"Nice photos," Melina said.

"Anthony Corelli makes a nice subject, especially when he's always so easy to track. Your establishment seems to be the place he prefers to spend his time," Irwin said.

Melina glanced at the woman. "The man has good taste. My establishment is top notch."

"So top notch that it was where he spent his last moments of life."

Melina's gaze shifted to find Parks watching her. His eyes narrowed as if he was sure he had something on her.

"I'm not sure what you mean."

Irwin broke in. "The last time Anthony Corelli was seen he was heading into your place of business. No one reported seeing him come out."

Rubbing her wrists, Melina noted she already had bruises forming around the tight cuffs. She took a long breath before she answered.

"As I've said before, there's no way I can possibly know every single patron that may or may not frequent my establishment."

"Well it's a good thing we have that covered then. The last time Anthony Corelli was seen alive was entering The Dollhouse. That combined with the room we found inside bleached from floor to ceiling, with no bed leads us to believe that he was murdered … by you."

So they'd finally played their cards.

Murder.

The prostitution and conspiracy charges were only a ruse.

A means to attempt to flush her out.

To see her crumble.

Too bad for them she wouldn't.

Melina gave a long exaggerated sigh before she laughed. Loudly.

"Is there something you'd like to share with us?" Irwin asked. Her right eye twitched in irritation.

"Your department is ridiculous. The fact that you're wasting tax payer dollars doing surveillance on the coming and goings of one man when there are real crimes out there being committed annoys me. It annoys me almost as much as you accusing me of murdering a man you assume that I know. I have a husband and a son that I adore and love. What woman would jeopardize that?"

Parks shook his head as he placed the pictures back into the folder. "He's trained you well. You sound like the perfect mob wife. Denial springs from your lips so smoothly one could almost believe you're telling the truth. Good thing for me I know better."

"I believe I've said everything I have to say," Melina said coolly.

"Suit yourself. Perhaps some time in lockup will make you reconsider the first degree murder charge we're adding to your rap sheet," Irwin said. She stood up and came towards Melina, motioning for her to stand up.

"I'm entitled to my phone call."

Parks too stood. "Indeed you are, but we'll decide when that is."

"Up, Maccari."

Melina glared at Irwin. They were deliberately denying her the rights that she was entitled to. But she wouldn't let them see how much it upset her. How worried she really was about the new charge they'd just leveled. Instead, she stood up and smiled.

"Lead the way."

Irwin grabbed her roughly around the arm and jerked her towards the door. Melina itched to knock the sanctimonious bitch on her ass, but she had more important things to worry about. Her phone call had been denied, and she had no idea if Mac even knew that she'd been arrested. Or that she was facing life in prison or worse, death, for something he'd assured her would never haunt them again. For once, her husband had been wrong.

A week.

Seven days away from her husband.

Her son.

This was bullshit.

Fucking bullshit.

It had felt as if she was swallowing sand when one of her guards had gloated about Mac showing up to see her and being turned away … repeatedly. Melina was certain that he was worried. It was one thing for her to be arrested. They'd faced that battle already. This was a whole new war. She was deliberately not being allowed to communicate with her husband and one way or another Melina vowed that there would be reckoning for all those involved. From the taunting guards, to Irwin and Parks who had taken it upon themselves to stop by her cell on alternate days in hopes that she would talk.

She hadn't.

She wouldn't.

Not even today.

Today the attorney Mac had hired would be speaking for her at arraignment. Despite not allowing her to call or see her husband, the pricks running the jail hadn't been able to deny her right to an attorney. Melina glanced at the man now as she watched him walk into the courtroom. Short but stoic with sharp black eyes, Jonathan Olivera, was a man of few words, but he got things done. Her arraignment had originally been scheduled for nearly a week later. Jonathan had threatened to sue the entire police department and jail staff and had her arraignment immediately rescheduled … today. She would be the first one before the judge. A blessing and a curse. He walked over to where she stood handcuffed near a waiting guard.

"Judge Allgood will be presiding over today's proceedings. He has a reputation as somewhat of a hard ass, but I will do everything I can to try and get you released on bond."

Melina nodded, but dread tightened around her heart.

It seemed she couldn't catch a fucking break. Jonathan motioned for her to follow him to the podium where they would wait for court to convene. She did, looking around as the room started to fill up rapidly. The state attorney had already taken her spot at the podium across from them. Tall, thin, and brunette, the older woman stared at Melina like she was something dirty on the bottom of the woman's shoe.

Melina pointedly rolled her eyes.

Her annoyance level rose as she noted members of the media slinking in with their cameras. They were like a bunch of damn hyenas waiting for something to feast on. In this case, it was her. Melina could see them practically salivating as they stared at her.

"Ignore them. I didn't think they'd bother to show up for an arraignment."

"They were at my last one. Sharks always smell blood in the water," Melina said.

Jonathan raised a thick brow, but before he could say anything else a door opened at the front of the room, and a uniformed bailiff walked out. The courtroom immediately became quiet.

"All rise for the Honorable Judge, Theodore Allgood."

The old, white-haired man took his seat in the front of the room and motioned for the bailiff. Melina knew the drill. The judge would look over the docket before he'd call for the first case. A minute later Judge Allgood did just that. He didn't even glance up when they called her name.

A good sign.

Maybe.

Then her charges were read.

That made him look up from his papers and scrutinize her. She didn't melt under his gaze, but simply stared back without blinking.

"And because of the seriousness of the charges leveled against her and the financial means Mrs. Maccari has at her disposal, the state moves to have bail denied. Mrs. Maccari is a flight risk," the state attorney argued.

"Mrs. Maccari is not a flight risk. What she is, is a wife and mother who never was allowed a phone call upon her initial arrest, and denied visits from her husband. She has an infant son at home waiting for her. Besides that, Mrs. Maccari does not even have passport. Circumstances being what they are, I believe my client is more than entitled to bail."

"These are serious charges. People like Mrs. Maccari pose a danger to society. If not a physical one, then definitely a moral one. It wouldn't set a good precedent if we allowed someone like Mrs. Maccari, to be free on bail. Bail denied. Clerk, call the next case."

Just like that, she was dismissed.

Just another case number.

Just another criminal in the eyes of the law.

Melina didn't say anything as Johnathan placed a hand on her shoulder.

"I'm sorry. I promise, I'll fight this."

"No need," Melina said.

She turned as a guard appeared to lead her down the center aisle of the courtroom, past all the gathering onlookers.

Another calculated move designed to remind her yet again, who really ran the show. Despite the whispers, Melina kept her head held high as she walked unhurriedly through the crowd. If they wanted to look, let them. Each step seemed to take her past someone more curious about her, than the proceedings that had already started again behind her. Melina didn't bother to hide the annoyance that boiled her blood until she met a pair of hazel eyes.

Mac.

Her heart skipped a beat.

Working to control her sudden, labored breathing, all she wanted to do was wrap her arms around her husband. His expression was grave as his eyes drank her in. Melina's steps deliberately slowed. The guard, Johnathan, and everything else forgotten. She wanted to run to him.

To feel his arms around her.

To feel his kiss.

To get lost in his scent.

But she couldn't. Instead she just stopped in front of him, her handcuffed hands held out in front of her. No doubt the cameras were trained on them, waiting for something to report. Some tidbit that they could turn into some salacious lie to garner more ratings for their subpar evening news.

"I'm sorry."

Melina shook her head. "Don't be. I …"

Her words were cut off when something caught her eye near the doors as they opened. A pair of sly eyes met hers as the door closed. Melina's nostrils flared and her hands clenched into fists. Truth dawned. In the midst of her incarceration, she'd given a lot of thought to her arrest. The real reason behind it, and why Anthony had been under constant surveillance in the first place.

Anthony Corelli was an "alleged" crime figure, but he was hardly the highest profile Cosa Nostra member in New York. There were others that the cops could be watching more closely, but they hadn't. Instead they'd chosen Anthony, specifically him coming and going in and out of her establishment. And there was only one reason he'd been there so frequently in the first place.

Yes.

Everything was clear now.

"Get moving," the guard growled at Melina, grabbing her arm.

Mac made a move towards the guard, but Melina shook her head.

"Beware of those who have offered help and kind words. It was here that our ruin was already set in motion," Melina warned.

And then she was dragged away by the guard,

towards the doors and out of the courtroom leaving her husband behind. As the doors closed behind her, Melina was left with one last glance at Mac and Johnathan. She could only hope that Mac would piece together the meaning behind her cryptic words and understand what needed to be done next to save their family.

CHAPTER FIFTEEN

Mac stood frozen in time as his wife was taken away from him yet again. It seemed like something in life was always scheming to take her away from him. When she was gone, his world was not right. Off-center, axis tilted, and on shaky ground.

He hated it.

All around him, noise continued to grow. The gathered reporters asking questions, and hoping for some scrap of information to be tossed their way. Like vultures. The judge, irritated that his courtroom had been turned into a three ring circus, banged on the large desk and again shouted for the next case.

Mac was just … frustrated.

Exhausted.

So alone.

"Did you catch those last words?" the lawyer asked.

Mac passed Johnathan a look. He was a good defense attorney—worth his weight in gold, according to anyone Mac asked. His win to loss ratio was twenty to twenty-five. There wasn't another defense attorney in the state with that kind of margin.

He did *not* want Melina to fall on the losing side.

Mac could not afford for her to.

"Did you catch what she said?" Johnathan asked again.

Beware of those who have offered help and kind words. It was here that our ruin was already set in motion.

"I did," Mac replied.

In fact, Melina's words wouldn't get out of his damn head. All that she said, from beginning to end, rattled around in his mind. He took it in like gifts and soaked it up. He had no other choice. The fucking police weren't giving his wife her basic human rights in jail.

"What did she mean?" Johnathan asked.

Mac shook his head as he eyed the reporters. "I don't know."

He hadn't had the time to figure it out. It was still new words to him—something *important*. For all that she could have said to him, she chose something like that. Something vague when put against their current circumstances with no name attached, yet *very* pointed in meaning.

Beware of those who have offered help and kind words.

Who, though?

Who betrayed them like this?

A reporter came a few steps closer to Mac, and suddenly his fingers itched at his sides. He greatly wanted to take that fucker's camera and smash it into bits when he threw it on the goddamn floor. Mac had already been pre-warned about the profile of Melina's case, given the state of the Pivetti Organization, and the amount of attention that had been on it as of late.

This was expected.

He still hated it.

"I have to get out of here," Mac grunted under his breath.

Johnathan's hand smacked him on the back before the lawyer led him out of the courtroom. "Yeah, it's not like we can afford for you to have your own set of charges at the moment, now can we?"

"Ha, funny."

"I really wasn't joking."

"Even better," Mac deadpanned.

Outside the building, Mac found it less circus-like. He and Johnathan stood behind a pillar as some of the reporters flooded the outside. Already, they were setting up their cameras, ready to go on live for the five o-clock news with their up-to-date information on the case.

It was all bullshit.

"Even if it does go to trial," Johnathan said, dragging Mac's attention back to the man, "it'll be a hard one for them to prove without a body. It's damn near impossible to prove *murder* without a body, and no evidence of a killing."

"The Dollhouse room," Mac reminded him.

"Technically, circumstantial. Like most of their case."

"It's unlikely they've gotten this far with *only* circumstantial evidence," Mac pointed out.

"True. In cases like these, they almost always have a witness or two."

"A direct one?"

Johnathan pursed his lips. "A mole, yes."

"We call them *rats.*"

"Yes, well, should you find said rat," Johnathan murmured, "It would be very wise to be rid of it. However, I would not want to know that was the case."

"I think you're wrong," Mac said, blowing out a hard breath.

"Hmm, about what?"

Mac nodded towards the circus of reporters. "In America, there have been far too many court cases tried on the steps of a courthouse instead of *inside*. Cases where a husband had a solid alibi, witness collaboration, no evidence of a crime, yet he was still the one put behind bars and crucified by public opinion when his wife's body washed up on a shore. Or a child's parents, indicted and almost charged because *public* opinion felt they were the guilty party simply because their red-rimmed, swollen-from-crying eyes could no longer produce tears for a camera five times a fucking day."

Johnathan cleared his throat. "Those are not no-body cases, Mac."

"Fair enough, but I don't think they needed to be. I don't think this one needs to be, either. Body or no body, it is the media and the amount of attention that can convict my wife on these steps before she ever gets her day inside that building. Make sure that doesn't happen."

"Perhaps you should help me out, then," the lawyer suggested.

"I will be doing just that."

It was a fucking guarantee.

"Ma, you don't have to—"

"It's fine," Cynthia interrupted with a wave of her hand.

She didn't even look up from the counter she was wiping down. Every day for almost a week, his mother had shown up in the morning with food in hand, or bags of groceries to cook, and ready to clean.

Or do something—anything.

Sometimes, she came alone. Other times, she brought his sister.

Mac was grateful, of course, and he loved his mother to death. He knew exactly what Cynthia was trying to do. She barely mentioned Melina's current predicament because she had not been raised to do that sort of thing, but she was helping and supporting Mac through a difficult time in her own way.

"I made two of those casseroles so you could have an extra," Cynthia said as she wrung out the dishcloth. "It's wrapped and in the freezer. Directions are written on the top."

"Okay," Mac said.

"It's good up to six months in there, if you need it."

"Ma, it's going to be fine. You know that, right?"

Cynthia turned on her heel, and eyed the napping baby boy in Mac's arms. "Will it?"

"We're working very hard to make sure it is."

"I'm sure you are, my boy."

Mac looked over his son's peaceful expression. It was the only time the boy *was* peaceful at the moment. Marquise absolutely knew something was wrong in his small world. He absolutely knew someone important to his entire life and being was missing. Each time someone walked into a room, Marquise would light up. Quickly, that joy would fade when his son looked behind the new person in the room only to find his mother wasn't following behind.

And then the wailing would start.

It was taking longer and longer to soothe Marquise during those spells. Each time his mother did not come when he thought she would, his tiny heart broke a little more.

Mac was dying inside.

For himself.

For his son.

For his *wife*.

"It will get easier for him," Cynthia said softly.

Mac looked up from his son. "Will it?"

"It did for you."

"Is it the same thing?"

"Not at all," Cynthia said in a long sigh, "but as a baby, at that age, your father was still very much around when he was not piddling our money away or sleeping off a hangover in someone else's bed. You adored James. Lit up like a little angel whenever he came into the room."

"You never told me that."

"You would not have wanted to know."

"Fair enough," Mac admitted.

"And then he came less and less," Cynthia said, "because we fought more and more, and his behavior became worse and worse. You would perk up at every person, and smile wide the way your father always liked, but it was very rarely him. You taught yourself not to get excited. You perked up less and less. There came a time when it was your father, but you were more interested in the noisy toy on the floor than your father asking for a smile."

"That's ... awful, Ma."

Cynthia smiled a sad sight. "Isn't it? My heart hurt for you, and then again, for your sister."

Mac used the pad of his thumb to stroke along Marquise's chubby cheek. "My father chose to do those things, though. This isn't the same."

"Resentment can feel the same, especially when you are a young child who does not even understand what you feel *is* resentment."

Well, then Mac would make sure his son didn't feel that at all. Or rather, that he didn't have time to feel it.

Knowing he wasn't going to get his mother to leave anytime soon, Mac decided to go put Marquise in his crib and help Cynthia finish up cleaning. It wasn't like he had anything better to do at the damn moment. A distraction was always good.

He turned to head out of the kitchen.

"Did she do it?" his mother asked very quietly.

Mac hesitated in his steps. "Ma—"

"I watch the news. I hear things from friends. I may not be a mob wife *now*, but I am still very much on the outskirts of that world, Mac. When I ask things, I would like an answer. When I ask, I intend to know."

"Sure, but ..."

"Did she do it?"

"Only because I couldn't," Mac finally said.

"I always thought there was supposed to be a reason why women did not involve themselves in their men's affairs. Especially *Mafiosi* men."

Mac laughed dryly. "Melina is not like most women."

"No, I suppose not."

"Where's the *principe* today?" Enric asked. "I have to give my godson extra attention with his mother gone, don't I?"

Mac rolled his eyes upward, but smiled all the same. "Victoria took him out, actually."

"She's not bringing him back, or what?"

"I'm sure that's crossed her mind."

"Yeah, well, I wouldn't know."

Mac glanced at Enric as the man wheeled his chair next to the table. Leaning on the island, Mac had a good view of the obvious displeasure in Enric's features. He was not good at hiding how he felt in regards to Victoria, it seemed.

"My sister blow you off, or what?"

Enric frowned. "Doesn't matter."

"If you say so …"

"I said so," Enric replied.

So be it.

"How's Melina?" Enric asked after a moment.

Mac sighed. "I haven't seen her since the courthouse a few days ago. She was finally allowed to call Johnathan. She didn't feel safe to talk as they had detectives on either side of her. She did tell him the same thing she told me, though."

"What is that?"

"Beware of those who have offered help and kind words. It was here that our ruin was already set in motion," Mac said, not able to forget the words. They slipped out far too easily. "I'm still trying to figure out what she's attempting to tell me."

"Someone you trusted betrayed you. Someone close to you, maybe."

Mac frowned. "That leaves you or her, doesn't it? Given what I know about you—that's ridiculous. And I am pretty sure my wife did not set herself up to be charged with first degree murder. Not sure I could include my mother or sister in there, considering."

Enric cleared his throat. "Okay, so it's a little more confusing than it appears on the surface."

"Very," Mac said dryly.

"We'll figure it out, boss."

They didn't have much choice.

Melina's freedom was on the line.

"What's the word on the street?" Mac asked. "Give me some news worth chewing on, Enric."

"Scrambling men. Rumors flying. Confused Capos. I mean, nothing unusual considering the current state of the family."

Yes, a *famiglia* without a boss. A *famiglia* without a fake king on the throne. A *famiglia* waiting.

Mac smiled. "That's good, then."

Enric cocked a brow. "*Good?*"

"A fragile organization with men who are unwilling to immediately jump at the chance to manipulate and *organize* is the easiest to make submit. That is why the strongest and most cunning men always sit at the top, and hold the power positions. Those positions are the ones that decide who moves, and who stays still. Think about it, Enric. Would you rather your equal be sitting lower on the totem pole, unhappy as a Caporegime without an opinion, or sitting slightly below you where you can give him a bit of control and voice to satisfy his … nature?"

"I see your point." Enric turned a bit in his chair to face Mac. "Who will you choose to sit next to you?"

"I have a bit of time."

"You haven't decided?"

Mac shrugged. "There are very few people I trust in this *famiglia*, to be honest."

"Sure, but a boss still needs his right and left hand."

"Maybe I have chosen," Mac said, "but things are complicated at the moment."

"How so?"

"Well, for one, my wife is behind bars."

Enric's brow furrowed. "That has nothing to do with you choosing an underboss and consigliere."

"It does when the only person I would consider having as my *consigliera* is currently in lockup, and awaiting trial."

"*Consigliera*. Feminine form. As in a woman." The younger man stiffened. "You can't have a woman—"

"First, I can *do* whatever I want," Mac interjected firmly. "I can—and I will, if I need to—go back into the history of every Cosa Nostra family in North America to show consiglieres are not always *only* made, Italian men. There is a long history of Dons choosing their closest, most trusted friends as their advisor. Men, sure, but unmade men. Men that were not of Italian descent. Men that were not even criminals."

"Yeah, but that was the thirties, forties, and fifties. That was men, not women, boss."

"And this is my century, and my family. I will choose the best person for the position, and that person is my wife. The men don't have to particularly like it. They simply have to respect it. There has never been a better moll for a man than mine—every inch a queen, and I intend to put her higher than any man that would consider slighting her for who she is. It's one thing to be a man's gun or gangster moll, it's another thing to be the *Madame*.

"I do not need Melina's focus to be on the betterment of *la famiglia*, but rather, the betterment of me. That's where her attention has always been."

"It's hard not to respect Melina," Enric said. "Considering everything."

"Exactly." Mac pulled open a drawer on the island, and took out a few items he had stashed in there earlier when Enric messaged that he was dropping by. Enric, distracted by the window overlooking the yard, didn't see what Mac had pulled out until he set the items on the table. "I also chose my underboss, Enric."

Enric glanced down at the items.

A knife. A single bullet and a gun. A lighter. And the picture of a saint.

"Me?" Enric asked.

"You."

"But I'm not … a made man."

"Give me a few minutes," Mac said with a smirk.

Mac pulled out a chair, and turned it so that he could sit and face Enric. "A while back, your father extended me a great courtesy."

Enric was still looking at the items on the table. "Did he?"

"He chose to give me the button in private. A moment that was shared between only him and I alone. He made it clear that he did not need the opinions or pageantry of other made men and traditions to make his choice where I was concerned. He knew where my loyalty was, and the kind of man I was."

"You can't … give me my button," Enric said quietly.

"Why can't I?"

"Well, what use am I like this?"

Mac didn't even look at the wheelchair Enric waved at. "Far greater than you give yourself credit for."

"Only bosses can make a man in the family."

"And I am unrecognized," Mac supplied.

Enric nodded. "I mean, *I* recognize you."

"Then I'm not unrecognized, am I? Not to the person who matters at the moment. Luca was kind enough and smart enough, to see things in me that I didn't even see, Enric. I see those same things in you. Your circumstance doesn't make even the slightest difference. It never has to me."

"I …"

Mac picked up the knife, and spun the tip against the pad of his thumb until a single red drop slid against the blade. "Is this what you want? That's all you have to answer."

"All I ever wanted was to be a made man."

"Then the rest is details." Mac held out his hand. "Palm up, Enric."

It took another second, but Enric lifted his hand to set it palm up inside Mac's. "I guess this will save you some effort in the family, huh?"

"For what?"

"People trying to gain false favor to get a position closer to the top," Enric supplied. "Or rather, people trying to get closer to you only to stab you in the back."

Mac hesitated as he pressed the blade into Enric's palm. Something clicked in his mind all at once. Like a vault door closing shut with a bang as all the tumblers fell into place. "*Her.*"

Enric looked up. "What?"

"It's not *me* someone betrayed. I kept thinking she meant *me* … or us, even. She meant her. Only her."

"Melina?" Enric clenched his hand around the blade, saying, "But she trusts even fewer people than you do, boss."

"*Offered help and kind words*," Mac repeated. "Help and kind words. It started there, she said. That's where it began."

"You're not making sense, and—"

"Melina made a friend in prison the first time. A friend that sought her out after release. She felt she could accept the woman as a friend because she was the only one who offered her kind words and some kind of help behind bars. She made it bearable for Melina. This is someone Melina has progressively brought closer and closer over time because she trusted her. That same woman …

Anthony's preferred piece of ass at The Dollhouse. Actually, the *only* piece of ass he gave any attention to at the joint. Next to trying to cozy up to my wife. Anthony believed he was going into The Dollhouse the night he was killed to *see* that woman. Melina was simply a nice surprise for him when he got there. He would have been in contact with the one he thought he was going for, though, surely."

"Erika?" Enric asked.

"Erika."

"You think she's an agent or something?"

"I would be willing to bet my life on it," Mac muttered, "and right now, it's literally Melina's life on the line for it."

"What the hell are you going to do about it, then?" Enric had clenched the knife so tightly, that blood had already began to trickle down to Mac's hand. "If she is an agent, they'll likely have her locked down in a safe house, or even back to normal life far away from here until she's needed at trial."

Right now, Mac was going to make a man.

Later, he was going to start smoking out a rat.

Mac beat on the apartment door for the third time. This girl—Rena—was one of his last hopes to figuring out either where, or who, the mysterious Erika was. Quite a few of Melina's Dollhouse girls had been locked up on prostitution charges the night of the raid, but a few had not been working, and escaped the cops' clutches.

The few that Mac had already talked to didn't have very much to tell him, and at times, seemed wary of his questions. For the most part, it seemed Erika was elusive to the women she worked around. Quiet, and didn't often offer information about herself or her life. She hadn't

BETHANY-KRIS
ERIN ASHLEY TANNER

attempted to make friends with any of the girls, and never invited them back to her place for even something as innocent as a drink.

For the women who were wary of his questions, Mac understood that, too. They were likely concerned about the status of their own freedom. It was a real possibility that at any time, detectives might show up at their doors— if they hadn't already—with questions to ask or warrants to serve.

They had every right to be concerned.

Mac still needed his answers.

Again, he beat on the apartment door. Behind it, he heard someone stumble and cuss before the door was yanked open. A wild-eyed, wet-haired blonde glared at him. Her fist clenched into the towel wrapped around her body.

"What?" she barked.

Then, she met his gaze.

"Mac."

"Rena," he said with a smile. "Sorry to interrupt."

"Is something happening with Boss Lady?"

"No, but I have some questions. Do you have a few minutes?"

"I'm actually running late for a class at the college," Rena admitted.

"It'll be quick, I promise."

"Shoot, then."

"Erika, from The Dollhouse. New Yorker. Seemed close to my wife. Didn't make a lot of friends with you girls. Anything you can tell me about her?"

"Not really. Like you said, she didn't make friends with any of us. Sometimes when someone is close to the boss, you tend to stay a healthy distance from them anyway."

"Even a boss like Melina?"

Rena shrugged. "I mean, not really, but Erika gave some of us strange vibes, too."

"What do you mean, *strange?*"

"Judgey, maybe? Like okay, sweetheart, you're hooking in the club, but turn your nose up at us when we smoke a little kush in the back? Kind of like that, I guess."

"That all?"

"Well … once she sat her phone down and the screen hadn't faded out. I saw a text that used the name Kiera. I thought the person must have had the wrong number, but Erika's reply was something like, *yep.* So, maybe not?"

"As in, they called *her* Kiera?"

"Yeah," Rena confirmed. "Also, you called the girl a New Yorker. Definitely not, Mac."

"What makes you say that?"

"You have heard her talk, right?"

"Sure, but you have heard a dozen New Yorkers talk, right?" he shot back with a chuckle. "This place is a fucking melting pot of people. Accents and inflections come and go. Hell, my Brooklyn accent has basically become non-existent over the past three years."

Rena rolled her eyes upward. "Okay, fair enough, but that's not what I mean. Certain words and terms, you know, come from certain places. Erika had a few inflections like that—Chicago, for sure. I only know that because I dated a guy from Chicago. Major asshole, but cute as fuck any other time."

"Chicago, you're sure?"

Rena nodded. "But that's all I know, Mac."

It just might be enough for him to start looking somewhere, though.

Mac could do that.

"Thank you," he told the girl.

Rena shifted in the doorway. "Is Melina going to be okay? I mean, she'll get out, right?"

"Yeah," Mac assured, even though sometimes he didn't feel like it himself, "she's going to be just fine."

Kiera Tompson.

Single. No children. No husband. Member of the Chicago Police Department for five years. Undercover agent for ... ha, a laughably short amount of time.

Finding information on the so-called *Erika* was not so hard to do when Mac started digging. The girl was not a trained undercover cop—in fact, she was a barely passable one.

What Kiera was ... was sadly amusing. A young cop fresh out of her rookie blues, one that would be unrecognizable to a New York native like Mac, Melina, or someone else in the Pivetti Organization because she came from Chicago. A girl who, at the time, had no children or husband that she would feel separated from, or pining for while undercover.

Mac suspected that was why young Kiera "Erika" Tompson had been sent from Chicago. A young woman given a hard past for his wife to relate to, or even ... sympathize with. Someone who could worm her way into Melina perhaps easier, or a bit faster, than someone else might have.

No matter what, Mac would not fault his wife for the friend she thought she had made in Kiera. Or ... Erika, whatever. Mac, more than anyone else in his wife's close circle, could certainly understand how suffocating their life could be. How lonely things sometimes seemed. How alone one could feel standing in a room full of people.

To want a friend—a single, trustworthy friend—in the midst of untrustworthy people was understandable.

Mac lifted his head at the sound of a key jiggling in a lock. At his sides, his gloved hands pulled the items from the inside of his suit jacket that he had kept hidden. Quickly, he spun the silencer into the barrel of the Beretta.

At the end of the apartment's hallway, he was hidden by the shadows leading into the main room and open kitchen.

Kiera entered her Melrose apartment, and locked the door behind her. It wasn't until she had kicked off her shoes, tossed her bag aside, and was halfway down the hall before she noticed Mac standing in the shadows.

For a split second, her gaze dropped to his gun then back up to his face. He smiled at her, feeling a blinding coldness seep into his fingertips at the same time. The young woman glanced over her shoulder at the door, and then quickly back to Mac.

"You could try to make a run for it," Mac said, "but I am a fairly good shot, and a very quick draw. Weigh the risk and rewards of a second shot should I miss a death-shot or a quick death should you stay still."

Kiera's gaze narrowed. "You fucking—"

"Bastard, asshole, cocksucker? I prefer Mac, thanks. Which do you prefer?"

"I beg your pardon?"

"Erika or Kiera, which one?"

"I ... what does it matter?"

"It's a matter of my curiosity," Mac said with a shrug. "You know, you're not a very good undercover cop, sweetheart. You messed up a few times. Left enough breadcrumbs for me to put together and lead me to Chicago. To *you*. Shame, they might as well have tossed you under the bus, really, seeing as how you're barely fresh enough to be out of the academy."

Mac waved his hands wide. "And here I am, in Chicago to pay you a visit. Do you know, it's taken me three weeks to put this together and find you? That doesn't include the time my wife was already behind bars before I put together that it was you who got her there."

"*She* got herself there," the woman snapped. "She's a criminal, like you are."

"Ouch." Mac put a hand over his chest. "Hit me where it hurts. Right in the damn heart."

"You don't have a heart."

"Not for rats like you, anyway," Mac said with a grin. "So, the guards they have posted at the front and back door will probably find you in the morning, if you are curious. I've watched you for a couple of days, and they only get twitchy if you're not out of the apartment by seven. If you wondered, someone left a fire escape pulled down on the west side of the building, and I climbed up to the roof. Beat the lock off the door, slipped down here, and picked your shitty little lock."

Kiera's eyes blazed. "Rot in hell."

"I'm too Catholic for Hell. Catholics don't *do* Hell." Mac cocked the hammer back on the gun, and tipped his head to the side. "What was the ultimate goal? Melina, or the Pivetti Organization?"

"Does it matter?"

"As I said before, it's a matter of my curiosity."

"Anthony was feeding information on the family. As far as I knew it, they were planning on giving him some kind of deal for his information. He would stay out of prison, the rest of you would go in. That was the goal."

"Melina taking him out kind of fucked that up, huh?"

Kiera didn't reply.

Well … no need.

Mac pushed off the wall, and raised his gun to aim. "You didn't answer me. Which name do you prefer, Erika or Kiera? I want to get it right when I explain it all to my wife."

"Fuck you, Mac."

"Wrong answer."

Other than a quiet pop, the gun barely made a sound when it fired. In fact, Kiera's body hitting the floor made a louder thump. Dead eyes stared up from the woman's body. Mac didn't give it a second look as he stepped over her.

Without their direct witness, the state would have nothing on his wife. Nothing tangible, anyway. The prostitution charges on the girls and the ensuing solicitation charges against the men could be easily fought or cleaned away. The murder charges on his wife were nonsense with no body, and no person to say they knew she had done it.

Simple.

Now ... to wait.

CHAPTER SIXTEEN

Melina stared up at the ceiling. She hadn't even bothered keeping up with how many days passed since her bail had been denied at arraignment. Judge Allgood had said she was a danger to society, but she knew the real motive behind his decision. He wanted to make an example out of her. By refusing to allow her to be released on bail, the judge had used her to send a clear message to anyone connected to the mob. They would get no justice. To be honest, she hadn't been expecting any.

It would've meant everything to go home to her family.

But Lady Justice had never cared for her, and so here she remained stuck in a cell. Melina hadn't been able to stop thinking about the hard regret that had been on Mac's face as she was led away. It didn't take a rocket scientist to see that he blamed himself for her current incarceration. She hated that she hadn't had more time to give him some comfort, and let him know that none of this was his fault. Instead, all she'd been able to offer was a cryptic warning.

With cameras around ready to capture her every move, and microphones waiting to pick up any little slip, she had no choice but to be creative with her warning. She only hoped it would be enough to put Mac on the right path. He had to fix this or this cell would be where she spent the rest of her life. All because she'd dared to trust.

Now she was paying the price for letting her guard down.

To see the woman she'd considered a friend, basking in the ruin that she'd brought to her family's doorstep was a shock. To say the least. The realization of how deeply she'd been betrayed had nearly made her heart stop. She'd believed every lie Erika had fed her about her past, and felt sorry for the bad breaks the woman had. It was why Melina had invited the woman into her life, and trusted her with so much.

Only to be betrayed.

But no betrayal came without a cost, and one way or another Erika would get exactly what she deserved. No doubt the woman had been an undercover plant, specifically sent to target her. And Erika had done a damn good job of it. Too damn good. Melina balled up her fists, wishing that she could be the one to unleash her wrath on her former "friend." A bullet between the eyes was exactly what the bitch deserved, but all Melina could do was wait for Mac to put things in motion.

Mac.

Seeing him in the courtroom had been like giving a dying man a glimpse of Heaven before he went straight to Hell. They'd been apart for longer than this when she'd been arrested close to two years ago. Things were different this time around. She and Mac were bonded even closer than ever now. Having a child together did that. It made you realize just how much another person's existence affected your own. How it made life easier to live, knowing you had that someone beside you that made every moment worth living. Every day worth looking forward to. Melina was ready to sell her soul to have that feeling once again.

"Maccari, let's go."

Melina got up from her bunk, and moved towards the barred entrance of her cell. A guard motioned her back as he unlocked the door.

"Where am I going?" she asked.

"Emergency hearing. That's all I know."

Melina presented her wrists, waiting for the guard to slap on a pair of handcuffs but he shook his head.

"No need. I've watched you since you've been in here. Causing a scene is not your style."

"You're right. Thank you."

The guard nodded as he locked the cell doors back, and started moving with her down the hall. Unlike most of the guards that worked in the jail, this one hadn't been an asshole. She'd remember that if she ever ran into him outside of the jail. He moved at a brisk pace taking her from behind the locked doors, and down the hallway that lead towards the front of the jail. As she walked, Melina wondered what the hearing could possibly be about. The judge had already denied her bail request. There was nothing now to do but wait for her inevitable trial.

Melina remained silent as she was escorted to a large conference room. Everything about this was out of the ordinary. Inside waiting was Johnathan.

"Everyone else should be here momentarily," the guard said before he shut the door and exited the room.

"Melina. You look well considering the circumstances."

"Cut it out, Johnathan. Why are we here instead of at the courthouse? What exactly is going on?"

The man faced her with steely resolve. "I'm about to secure your freedom, once and for all."

He motioned for her to have a seat at the conference table in front of him.

"I really hope so," Melina said as she sat down.

Johnathan took a seat next to her, and it wasn't long before the door opened admitting the same thin, snooty looking attorney who'd been at her arraignment.

"Mr. Olivera, I don't know what you're trying to pull, but I intend to lodge a formal complaint with the bar."

"Miss Townsend, you are welcome to do whatever you want, but after this meeting I would reconsider my threat if I were you."

The woman glared at Johnathan, but said nothing further as she took a seat across from them and opened up her briefcase. The room was silent as they waited for the judge to arrive. Melina had no idea what exactly her attorney had been up to since her arraignment, but the man was plainly confident and unbothered by the State Attorney's threats. Clearly, he had something up his sleeve.

Judge Allgood entered, and took a seat across the table from State Attorney Townsend. He gave Melina the quick once over, and she returned his gaze without flinching.

"This had better be good, or both you are going to be looking for a new line of work."

"I can assure you, Judge Allgood, whatever this is was not my doing," Townsend said.

"Mr. Olivera, it is highly irregular for the chief judge himself to call me, and demand that I come to the jail immediately. Please tell me what this is all about."

Melina glanced at Johnathan who opened up his briefcase and slid a red folder across the table to the judge.

"Your Honor, there are a number of reasons for this informal hearing. For starters, my client is ready to exercise her right to a speedy trial. She has been jailed for two months, and has been unable to have phone or visitor privileges. Both are a clear violation of her rights, and at this time she is ready to proceed with the case against her."

"An emergency hearing was hardly needed for that," Attorney Townsend said.

Melina wanted to wipe the smirk off the woman's face.

"That is her right," Judge Allgood said. "Is there something else?"

"Yes, Judge, there is. The evidence against Mrs. Maccari has been, and remains, circumstantial. Now, the prosecution was supposed to have a key witness who supposedly could corroborate and give a firsthand account tying my client to the murder of Anthony Corelli. But word has reached me that this all important witness is dead. With no witness there is no case."

Melina bit her lip in an effort to school her reaction. Her husband had realized Erika was the one who set her up, and he'd acted accordingly. The bitch was dead. No wonder Johnathan appeared so confident.

Judge Allgood cut his eyes to the state attorney. "Is this true, Miss Townsend? Is your witness dead?"

The woman swallowed hard before she answered. "Well—"

"It is a yes or no answer, Miss. I am not asking for details about the witness, only a yes or no."

"Yes, Your Honor."

"And how long have you known your key witness was dead?" the judge pressed.

"Almost two weeks."

"Do you have any other witnesses who can corroborate the charges against Mrs. Maccari?"

"No, Your Honor."

Melina finally allowed a smile to slip, as Judge Allgood glared at the state attorney who now refused to meet his eyes.

Johnathan sat back in his chair. "My client has the right to face her accuser, but especially in a case like this. Does she not?"

"I am quite aware of what the justice system demands," the judge barked.

"Good. And, Your Honor, if I might also add, the reason Chief Judge Walden insisted you come immediately to this hearing, if you call it that, is because evidence has been uncovered that Miss Townsend has been trading sexual favors to get her warrants signed. For instance, my client's warrant was signed by Judge Peters, only the good judge didn't sign it, and had no knowledge of it. His judicial assistant, a Mr. Ryan Lockhart, signed it after some coaxing from Attorney Townsend."

"That's a lie!"

The woman stood up staring wide-eyed at Johnathan across the table.

"In this case, I have truth on my side. The warrants that lead to Mrs. Maccari's arrest were fraudulent and improperly executed. Yet another reason why she should be freed immediately, and all the charges against my client dropped. You'll find everything you need in that folder, Judge Allgood," Johnathan said.

"Judge, you can't really believe—"

The judge held up a hand, silencing Attorney Townsend. Melina watched him as he read over the papers Johnathan had assembled in the folder. Beside him, the state attorney fidgeted in her seat, eyes darting back and forth between Johnathan and the judge. A few minutes later, Judge Allgood pulled a pen from his pocket, and quickly signed two sheets of paper before he closed the folder and slid it back to Johnathan.

"Mrs. Maccari, consider yourself a free woman. Miss Townsend, consider yourself under arrest."

Judge Allgood stood, and opened the door behind him calling for the guards. Two rushed into the room, and Melina sat momentarily stunned as the judge had the state attorney arrested, cuffed, and hauled from the room over the woman's loud objections. The judge summarily followed behind them, leaving Johnathan and Melina alone. She turned to him.

"I don't know how you managed to pull any of this off, but I can never thank you enough."

Johnathan shook his head. "No thanks needed. Just doing my job. Now, let's get this paperwork filed and stamped so we can get you back home to your family."

Yes. Back home with her husband and son.

The one place in the world where she would always belong.

Home.

Melina could hardly believe she was really here.

"Are you sure you don't want to come in, Johnathan?"

"No. You go on and enjoy your family. I'm sure you and Mac have a lot of catching up to do."

She nodded. "Yeah, we do."

Impulsively, she leaned over and kissed him on the cheek before exiting the car. Moving briskly, Melina was up the stairs that lead to the front door. She'd barely made it to the last step when the door was flung open.

"Melina."

"Mac."

His arms wrapped around her, crushing her to him in an embrace so tight she could barely breathe, but she didn't care. She held him close, breathing in his scent.

"I've missed you, doll."

"I've missed you, too, Mac."

Melina had barely gotten the words out before Mac's mouth was crashed down on hers. His kiss tasted of desperation. His tongue darted into her mouth, and Melina moaned, drunk on the taste of him. Heady and drowning in desire.

And then she heard her son's cry.

"Sounds like someone needs his mother," Mac said. He kissed her nose and then her forehead.

"His mother needs him, too. Where is he?" she asked.

"In the living room. I had him napping in his playpen next to me."

Melina quickly moved past her husband, and down the short hall into the living room. And there she saw him, lying on his side kicking his legs against the side of the mesh pen as he cried.

"Marquise."

She approached the crib, and leaned over reaching for her son. His crying stopped immediately, and the biggest grin spread across his face. His little arms reached upwards for her, and Melina picked him up pressing her face against his. She pressed kisses all over his face, inhaling the soft, sweet scent of him. Tears welled up in her eyes, and she let them fall. Marquise cooed, and Melina melted as his little fingers touched her nose and cheek.

"There is nothing like the bond of a mother with her child," Mac said.

"I've missed him more than I thought could be possible."

Melina smiled through her tears as she took Marquise, and sat down with him on the couch behind her. He held one of her fingers in his fist as he continued to coo and smile at her.

"And he missed you. I was afraid some days that he would never stop crying. Whenever someone came into the room his face would light up, and then when he saw that it wasn't you, that light would just disappear. It broke my heart."

Mac sat down beside her, pulling Melina into his arms as she held their son.

"A mother should never be separated from her child," she said to Mac before transferring her attention back to their son. "Momma's so sorry she had to leave you. I promise it won't happen again."

Marquise's eyes stretched wide, and Melina laughed as a small spit bubble formed on his lips. He continued cooing at her.

"I won't pretend to understand everything that you've gone through because of me, but I can promise you that I'll spend the rest of my life making up for it."

"There's nothing to make up for, Mac. I knew what I was signing up for when we married, and committed myself to building a life with you. I don't blame you for any of this. Honestly."

She freed one hand from holding Marquise to touch her husband's face. His hazel eyes watched her intently, searching her face.

"You really mean that," he finally said.

"Of course, I do. You're my husband, and I love you. Nothing has changed."

Mac's attention shifted as Marquise squirmed in her arms. Together they looked down at him. He rubbed their son's head as she held him.

"Everything has changed, doll. We'll soon be in positions we never thought we'd be. Our lives are never going to be the same."

Melina looked down at their son who had fallen asleep in her arms. His cheeks were soft as she rubbed her finger against them. Marquise was growing up right before their eyes. She never wanted to miss another moment of his life.

"And what position is that?"

"No need to worry about that now, doll. All that matters is right here and now."

"You're right. There's more than enough time to worry about tomorrows."

Melina moved closer to Mac, leaning against him. She relished in the nearness and sanctity of her family. Nothing mattered but this moment, and for now it was enough.

Melina walked into the bathroom, and smiled to herself when she saw the lit candles placed around the room. The tub was filled nearly to the brim with sudsy bubbles just waiting for her.

"Get in, doll, before the water gets cold."

Melina turned to find Mac standing behind her

completely naked.

It was a sight for sore eyes.

"And might I assume from your current state of undress that you're going to join me?"

"As soon as I get you naked."

Mac moved swiftly, hauling her to him. His kisses rained down on her face as he pulled up her dress. Melina moaned as he tore at her panties before plunging a finger inside her. How she'd missed him. Missed this. Her thighs opened wider offering him access to what belonged only to him. Always only to him.

"God, I've missed you," she whispered.

"I can tell, doll."

Melina groaned at the soft, wet sucking sound her body made as it greedily devoured his finger inside her. As his thumb brushed over her clit, she sucked his bottom lip between hers. Mac damn near growled.

"I like that sound," she teased.

"I think I'm going to do something about that."

Before Melina knew what Mac was about, he was on his knees and her bottom rested flat on the bathroom counter. The first lick of his tongue on her pussy nearly made her come off the counter. Her thighs fell completely open, and her hands threaded through his hair as he ate at her greedily. Every lick of his tongue brought her higher and higher to Heaven. His lips closed around her clit, sucking hard and fast. Closer and closer her orgasm hovered towards her. And she was falling over the edge, lost in a wave of roaring pleasure. Her head rested against the glass mirror as she struggled to catch her breath.

"I can safely assume from the honey dripping down your thighs that I did something right."

Mac stared at her from between her thighs, merriment dancing in his eyes.

"Indeed, and I can't wait to see what else you have in store for this evening," Melina said.

"Well then we'd better make good use of this bath

tub, shouldn't we?"

"Mac, I wish you would tell me why you wanted me to accompany you. I know that this meeting is about securing your position as the new boss. I don't understand why any of that requires my presence."

"I must not have done my job adequately last night if this meeting is all you can think about," Mac teased.

"After last night I'm surprised I can even walk straight. No worries there."

"Good to know. Now I can take this meeting with a clear mind. You ready?"

Melina nodded as Mac held the door open for her. She stepped inside and found the room filled with men, some sitting at the long brown conference table in front of them. Others sat near the walls on fold out chairs. When Melina and Mac entered the room, they all stood up, except for Enric who eased out of his chair but was not able to stand up fully.

Mac gave a curt nod to everyone in the room before he held out a chair for Melina. She sat down next to him, and faced the men in the room who were studying her, wondering what she was doing there. Melina wondered the same.

"I want to thank each of you for coming today. Times have been uncertain for all of us, but I'm sure that after today things will look better. For starters, I think it is important that all of you know that the man some of you were looking to for leadership in our former boss's absence was a rat working for the cops. His aim was to take enough of us down leaving a vacuum of power and assuring him the boss's seat."

Her husband paused as the men started to whisper

among themselves at the news that had been imparted. Melina was shocked. Anthony, a rat. The man had put himself out as some paragon of old Cosa Nostra values. Hell, the way Anthony had tried to paint things the only clear choice to lead in Luca Pivetti's stead was an old fashioned man like him. To find out he was a rat trying to destroy his own family for power, made him even more of a disgusting prick than she'd thought.

"How can you be sure of this?" one man toward the back asked.

Mac carefully pulled out two rings from the inner pocket of his jacket, and slid them down his fingers. One, Melina recognized had been Luca's. Another, Anthony's.

Then, he set a small recorder down on the table, reached over, and pressed play. Erika's defiant voice and Mac's cool, calm tenor echoed over a device. A final conversation, she realized. It ended shortly after a gunshot and footsteps.

Mac waited for the recorder to click before he looked over the men again.

"I'm sure some of you recognize that woman's voice, and who we thought she was. Anthony Correlli was a rabid dog, who finally got put down. This is the last time we will ever speak of him. Right now, we have better things to talk about. When I last spoke with Luca, it was clear that he wanted his line of succession to fall to me." Mac waved at Enric and said, "You have his oldest, and only, son here to question on that front. I have his ring, given willingly to help speed this process along. But should any of you choose to make it hard on me that I fully intend to carry out his wishes, I will make it very hard on you to *live*."

No one spoke up.

Mac smiled. "We've had a lot of issues lately in this business, haven't we? Too much police attention, too many arrests, and other bullshit we don't need. That'll all come to a stop. With the right boss, the proper rules, and careful attention to detail and business, it will stop. I promise. Take care of me, and I will take care of you."

A few confirmative murmurs passed through the men.

Approval, maybe.

"As my first order of business, I have a few key appointments to make."

Melina watched as Mac paused, studying the room. She didn't trust some of the men assembled. After all, she was sure that some of them had been supporters of Anthony, and there was no doubt that they still harbored some bitterness about Mac's rapid rise. She waited for someone to speak. To say something untoward, but no words came. Maybe a stable future was within her husband's grasp.

"A man cannot hope to be a successful boss without having people in his corner that he can trust. People that have proven themselves loyal time and time again. For my underboss, I choose Enric Pivetti."

Melina's gaze shifted to Enric. He sat unmoved, a signal to her that he had known about Mac's intentions.

"Only a made man can be underboss," a dark haired man sitting near the wall said.

"He was made … by me. Besides that fact, there is not a man among you braver or more dedicated than Enric."

"He's a cripple," someone else spoke up. "That's not concerning to you that he might be seen as an easy target or—"

A loud pop echoed, followed by shattering glass. The man who had been insulting Enric while he sat in the same room with the young man now held shattered remains of whatever glass object he had been holding. Blood from where the shards cut him started trickling down his arm.

On the other side of the room. Enric sat still as stone with a gun pointed at the man. "Call me a cripple one more time, Carl."

"Well, I just … meant that—"

"One more fucking time."

Mac chuckled. "Do you need a moment to clean up your arm, Carl?"

Carl swallowed hard, and shook his head. "No, no. I'm quite fine."

"I'm aware that Enric has his *challenges*. So do the rest of us. No man in this room is perfect. His job as an underboss is to protect me, and manage the rest of you. To be my go-between. Nothing more, nothing less. He already does that. He has friends in every single one of your crews. He's what you might call a *smart boy*."

Enric snorted, but stayed quiet.

Mac waved a hand, saying, "And that brings me to my next appointment. As consigliera, I choose my wife Melina."

Melina had to fight to keep her mask of indifference in place. Consigliere or consigliera was something she'd never expected. How could she? From everything she knew Cosa Nostra had never been open to women and now her husband had just turned everything on its head.

"A woman as consigliere? It's unheard of," one man said.

"First, tack the *a* onto the end of that and give her the respect of the feminine form. After all, there *is* a reason there is a feminine form of the word, no? Gentlemen, I think some of you forget the real purpose of that job. It is an advisor to the boss. A person that he can absolutely trust to give him the best advice and see to his own interests. But above all a consigliere—or consigliera—is absolutely loyal to the boss, and no one has proven that more than my wife. She has endured jail time, assassination attempts, and things no woman should have, and for that I honor her. Any man that dares to even think to disrespect her will meet with my rage."

"Now, are we all in agreement?" Mac asked with a flick of his wrist in the men's direction.

Melina had the feeling none of the men really had a

choice, but at this point, a boss like Mac was probably the best option.

Eventually, one by one, confirmations rang out.

With his peace having been said, Mac rose and offered his hand to Melina. She took it, allowing him to help her from her seat. The room remained quiet as Mac opened the door leaving the men and the clandestine meeting behind them.

"You might have warned me," Melina said.

"And miss out on the shocked expression on your face? Never."

"Will they accept me, Mac? I don't want to be the cause of more problems for you."

Mac stopped and grabbed her hand. "You won't. They will accept you because I have ordered it, but in time they will come to see what a valuable asset you are. They will respect you."

"Your confidence is inspiring."

"You are inspiring, doll. I know that whatever the future holds, it will be better for all of us with you at my side in all things. I need you, Melina. Together we can change this *famiglia* for the better. Will you take the position? Did I mention there are some very nice perks that come with it?"

Melina laughed as she wrapped her arms around her husband. "What kind of perks?"

"Whatever you want. I'm open to negotiations."

"Well then, I'd say that you've got yourself a new consigliera."

Their lips met in a kiss of fire and passion. For once there was nothing to worry about. Nothing to fear. The world was theirs, and the future brighter than it had ever been.

EPILOGUE

Mac sat behind his desk with his elbows resting to the top. What he should have been doing was going over some illegal cigarette and liquor shipments he was supposed to be sending into Canada next month. But no. His work for *la famiglia* had to be pushed aside because his children were testing every single one of his limits today.

Every single damn one.

Leaning forward, he stared hard at his two sons, and his youngest child, their only girl. Their thirteen-year-old girl, Isabella.

"Now, once more," Mac said, trying to keep a calm demeanor. "Marquise, Luca, try that again, but with the truth this time."

Seventeen-year-old Marquise glared at the wall.

Luca, at fifteen, kept his arms crossed over his chest.

Isabella snapped a wad of gum in her mouth.

Teenagers were God's way of punishing a man for all his misdeeds. Mac was sure of it. He no longer believed that Hell was a punishment for sins, but rather, these monsters people gave cute names to, raised and loved them, only to have them turn when puberty hit.

He wished he was being dramatic.

"Okay, then the Italy trip is off," Mac said, leaning back in his chair with a shrug.

"No," Isabella shrieked. "Daddy, no, please don't

cancel the Italy trip. *Please*."

"Weak," Marquise said out of the corner of his mouth.

The closest thing Isabella could find—a pillow, and a book Melina had left on the side table—went flying. The pillow hit the wall, and the book hit Marquise right in the side of the head. Marquise was already reaching for something else to throw.

Good God, forgive me for whatever I have done to deserve this, please.

Mac's prayers usually went unanswered.

"Don't you call me weak, you fucker!"

"You are weak," Marquise shouted back. "Dad would never cancel that trip because he's going to see—"

"Shut your mouth right now," Mac warned, "we don't say those names in this house, Marquise. Rules for their safety, you know that."

"She's still weak, though."

"I'll show you weak!"

"*Bella!*"

Mac's daughter stilled on the couch, and her gaze darted to him. "Well, he insulted me."

"You did hit him in the head with a book."

"Daddy!"

Between the oldest and youngest Maccari sibling sat a quiet Luca. It never failed to amuse Mac how his middle child never presented anything close to the middle-child syndrome.

"A guy was bothering Bella," Luca said, "and she let us know, so we beat the shit out of him."

Mac's brow raised at that omission. "That's why you beat him up?"

Marquise grumbled something under his breath, and his fist shot out to punch his brother in the thigh. Luca barely reacted.

No, Luca was smart.

He would wait for *later* to get his brother back.

He always did.

"Yep," Luca said, "and I would do it again."

Marquise shrugged. "We only got suspended because he tattled like a baby."

Mac rubbed at his temples, willing his oncoming migraine to go away before it got too bad, and he had to take a pill for the damn thing. "Okay, boys, I get it. Couldn't you wait until after school when he was off school property?"

"Not really," Luca said.

"Next time, do *that*."

Now that all Mac's children were in the same high school, he thought life would be less complicated. That was not the case. His children had a wonderful way of making days difficult just because they could.

Most times, he didn't mind.

He also didn't want two out of three in his home for the next seven days before March break came up because they couldn't *behave*.

"Isabella, thank you for going to your brothers and not gutting the boy the first time," Mac said.

Isabella preened at her father.

She was shockingly like her mother. Melina's pretty eyes, delicate features, his olive skin tone, and dark, wavy hair. But beyond the physical appearance, their daughter was Melina all over. Attitude, swagger, and style. She took no shit.

Melina was proud.

Isabella mostly gave Mac mini heart attacks.

"You may go," he told his daughter.

She stood from the couch. "Is the Italy trip—"

"Don't you push it right now, *bambina*."

Out his daughter went.

Once the door was closed, Mac turned his gaze on his two sons. Neither of them seemed to want to look him in the eye at the moment.

He was not even surprised.

"Marquise, Luca, eyes on me right now."

Both boys looked to him.

"Marquise, kiss your trip to Chicago with Enric to meet the Outfit boss goodbye."

"What, but—"

"Luca, same goes for you."

"Dad, that's not—"

Mac held up a single hand. "Also, weekends are gone for the next two weeks. Get ready to stay at home and make your mother feel like a queen. Marquise, you can cook supper tonight. Luca, you can help your brother tonight, and your mother and sister cook tomorrow. The garage is a mess, work on cleaning that out and organizing it during your suspension. What else?"

He considered anything else he could pile onto the punishments.

"Head into the library and pick three books each—make sure they're at least an inch thick or more. I want them all read, and a verbal report on the contents. Don't ty to fuck me around with some Wikipedia shit, I *will* know."

Quietly, Marquise asked, "Is that all?"

"For now," Mac replied, "but I reserve the right to add things to it. Let's put this this way, boys. Your mother and sister really want to go on that Italy trip, so make sure they get there by following through on your punishment for this. You know the rules—school comes first *always*. You keep family and business out of those hallways. Marquise, you have a few months left to be in that damn school, make it easy on yourself. Luca … you know what, just stop altogether. Stop."

"What about Bella?" Marquise asked. "Is she getting punished?"

"Her fists didn't break some boy's face into the ground, Marquise. Jesus Christ."

Luca muttered under his breath.

"What was that?"

"I said that's only because she came to us," Luca said

louder. "Had she taken care of the guy, he probably wouldn't be able to make babies."

"Right, because she's a smart cookie. Unlike you two. See, she got you two to do her dirty work for her. She escaped punishment. You both think I don't know the tricks your sister pulls, but this is not my first rodeo. So which two between the four of us are not the sharpest tools in the shed? Your sister, who has her tricks; me, who knows them, or you two, who keep falling for them?"

Neither of his boys spoke up.

Again, not surprised.

"Nonetheless, she still didn't do anything wrong. The only reason you're both not spending the next week picking up garbage off the side of the highways is because it *was* your sister. I respect that—would have liked it a lot more had it been off school property, and not on school time."

With a wave of his hand, Mac dismissed his boys. The two went without a look back.

Frankly, he was never going to take away their Italy trip. He looked forward to it more than anyone. They still needed a good scare every once in a while.

Kept them all in line.

Mac stood in the kitchen entryway, and watched his teenage boys share punches on the floor. Marquise currently had the upper hand, but that was only because he had five inches and twenty-five pounds on Luca. It wouldn't be long before Luca equaled his older brother in strength and size.

"What are they doing?" Melina hissed as she came up behind him.

"Fighting."

"Obviously, Mac. *Why*?"

"Because they were cooking together."

Melina let out a hard breath, and glared at the ceiling. "Why would you even bother trying to get them to cook together?"

"I didn't think it through, really."

"Clearly. Why the cooking?"

"They beat up some kid because their sister manipulated them into doing her dirty work again."

Melina smirked at that admission. "She's so sneaky."

"Thinks she is, anyway. I'm on to her."

His wife seemed to decide quickly that she had enough of her sons fighting on the kitchen floor. Walking a couple of feet into the room, she clapped her hands three times loudly in quick succession. It almost sounded like firecrackers going off.

"Okay, that's enough, you two. Enough, I said!"

Melina grabbed Luca by the collar of his shirt, and Mac stepped in to help with Marquise. The two of them pulled the battling teenagers apart. Marquise spit curses at his younger brother while Luca hurled promises of violence.

Mac had no idea when, if ever, these two would be able to get along for more than a few minutes at a time. Clearly it was possible, considering the two had beat the hell out of a guy and worked it out without killing one another. Why couldn't they figure out the same kind of thing when they were at home, or elsewhere?

Shit.

They would even fight in *church*.

"That is enough!"

Melina's shout echoed in the kitchen. Both boys quieted and stopped fighting instantly. She glared between the two boys. Mac hid his smile and bubbling laughter by looking away.

It never failed.

Him, the boys would push and test.

As much as they could, anyway.

Their mother?

Nope.

Melina let go of Luca, pulled two kitchen chairs from the table, and set them in the middle of the room so that they faced once another.

Pointing at the chairs, she said, "Sit, right now."

"But, Ma—"

"Luca, I said *sit*."

Marquise and Luca each took a seat. The two glowered and scowled at one another. Melina simply shook her head.

"I will finish cooking. You two can sit there and stare at each other. To make time go faster, give each other compliments."

Marquise scoffed. "You're fucking kidding, right?"

"Use that word to me one more time, Marquise. Do it."

He looked away.

Melina checked her watch. "Start now."

God, Mac loved his wife.

Queen of his house.

The fiercest mother.

Really, his kids were lucky. Melina actually gave a shit.

At the stove, Melina called over her shoulder, "I don't hear any compliments."

Luca bitched under his breath before saying, "You don't punch like a girl."

Marquise replied, "And you don't look like one."

God save him.

These kids would kill him someday.

"Keep going," Melina urged without ever looking back.

"You're … basically not a piece of shit," Luca said.

Marquise shrugged and said, "I guess neither are you."

Progress, Mac told himself. *Accept the progress.*

Even if it was barely there progress.

"Nice place to be, isn't it?"

Mac looked to his left, and nodded at the man resting in the lounger beside his. "Where is that?"

"The top," Luca Pivetti said.

The man proceeded to sip from a glass of wine as he watched the teenagers make a mess of the Four Seasons' pool. Italy was a wonderful place to visit no matter the time of year. It was an even better place to visit when a person could meet up with old friends.

"The top is a very nice place to be," Mac agreed.

Luca smirked. "I know. How's my son?"

Mac was aware that Luca and Neeya met up with their children a couple of times a year, usually at difference places each time. No one ever discussed those meetings, or when the next one would happen. Mostly because of safety.

"Enric is … good."

"The first time I met up with him after he could walk again …" Luca trailed off with a laugh, and then added, "He came walking up to me with a big smile, and I have never been prouder."

"Shame you missed the wedding."

Luca gave Mac a look from the side. "We've missed no weddings. You simply haven't seen us."

Ah.

Mac chose not to ask more.

"We come and we go," Luca murmured, "and it has to be this way."

"Maybe not forever."

"Maybe not, but for right now, yes."

Marquise jumped off the diving board, and soaked his

brother with a tidal wave of water. Neither of the two brothers seemed to notice their sister was chilling at the shallow end of the pool with a tan, too-old-for-her boy.

"Someone made a friend," Luca noted.

Mac forced himself not to get up out of the lounger.

Only because Marquise finally noticed his sister and her friend.

"Not for long," Mac said with a chuckle.

A shadow darkened Mac's rays of sunlight a second before his wife dropped into his lap. She dotted his face with sweet kisses that made him smile.

"Hey, doll."

Neeya stood on the other side of Luca, and exchanged the man's wine glass for a highball of whiskey. "You look comfortable."

"Working on my tan," he told her.

"I bet."

"We were going to head to the spa," Melina told Mac.

He nodded. "Okay."

"Won't you miss me?"

Mac pressed a quick kiss to Melina's pouting lips. "Do you want me to follow along and glare at anyone who looks your way?"

"It *is* a nice thought."

Luca snorted beside them. "You two are sickening."

"You are not any better," Neeya told him, "so climb right down from that high horse, Luca."

Mac ignored them because his wife was still looking at him and smiling.

Everything was always better when Melina smiled.

ABOUT THE AUTHORS

Bethany-Kris is a Canadian author, lover of much, and mother to four young sons, one cat, and three dogs. A small town in Eastern Canada where she was born and raised is where she has always called home. With her boys under her feet, a snuggling cat, barking dogs, and a spouse calling over his shoulder, she is nearly always writing something ... when she can find the time.

Find Bethany-Kris at:
Her website www.bethanykris.com or on Facebook at www.facebook.com/bethanykriswrites on her blog at http://www.bethanykris.com/blog or on Twitter - @BethanyKris.

Sign up to Bethany-Kris's New Release Newsletter here: http://eepurl.com/bf9lzD.

A proud alumna of the University of Central Florida and Florida State University, Erin is the creator of romances that are a tad bit reckless. With paranormal, organized crime, and mafia soap operas under her belt, Erin looks

MADAME MOLL

forward to continue writing in all the genres she so loves.

Find Erin Ashley Tanner at:

Her website:
www.erinashleytanner.wix.com/erinashleytanner
or on Facebook: www.facebook.com/ErinAshleyTanner
on her blog: https://erinashleytanner.blogspot.com/
or on Twitter- @ErinTheAuthor

ACKNOWLEDGMENTS

Many, many thanks to all the ladies who helped make this series for Mac and Melina possible with Erin and I. Our editors who worked on the series—Nina and Eli. The ladies who beta'd or proofread the books. All the reviewers and bloggers that shared their love for this couple. A huge thanks to our readers for loving this couple. More to come from this world soon, loves. And to Erin, so much love and thanks for taking a leap with me and writing these books.

—Kris

Mac and Melina would never have come to be if Kris hadn't asked me to write with her. This has been such a fun journey together creating this new world. Major shout out to Kristen for this fun collaboration and I look forward to more books and expanding this world together.

—Erin